PREDICTABLE VIOLENCE

Gillean Campbell

Copyright Notice

Version_3

Other Books by the Author

The Ideal Victim is an utterly gripping and compelling detective thriller in the style of the movie Se7en. Fans of Robert Bryndza, Robert Dugoni, and Angela Marsons will be hooked from the very start.

If Michael the avenging angel is watching, you're already dead...

When a typed message quoting the Bible is delivered to Detective Dani McKenna, she discovers a calculated serial killer - stalking his victims before choosing the right moment to strike.

What is the dark secret that Dani's been hiding for years? Could it be the reason for the murders?

When the case threatens Dani's sanity, she must battle her own personal demons as well as catch a killer who's getting ready to end yet another life. But the victims might not be the only ones being watched... Dani's own life could be on the line.

Contact the Author

To contact Gillean directly, you can email her at **gillean@gilleancampbell.com**.

Visit her website at **https://gilleancampbell.com** and read more about how she writes.

Follow her on Twitter **https://twitter.com/authorgilleanc**.

Friend her on Facebook at **https://www.facebook.com/gilleancampbellauthor/**.

Dedication

To **Deborah & James,**

My children, my first-line copy editors, my everything.

Table of Contents

PROLOGUE

The light shining in Greg Brown's eyes was so bright that it burned his retinae. He was confused. Was he asleep or awake? He was sure he was awake and that this was not a dream. But where was he? As he tried to look around, he realized that he was naked. He was lying on the carpeted floor in a room, looking up at the ceiling. He couldn't blink his eyes or turn his head. And, he was dizzy and tired. So very tired.

Mentally attempting to shake the cobwebs out of his mind, He tried to remember what happened to him. The answer was right there, but he couldn't quite bring it into focus. And there was pain, so much pain. It was getting harder and harder to breathe. Sweat trickled down his forehead and into his blonde hair. Brown tried to yell for help, but he couldn't open his mouth. He couldn't move his arms and legs either.

Just then another person walked into his sightline. That person stood looking down at him. He tried to ask for help, but the muscles in his mouth wouldn't form the words.

Finally, the person standing above him said, "Are you in pain? How does it feel? I hope it hurts like nothing you've ever felt before, you disgusting excuse for a human being." The person smirked. "The pain's going to get worse, too. Then you're going to slowly suffocate to death. And, I'm going to stand right here until you take your last breath."

Brown's eyes showed confusion. Who… who's that?

"Focus, asshole. I want you to remember who I am and what you did." The person knelt by Brown and slapped him across the face. "Think… Think really hard… Come on, concentrate… Do you remember now?"

He fought through the haze in his brain. He concentrated on the face of the person over him. It all came flooding back. First recognition, then fear showed in the dying man's eyes.

"Good… You piece of shit. I want you to know that you died for what you did and that I'm the one that killed you."

CHAPTER 1

Detective Mackenzie Anderson stood across the street from the Skaus Lake Police Department. She saw that the small, red brick building was nestled between Lu Lu's Cut 'n Curl and Happy Jack's Hardware. Walking inside, Mack saw that the hallway to the left led to the water department and the building inspector. Because Skaus Lake was such a small Idaho town, there were signs that announced dog tags and yard sale permits could also be purchased there. A right turn led to the town's police department.

Inside the small lobby of the police department, she saw a battered, wooden, L-shaped counter that served as a desk for the woman sitting behind it. "I'm Detective Anderson. I believe Chief Davis is expecting me."

The woman's pale gray eyes widened, taking in all of Mack's five feet eight inches. The woman jumped up from her chair. "Of course. If you wait here a moment, I'll go find the chief." The receptionist's tennis shoes made little noise as she hurried down the corridor directly behind her desk.

While Mack waited, she took the opportunity to look around a bit. The woman's desk held a two-way radio system console, computer, four-line display speakerphone, typewriter, and a great deal of paperwork. But what caught her eye was a framed photograph sitting on the desk. While the woman looked like your typical grandmother, with short curly gray hair and kind eyes, the picture showed her at a party with an enormous cigar in her mouth and a glass of red wine in her hand. Smiling, she decided that she was going to like the woman.

A minute later, the woman returned with Chief Davis following behind. He was in his late fifties, with buzz cut graying hair and drab brown eyes. His paunchy stomach jiggled as he vigorously shook hands with her. "Detective Anderson, I'm John Davis." Turning to the receptionist, he said, "This is Barbara Miller. She keeps this place running."

Mack smiled. "Nice to meet you both."

Barbara patted her on the arm. "I figured you didn't have time to book a room, so I made a reservation for you at Elaine's Bed and Breakfast. It has private baths, and it's close by."

"Thank you. I left in such a hurry this morning, I didn't even think about where I'd stay."

"Barbara was born in Skaus Lake and has been working at the police department for longer than anybody else here. So, if you have questions about the town, she can most likely answer them." Davis paused. "Let's go into my office so we can chat, then I'll introduce you to the rest of our team."

He led the way to the only office off of the corridor. He pointed to the room next door. "This room's for interrogation, interviewing witnesses, and the like."

Mack could see that at the end of the corridor there was an open bullpen area with four desks and a large conference type table.

A wall in the office held framed photographs of his time as police chief. One picture showed him shaking hands with the governor. Another showed him shaking hands with the city's mayor. She thought the smile on his face in most of the photographs seemed like it was pasted on. The pictures on the opposite wall were of Davis' wife, children, and grandchildren. There were photographs of him and his family camping and fishing together. In contrast to the work pictures, the smile on his face in all of the family photographs seemed genuinely happy.

He motioned for her to sit in one of the two chairs in front of his cluttered desk. He took the other seat, grunting as he lowered himself. "Thanks for coming so quickly."

"No problem."

"When I called your captain to request help from the state police, he said he'd send his best investigator, Mack Anderson. I have to admit, I thought you'd be male. Barbara was a little surprised too."

She shook her head, smiling slightly. "To tell you the truth, I think Captain Wilson gets a kick out of shocking people like that." She leaned forward in her chair. "I hope my being female isn't a problem for you."

"Not at all! I wouldn't care if you were purple with pink stripes, as long as you can help us solve these homicides. We have one officer that handles all of our white collar crimes, narcotics, robberies, investigations. That kind of thing. But we've never experienced anything like these triple homicides before." He sighed. "Also, I'm concerned about the personal connection between our officers and the victims. Some of them were friends. Some of their children went to school together. We need an investigator that can take an unbiased look at this nightmare."

"I'll do everything I can to help."

He pushed himself out of the chair. "That's all I can ask for. Let's go meet the rest of the team."

In the bullpen area, two uniformed officers stood when they entered.

"Gentlemen, this is Detective Mack Anderson from District One Investigations. As I told you, I've asked the state police to help us with the murder investigation. Detective Anderson will take the lead."

Davis turned toward one of the officers. "This is Lieutenant Charles Swartz. Charlie heads up our patrol division. We have two additional patrol officers, Dave Barlow and Bob White. Bob's securing the crime scene, and Dave's patrolling. I asked Charlie to suspend his patrol for now so he can support you during the investigation."

Charlie was a big guy, standing six feet five inches tall and weighing two hundred and fifty pounds. Despite his size, his round face and broad smile screamed 'teddy bear'.

She pushed a stray auburn curl back into her low ponytail and shook hands with him. "Appreciate your help."

Davis placed his hand on the shoulder of the other officer in the room. "And this is our senior officer, Nick Moore."

She held out her hand. Taking it, Nick intentionally squeezed hard. She couldn't decide if he was unhappy that she was there, or if he was just a jerk. He was six feet tall, so she only needed to tilt her head back slightly to look him in the eye. Her hazel eyes remained neutral. "Nice to meet you."

He let go of her hand and mumbled, "You too."

She quickly looked him over. He seemed to be a few years older than she was, maybe twenty-eight or twenty-nine, and he was thin and wiry. He shaved his head, but not his face. His strawberry blonde beard was neatly trimmed. His dark brown eyes were currently glaring at her.

Davis broke the tension. "Nick responded to the homicide call and secured the crime scene. He can fill you in on all the details. So, unless you need something else from me, I need to go assure old Mrs. Austin that we'll find Mimi, her lost poodle." He sighed and shrugged. "Life goes on."

She nodded, and Nick said, "We've got it."

The senior officer motioned with his head. "This is the desk where you can work. The one facing it's mine."

"I hope I'm not kicking someone out of their workspace."

He shook his head. "Since Bob and Dave aren't in the office much they share a desk." He paused a few seconds. "I guess you're going to want to check into the place where you'll be staying."

"I'd just as soon go straight to the crime scene."

"Glad to hear it. I have all my equipment in the trunk of my cruiser, so let's get going."

Before following Nick out the back door, she said, "Nice to meet you, Charlie."

He hitched his pants up over his slightly protruding belly. "You too, Mack."

As they walked to the parking lot behind the building, Nick said, "We're luckier than most small-town police departments in Idaho. Charlie and I both have a vehicle dedicated to us, and Bob and Dave each have a motorcycle that they use for patrol. Since the town lies along the shores of an eleven-mile-long lake, we also have a patrol boat. Even though the town's year-round population's less than eight thousand, we have more than double that in tourists each year. That translates into a higher crime rate."

"I believe this is the town's first multiple homicides. Is that correct?"

"That's right. There've only been two other murders in town in the last fifty years. Both before my time." He glanced at her. "Have you investigated many homicides?"

"Thirty-nine. Not including these three." She sighed. "Too many. Way too many."

CHAPTER 2

Unlike Mack's unmarked Dodge Charger, Nick's was dark blue with the Skaus Lake Police Department's logo on the sides in bright yellow.

As he drove, he gave her an overview of the murders. "At seven thirty-eight this morning we received the emergency call from seventeen-year-old Susan Brown. She'd spent the night at her girlfriend's house. Susan came home to find her forty-year-old mother Patricia, her fifteen-year-old brother Alan, and Alan's friend Jack Caldwell dead on the living room floor. Susan's thirteen and eleven-year-old brothers, Tom and Will, were upstairs asleep. They didn't hear a thing. Tom's friend, Ethan Williams, was spending the night. He saw a man in the house. Ethan's our only witness so far."

She pulled a spiral notepad out of her oversized black leather handbag and took notes as Nick talked. "Was Patricia divorced?"

He shook his head. "No. Widowed. She moved to Skaus Lake with her four kids two years ago. Patricia was born and raised here. Her mother, Grace Franke, still lives in town. Patricia moved back home after her husband unexpectedly died of a heart attack."

"Sad. First, the children's dad dies. Now they've lost their mom and brother." She looked at him. "Where are the children now?"

"I took Ethan home, and I took the Brown kids to Grace's house. The chief broke the news to Grace before we got to her house. He also informed Ida and Frank Caldwell, Jack's parents. Dave will be going by to see the kids today to ensure them they're safe. The kids were worried that the murderer would come back for them."

She nodded. "Perfectly understandable."

"While he's there, Dave's going to set up a time for the kids to come into the station tomorrow, so that you and I can interview them. He'll also go see Ida and Frank and set up a time for them to come in. Dave's good with people."

~~~

The crime scene was located seven minutes from downtown, in a secluded subdivision surrounded by forested land. The Browns' house was the second of six on a short, dead-end street that started at the lakefront and meandered uphill. Each house sat in the center of a lot. None of the properties were fenced, but each lot was bordered by large evergreen trees and shrubs that provided privacy. The yards surrounding each house were beautifully landscaped with grasses, giant boulders, and decorative perennial flowers. A circular paved driveway led from the street to the front of each house and back. A large fountain or pond decorated the center of each driveway.

"This is a nice neighborhood," Mack said. "What did Patricia do for a living?"

"She didn't work. Patricia told my wife that her husband left a sizable insurance policy when he died. From what my wife said, I gather that Patricia didn't need or want to work. She felt it was better to be home with her kids to help them with the passing of their father."

She nodded and jotted down a few notes.

As they approached it, she saw that the house was sprawling, with a large front patio that faced the lake. There was also a side patio that afforded views of the lake. The home was clad in redwood. Broad flagstone steps leading up to the front door. Square pillars, faced with river rock, flanked the front door and held up a small second story balcony. Colorful potted flowers of differing varieties sat on the patios and the front steps.

The entire property was cordoned off with yellow crime scene tape. Nick parked on the street. A uniformed officer walked over to the police sedan. They stepped out of the car. "Bob, this is Detective Mack Anderson."

Bob's face made him look like he wasn't old enough to drink, much less be a police officer. He had blonde hair and green eye. He was tall and thin.

She shook his hand. "Nice to meet you."

15

"You too, ma'am." He tipped his four-corner-pinched hat.

Nick said, "As soon as the coroner gets here, we'll be working the crime scene inside. I'd appreciate it if you could continue to keep guard."

"No problem."

A minute later the county coroner pulled up in a black van. Getting out of the vehicle, Oliver Cooper said, "Mack, I should've known I'd find you here. Nice to see you again… Although, I wish it were under different circumstances."

In Idaho, the county coroner's position is an elected government official. Cooper was not a physician, so she wasn't surprised when Dr. Joe Bonner, the coroner's chief deputy, arrived in a separate van.

She shook hands with both men. "Oliver, Joe, this is Officer Nick Moore. I'll be working the homicides with him."

Cooper said, "I hope you haven't been waiting too long for us."

"Not at all," she said. "We just arrived ourselves."

"Good. Joe will take charge of the bodies and work the autopsies with our forensic pathologist. This case takes precedence, so our office will have the results to you as soon as possible."

Nick nodded. "We appreciate that."

"I'll leave it to you. If you need anything from me, just call."

As Cooper drove away, Nick looked at his watch. "It's almost ten-thirty. Let's get started. We have a long day ahead of us."

Mack said, "If it's okay with you, Nick, I'll handle the narrative, photos, sketches, and blood patterns, while you handle latent prints and evidence collection."

He mumbled, "Whatever."

She inwardly rolled her eyes. "Where did our witness say he saw the suspect?"

"In the kitchen."

16

She nodded. "We'll need to vacuum the living room, kitchen, and any adjoining areas."

While Nick and Joe retrieved their equipment, Mack grabbed her field bag from the back seat of the sedan. She took out a spiral notebook and pen and placed her field camera's strap around her neck. She put a small tape recorder and extra blank tapes in one pocket of her cargo pants. Everything else she would need went into the other pockets of her pants.

The three collected their equipment, then donned protective coveralls with a hood, gloves, and shoe covers.

She asked Nick, "Has anyone been inside since you responded to the 911 call?"

"Nope. Nobody."

"Okay," she said. "Here we go."

CHAPTER 3

When she entered the house, the overpowering metallic smell of blood smacked Mack in the face.

The three victims were lying face up, side by side, on the wooden floor of the living room. The bodies were oriented so that their feet were toward the front door. Their wrists and ankles were bound together with extra-wide duct tape. The same tape was used as an over-the-mouth gag.

"The middle boy is Alan Brown," Nick said. "The other boy's Jack Caldwell. And, the female on the left is Patricia Brown."

It was immediately evident that the victims were brutally murdered. Amoeboid shaped pools of blood spread out under and around their bodies. Patricia's yellow wool sweater was slashed numerous times, the yarn unraveling around each tear. Patricia's pale face, brown hair, and tan wool pants were covered with sprays of blood. Alan's blue long-sleeved t-shirt was ripped to shreds. Some of the cotton material stuck in the slashes on Alan's chest and abdomen. Alan's face and blue jeans were also covered in blood spray. Jack's throat was slashed. Blood was sprayed across his face and gray plaid shirt. Blood trailed down the sides of Jack's throat and pooled at the back of his head. Both boys blonde hair was matted with blood.

Joe quietly muttered, "Jesus."

Mack closed her eyes and took a moment to mentally prepare herself for what she was seeing.

Nick took a deep breath and exhaled slowly.

"I wonder if there's a purpose for how the bodies were laid out?" she asked. "Or maybe they were placed here to make killing them easier."

Nick mumbled, "Well, they definitely didn't all three fall down in that position."

Squatting by the bodies, Joe looked at their wounds. "Looks like we're looking for a long non-serrated knife of some sort."

Nick pointed. A large kitchen knife lay on the seat of one of the chairs in the living room. It was covered in blood the stained into the off-white seat cushion. "Looks like that's the murder weapon right there. The murderer left it sitting in plain sight."

"It was probably in the house," Mack said. "The murderer didn't bring it with him."

Nick started to process the weapon. "The blade's bent."

Joe shook his head. "Who the heck could be so angry at a woman and two fifteen-year-old boys that they used enough force to bend a knife?"

She said, "That's the million dollar question."

The living room was open to the dining area and kitchen beyond. An island separated the dining area from the kitchen. A laundry room and half bath were at the back of the house, to the right of the kitchen. The laundry room led into an over-sized two car garage with a shop area. The house had high-quality finishes throughout and was decorated in soft hues of gray and creamy white. Pictures of vibrantly colored flowers and birds hung on the walls.

Mack and Nick started in the living room, moved to the dining room, then into the kitchen. He vacuumed with the microparticle collection vacuum while she sketched the areas and took photographs. Then he dusted and took fingerprints from light switches, door knobs, the door itself, its frame, and the top of any flat surfaces.

In the kitchen, he found a knife set in a wooden block. "Set's missing the butcher knife." He fingerprinted, bagged, and tagged the items. Then he logged it on the evidence list.

French doors off of the kitchen led to a covered back patio, with beautiful views of the forested land above. "No sign of forced entry on any of the doors," she said. "Either a door was left unlocked, the murderer picked a lock, had a key, or someone let him in."

~~~

Nine hours later, Joe sighed loudly. "My initial examination of the bodies shows that Patricia and Alan died of numerous stab wounds, obviously. Jack bled out from his throat being slit. The victims died very early this morning. Of course, I'll be able to provide you with more specific information after the autopsies and analysis of any trace evidence that we find. I have all the photographic documentation, samples, and measurements that I need. How are you doing, Mack?"

"I have all the photos I need of the bodies." She asked Nick, "Would you supervise the labeling, packaging, and removal of the remains? I still need to finish sketching and mapping."

"Yep."

As Joe was leaving, Mack said, "Don't take this the wrong way, but I hope I don't see you soon."

"Same to you. Take care."

Nick walked back inside the house. "Finished yet?"

"I'm all done with these rooms for now. I'll need to come back to map blood spatter trajectory. There isn't time today. It's not going anywhere. It can wait until tomorrow."

"Bob's following the transport vehicles to ensure the bodies are properly transferred to the coroner's office. I asked Charlie to search the front and back yards and document any shoe prints. He's about finished."

"The murderer would have had a significant amount of blood on his clothes. Maybe he tossed them. We need to check around the neighborhood and in all the nearby garbage dumpsters."

He nodded. "Okay. I'll radio Dave and ask him to search as he patrols."

"Great. That will definitely help."

Mack and Nick worked their way through the laundry room and into the garage. She motioned with her head. "What do you know about these cars?"

He pointed. "The tan SUV's Patricia's and the blue Honda's Susan's. The Jeep in the driveway is Jack's."

"Since we have so much area to cover in the house, can you ask Charlie to vacuum and collect evidence from the cars if he's finished with the yard?"

"Yep." He relayed the request to Charlie on his radio. He pressed the remote on the wall and opened the garage door.

Charlie came into the garage with evidence bags and several pairs of latex gloves. Nick handed him the vacuum and three bags. One for each car.

A set of stairs off of the living room led to the second floor. Patricia's bedroom, walk-in closet, and bath were to the right. Susan's bedroom was across the hall from the stairs. Alan's bedroom was at the end of the hallway, on the right side. The two younger boys shared the bedroom across from Alan's. The four children shared one bathroom that was on the left side of the hall. All the rooms were painted the same pale gray with cream trim as downstairs.

Mack and Nick started searching upstairs in Patricia's master suite. Her cell phone was sitting on a bedside nightstand. Mack passed it to Nick. "Maybe something in here will give us a lead." Nick bagged and tagged the phone, adding it to the evidence log.

One corner of Patricia's room was set up as an office area. The cubbyholes of the large wooden desk were stuffed with envelopes, note cards, and stamps. There was no sign of a computer. Inside the desk drawers, he found files that held a mess of paperwork. There were numerous bank and credit card statements, the children's birth certificates, car registrations, and insurance.

"Let's take all of that," she said. "We can look through it later. You never know what might turn up."

He bagged the numerous items. "It's going to take us a week to sift through all this shit."

French doors across from the bed opened onto a small balcony the held two wrought iron chairs and a small side table. There was no sign of forced entry.

21

They looked through Patricia's closet, which held an abundance of clothes and many pairs of shoes arranged on a large rack. In the master bath, he bagged the medications.

The two moved to Susan's room next. It was neat and tidy. For a teenage girl, Susan didn't have many clothes.

Mack picked up a photograph that sat on the dresser. She held it out to Nick. "Is one of these two girls Susan?"

"Yes. The one with the dark hair. The other girl's Chrissy. The friend that Susan stayed over with last night."

"No pictures of a boyfriend." She looked around the room. "Most seventeen-year-olds have their own laptop. But there isn't one in here."

He shrugged. "Maybe all the kids shared one computer."

Next, they searched through the children's bathroom.

She said, "Tomorrow, we'll have to get prints and DNA samples from all the children for elimination purposes."

In Alan's room, the bed was unmade, and there were clothes strewn on the floor. There were no photographs. Nick bagged a laptop. They didn't find a cell phone.

She asked, "Joe didn't mention that Alan' cell phone was on him, did he?"

"Not that I recall. Joe said Jack's was in his right back pocket. Nothing about Alan's."

"There's a charger over here, so Alan had a phone," she said. "So, we have a potential missing laptop or two and a cell phone. Maybe the murderer was after electronics." Her brow furrowed. "If so, why not take Alan's laptop? And the TVs?"

He shrugged. "No idea."

When the two finished in Alan's room, they moved on to the younger boy's bedroom. The floor was littered with video games and clothes.

Nick suddenly stopped moving. "There's a big hairy rat thing in a cage over here!"

She walked over and smiled. "That's a hamster. We better take it and its food to the Brown children. They're not going to be able to get back into the house for a while."

"You carry it. The dang thing stinks."

By the time they finished inside the house, it was almost one in the morning. They worked the crime scene for over fourteen hours. Nick checked all of the locks on the windows and doors. After the two were outside, he put new crime scene tape across the front door.

"It's too late to take the hamster to the Browns," Mack said. "And, I can't have it in the hotel, so you'll have to take it home and drop it off tomorrow morning."

The look on Nick's face was priceless.

CHAPTER 4

Mack was relieved that Elaine's Bed and Breakfast was less than two blocks from the station. She was anxious to wash off the smell of death. As she pulled into the driveway, she saw that the building was a beautiful two-story Craftsman with a wraparound porch. The porch had large L-shaped brick piers and was protected by a roof with overlapping gabled dormers. The exterior was stucco with wooden accents. Several cheery flowering baskets hung on the porch.

Elaine herself checked her in. She was very petite, with short graying hair and gray eyes. She was bubbly and talked very fast. "You sure are lucky you're here in April. We have a carnival in March and a vintage car show in May. If you were here at those time, every place in town would be booked. Our annual events are regionally known." Without skipping a beat, she said, "I've put you in the Tulip Room, dear. It's one of our larger rooms, and even though you wouldn't know it now, it gets plenty of sunlight."

She thanked Elaine. She carried her small suitcase, briefcase, and handbag up the stairs to her room, which was at the back of the building. The inside was painted a pale shade of pink. Tulip wallpaper covered one wall. *Ah, the Tulip Room.* She looked around. The room had a sitting area at one end, furnished with two wing chairs and a round glass coffee table. The bed was on the other end of the room and was covered with a dark pink down comforter. The dust ruffle and numerous decorative pillows had different patterns consisting of several shades of pink. French doors led outside to a private balcony that held two wicker chairs with pink striped cushions and a small metal side table.

She hurriedly unpacked, then took a long hot shower. She stood under the water spray until she felt the stiffness in her shoulders begin to ease. She wrapped herself in one of the full-length white terry bathrobes that she found hanging on a peg in the bathroom.

Along with her clothes and toiletries, Mack always packed three bottles of white wine and two large bags of mixed nuts when she traveled for work. In the past, there'd been many days like today where she hadn't been able to stop to eat. She opened the wine and poured some into a paper cup from the bathroom sink. "Mmmm."

She took the wine and a bag of nuts out onto the balcony. Even though it was only fifty-one degrees, after being inside a crime scene all day, she savored the fresh, crisp air. The second story vantage point and the clear night sky provided a stunning view of the majestic Selkirk Mountains.

Having been born and raised in Idaho, Mack had spent a great deal of time hiking in the mountain range. The Selkirk's spanned the northern portion of the Idaho Panhandle, eastern Washington, and southeastern British Columbia. She never tired of the wild and rugged scenery.

Munching nuts, she looked at the screen of her cell phone and saw three voice messages. She was listening to the last one when the phone rang. She looked at the screen and saw that it was Evan. She swiped the answer icon. "It's almost two in the morning. Why are you awake?"

"I didn't hear from you, so I was a little worried," Evan said. "Did you get my messages?"

"Just now."

"How are you?"

"I'm fine."

"Really? Because I heard on the news that the victims included two children."

"I'm fine. Thanks for asking."

"How are the locals treating you?"

"The investigating officer isn't happy I'm here."

"So, nothing new."

"No, but I'll work it out."

"You always do."

She changed the subject. "How did your board meeting go?"

He chuckled. "There was no talk of replacing me as CEO, so I was happy with the outcome."

"The board knows what a mistake that would be. When you started working there, Innovations Inc. was in bad shape. You turned the place around."

"Thank you. I appreciate you saying that. But it was definitely a team effort."

She sighed. "I won't be back in Coeur d'Alene for a couple of weeks, at least."

"I'd like to see you while you're there. I can make the drive to you. It's only an hour."

"You know I'll be working long hours. There isn't going to be time for you to visit."

"What I know is that you won't rest until you've solved these murders. And every other part of your life will be put on the back burner."

"You knew that about me when you started dating me."

"True. But I thought that at some point you might enjoy spending more time with living people than dead ones."

"That's low, Evan."

He sighed. "I'm sorry. You're right. I didn't call to fight with you. I just wanted to hear your voice and tell you that I miss you."

"I don't want to fight either."

"Are you drinking that swill you call wine?"

"Very funny. You know I don't know anything about wine. I just drink what I like."

"I wish you'd let me buy you some good wine. I'd be happy to pick out something I know you'd like."

"Evan, please don't start that again. I've told you that I don't need or want you to buy me things."

"What's the point of having money, if I can't spoil you a little? You won't let me drape you in diamonds and furs."

She chuckled. "Those would look great with my Glock."

He laughed.

"I better get to bed. Talk to you soon." She severed the connection.

As was Mack's habit each night when working a murder, she pulled her laptop out of her beat-up briefcase and started documenting the case. She included a thorough account of the day's events, the Skaus Lake Police Department's organization, the victims, their family and friends, and any other details. She used a separate page for each person, including Nick's wife. She added a description of the crime scene, evidence collected, and initial findings. Then she emailed a brief summary to her captain at the state police. Finally, on separate pages, she typed each unanswered question. Motive? Opportunity? More than one murderer? How were three victims subdued? How could the two brothers upstairs have slept through the murders? Why were the three younger boys left unharmed?

When she finished, she poured herself another glass of wine and got into bed. She leaned back and tried to clear her mind. But flashes of the three bodies intruded into her consciousness. She drank the rest of the glass of wine and turned off the lights. The wine had its intended effect, and she drifted off to sleep.

The nightmare intruded into Mack's sleep as it often did. She woke with a start and groped for the light. Tears began to roll down her face. Finally getting the light turned on, she sat up in bed and shakily dragged in large gulps of air. Desolation wrapped its tendrils around her.

CHAPTER 5

Six Years Prior

"We're out of milk," Sean yelled from the kitchen.

"Okay," Mack mumbled from the dining room where she sat studying for the test in her 'Abnormal Psychology' class.

He walked into the dining room with Samantha on his hip. "Your daughter needs calcium to grow properly."

"Uh huh."

"Otherwise her bones won't develop, and she could get rickets and osteoporosis."

"Uh huh."

"Then she'll shrink and shrivel up and wither away." He chuckled.

"What did you say?" She looked up from the book she'd been reading. She smiled. "Wise ass."

"'Ise ass," Samantha repeated.

Sean burst out laughing. "What did you say, baby girl?"

Samantha beamed. "'Ise ass."

"Oh my God, Sean. Don't encourage her." Mack stood and hugged both of them. "I sure do love you two."

Sean kissed her. "How about you show me how much you love me tonight after this little miss goes to sleep?"

A grin spread across her face. "I'd be happy to do that."

"You know what they say. Too much studying makes Sean a horny boy."

"'Orny," Samantha said, smiling.

He burst out laughing again. "That's my girl."

Mack laughed. "The two of you are like duplicates."

Samantha looked like her father, with jet black hair and eyes as dark as obsidian. The only nod to Mack was Samantha's wavy hair. Sean's was stick straight.

"I'm going to take Samantha with me and walk down to the Quick Mart to get milk. Why don't you come with us?"

"I can't. I have to study."

"Oh, come on. A break will do you good."

"I can't, Sean. I have to study. My test's at seven in the morning."

"Okay."

She helped him load the little girl into the child carrier and onto his back. Samantha kicked and squealed with delight. Sean kissed Mack on the cheek. "Love you."

Mack stood at the front door of their apartment and waved as they walked up the street. It was the last time she would ever see them alive.

CHAPTER 6

When the alarm woke Mack the next morning at five, she put on sweats, a headband that covered her ears, and running shoes. She went out for a three-mile run around the small city.

Skaus Lake had grown from a muddy village on stilts due to spring floods, to a city of brick buildings, paved roads, tree-lined streets, and comfortable neighborhoods. The economy was based primarily on the lumber industry, ranching, and tourism.

She'd been living in a two bedroom townhouse, in the northern portion of Coeur d'Alene, since she graduated from the police academy. She'd purchased the townhouse because it was relatively close to work.

As she ran, she looked at the landscaped front yards of the homes in Skaus Lake. She felt a longing for her own yard. But then she remembered the maintenance required. She sometimes worked around the clock and barely had time to eat, much less do yard work.

She walked for a half mile before returning to the bed and breakfast. After showering and dressing, she went downstairs to the breakfast room. Elaine poured her a much-appreciated cup of coffee. She ate a heaping plate of scrambled eggs, bacon, and wheat toast from the buffet.

Elaine refilled her coffee cup. "How was everything, dear?"

She smiled. "Delicious. I was absolutely starving."

"I'm glad to see you eat so heartily. As thin as you are, I was afraid you might blow away in the Idaho wind."

~~~

Arriving at the police department a few minutes before seven, Mack found Nick already there. He was making a log of the names and numbers from Patricia's cell phone.

She said, "Good morning."

"Will's hamster's named Harry. In case you're interested."

30

She chuckled. "Can I get you some coffee?"

He looked up with a furrowed brow. "What?"

"I thought some coffee might help your attitude. So, I offered to get you some."

"Uh. No. Thanks… I think."

She pointed at the cell phone. "Anything interesting?"

"I just started. We can go over the log when I finish."

She nodded. "I thought I'd go back to the crime scene and map spatter trajectory."

Charlie walked into the room. "Need some help with that?"

"Thanks. That would be great." She turned to Nick. "I'll be back before our interview with Ethan."

Without looking up, he mumbled, "Fine."

As Charlie and Mack were walking toward his Ford Explorer Interceptor, a uniformed officer that she hadn't seen before got out of his personal vehicle. They walked over to the officer. "Dave, this is Detective Mack Anderson."

He shook her hand. "Nice to meet you." He grinned mischievously. "Although, after Bob went on and on about you yesterday, I feel like we've met already." Dave was attractive and had a dimpled smile. He turned serious. "How's the Brown-Caldwell case going?" As was the habit of most police officers, he called the case by the victim's names.

She shrugged. "Not much to go on yet."

"I haven't found any bloody clothes in the areas I've checked, but I'll keep looking." Dave shook his head. "I can't believe that something like this could happen here."

~~~

When Charlie started driving, Mack asked, "Did you find anything useful in the cars or the yard yesterday?"

He shook his head. "I didn't see anything of interest. In the yard, I measured and photographed the few shoe prints I found.

31

Not sure if they'll be of any help. The landscaping was so perfect that I imagine Patricia had a yard service."

"She did. We found bills from Freddy's Landscaping in her desk."

"I know Freddy. Good guy. I'll find out which of his employees did the Browns' yard. I can interview them to see if they know anything that could help." He glanced at her. "You okay with your accommodations?"

She smiled. "They're lovely. Thanks for asking."

"Elaine's a nice lady. Did you know that she's Barbara's sister?"

She shook her head. "No. I didn't."

"Elaine's a widow, but Barbara never married."

"I wonder why not? Barbara's an attractive woman."

"What my wife told me that Barbara's high school sweetheart was killed in the Vietnam War. Seems she never got over him."

"That's sad."

Charlie was quiet for a few seconds. "Nick treating you alright?

She shrugged. "Sure."

"Nick was pretty upset by the murders. Alan and Jack went to school with his son Mark. And his wife Rose was best friends with Patricia. He sure wasn't looking forward to breaking the news to his family. It was probably a rough night at his house last night."

"I didn't realize. He didn't mention it to me."

"My wife Linda's a teacher. She has Will Brown in her class. She sure was relieved that Will was safe. The school district's superintendent arranged for a therapist to come into both the grade school and high school to talk to students. Linda was glad for that."

"That's a good idea." Since Charlie seemed to be a fountain of information, she nudged him. "Do any of the other officers' children go to school with the Browns?"

"No. The chief's children are grown and live in Boise. Linda and I couldn't have any children." He paused. "That's why she loves teaching so much. Dave's children are only two and four. And, Bob isn't married."

When they arrived at the crime scene, Charlie sat in his vehicle for a full thirty seconds, staring at the house. Finally, he said, "Well, we better get this over with." The second they walked through the front door, his face went ghost white. His eyes darted around the living room. He covered his nose and mouth with his hand, whirled around, and lunged back outside.

Mack could hear Charlie throwing up outside. When he came back into the house, she asked, "You okay?"

"Uh huh."

"First murder scene?"

He nodded. "I didn't think it would be this bad."

"I've seen a lot of homicides, and this is one of the worst I've ever encountered. It's a hell of a way for you to get initiated."

CHAPTER 7

Six Years Prior

"Look, Mrs. Anderson," Detective Olin Tanner said. "We haven't come up with anything. Like I told you, we probably won't. And, we can't afford to continue to expend a bunch of man hours on this." It was evident from looking at Tanner that he and exercise were barely on nodding terms.

"I don't understand." Mack cocked her head to the side "Are you saying you're going to stop looking for the killer?"

"If something comes up, we'll follow through. That's the best we can do."

"You're not going to actively try to find the monster?"

"We don't have anything to go on. This was a random robbery."

She could feel something brittle inside of her exploding into pieces. "Some... random... robbery!" Her volume continued to rise. "My husband and two-year-old daughter were shot to death in that robbery, you asshole!! You worthless piece of shit. How the hell did you become a detective?"

Others in the large open room stopped what they were doing and started watching.

"I'm so sorry! Has my coming in here been disrupting your daily nap?"

A few of the other detectives snickered.

"Well, I don't give a damn about you, you lazy asshole! I care about finding out who killed my family!" She grabbed the front of his suit jacket.

Tanner's partner, Manny Trinidad, jumped up from his desk chair and pried her fingers loose. Holding her by her wrists, Trinidad pulled her away from Tanner. "Mrs. Anderson, I understand how upset you must be. I'm so sorry for your loss. But this isn't doing any good." Trinidad continued to steer her out of the room.

In the hallway, his words broke through her red haze of fury. "I'm okay. You can let go of me."

Trinidad dropped his hands from her wrists. "Sit down, please." He indicated a chair. "Are you okay to drive yourself home?"

She slowly sat. "I'm fine."

"Okay. Take a minute. Then go home. There's nothing you can do here."

Mack watched him walk away. She sat in the cold, hard chair staring at nothing. She felt like a new diary with completely empty pages. She was a vast black void.

From across the room, Gus Haskins watched her. He saw a woman with high cheekbones and a straight nose that led the viewer to the curve of her generous mouth. Even though he'd never met her, he recognized her. She was one of the living dead. Gus walked over and sat on the chair next to her. "Would you like to do something about it?"

She heard the man speak, but the words didn't register. She turned her head and stared at him. He was an older man with a ruddy complexion and a bulbous nose. "What? What did you say?"

"I can help you look for the man that killed your family."

"Do I know you?"

He held out his hand. "Gus Haskins."

She ignored the offer of a handshake. She wasn't in the mood for niceties. "What do you know about it?"

"I know as much as I need to know. So... are you going to curse the darkness or light a fire?"

"Who are you?"

"I'm a private investigator. It's up to you. You can sit here and remain lost, or you can get up and find your way." Gus stood and walked out the door of the Boise precinct.

Fueled by hatred... for the shooter, for Tanner, for the entire world... Mack followed. He walked north on the street for two minutes, then entered a Starbucks. He was only five foot five, so she didn't have any trouble keeping up with him.

When she opened the door, she saw Gus at the counter. She stood in the doorway like a statue, not knowing what to do... with life. He picked up a tray of coffee and pastries. He sat at a table near the front window. She moved over and sat in a chair across from him.

He placed a large vanilla latte and a piece of coffee cake in front of her. "Eat and drink." His voice exuded natural authority.

She sipped the coffee and took a bite. She chewed and swallowed mechanically. Like breathing, it just happened.

She started to say something, but he shook his head. "First we enjoy this lovely coffee and cake."

Without realizing it, she ate more than she had since Sean and Samantha were killed. Mack's mother had tried, but even she couldn't get her to eat more than a bite or two over the past two weeks.

He handed her a business card. "Be at this address at nine tomorrow morning."

She read it. "You'll start investigating the murders of my husband and daughter tomorrow?"

"No. You will."

CHAPTER 8

When Mack and Charlie got back to the police department at ten till nine, they found Chief Davis in the bullpen talking to Nick. Davis said, "Nick was just giving me a run-down. Barbara's arranged for a press conference at noon. I'd like both you and Nick to be there, so the public can put a face to the people in charge of the investigation."

She nodded. "Of course."

Barbara came into the room, interrupted them. "Joe and Alice are here with Ethan."

In the lobby, Nick introduced Mack to Ethan and his parents and explained about needing a set of fingerprints and a DNA sample for elimination purposes. Both of Ethan's parents said they'd been inside the Browns' house, so theirs' were also needed.

Her impression of the boy was that of a gangly puppy that hadn't grown into its feet yet. She asked, "Ethan, would you like your mom and dad to come with you to talk to Officer Moore and me?"

He looked at his parents. He shook his head. "I'll be okay by myself."

She looked between Joe and Alice. "Are you comfortable with us talking to Ethan alone?"

The two looked at each other. Alice nodded, and Joe said, "That's fine, as long as Ethan's alright with it."

Alice hugged her son. "We'll be right here if you need us, honey."

He blushed and mumbled, "Okay Mom."

Nick said, "Down the hall here."

After Ethan took a seat in the interview room, Nick said, "I'd like to record our talk in case I can't remember everything you tell us. Is that alright with you?"

"Okay."

Nick set the recorder on the table in front of the boy.

Mack moved a chair close to Ethan and sat in it. "We'd appreciate anything you can tell us about Friday night and Saturday morning."

He looked down at his lap. "Okay."

Mack and Nick exchanged glances. "Is Tom your best friend?"

"Yeah."

"What grade are you two in?"

He continued looking at his lap. "Seventh."

"You'll be in high school in a couple of years. I remember when I started high school. I was so scared. I must have changed clothes seven or eight times on the first day of school."

"I'm a little nervous, but not like some of the guys are."

"You're a lot braver than I was." She paused. "Does Tom spend the night at your house a lot?"

"Sometimes, but my mom always cooks meat and vegetables for dinner. Tom's mom gets pizza and burgers, so we like it better there."

"I love pizza."

"Me too. Plain cheese is my favorite. What kind do you like?"

"Pepperoni's my favorite. Did you have pizza at Tom's Friday night?"

"No. Susan made spaghetti and garlic bread, 'cuz Chrissy was eating with us, and that's her favorite. I like garlic bread, but spaghetti sauce not so much." He glanced at her and smiled shyly. "I ate five pieces of garlic bread. Tom said I was going to turn into one."

She leaned in ever so slightly and smiled at him. "What did you and Tom do after dinner?"

"We played a video game."

"Which one?"

"League of Legends." Ethan looked up at Mack. "Do you know it?"

"Isn't it a multiplayer online battle arena game?"

He turned toward her. "Yeah! Players assume the role of a summoner that controls a champion with special abilities. We battle against a team of other players. The goal's to destroy the other team's Nexus. That's a building at the center of their base."

"It sounds fun."

"It's seriously on fleek!"

She smiled. "How long did you and Tom play after dinner?"

"Not very long at all. Usually, we play until, like, midnight. I wanted to play longer, but Tom was real tired, so we went to bed."

"Did you go to sleep as soon as you got in bed?"

"No. I couldn't fall asleep 'cuz my stomach hurt from all the garlic bread."

She leaned in a little more. "Did you barf?"

He smiled. "No. I just lay in bed for a real long time. Then I heard noises downstairs."

Mack was thankful that Nick didn't interrupt. "What kind of noises?"

"I thought I heard doors opening and closing. I hadn't heard Alan or Mrs. Brown for a while, so I thought they'd gone to bed. I was curious, you know, so I got down from the top bunk to check it out. I peeked around the corner of the hall and over the banister. I saw a man walking around."

"Can you tell me what the man looked like?"

He shook his head. "I couldn't see his face."

"Could you see what color his hair was?"

"No. It was completely covered by the black hoodie he was wearing."

"Did he seem tall or short to you?"

Ethan shrugged. "Kind of medium? Sorry, I'm not real sure."

"That's okay. Don't worry about it. Could you tell if he was thin?"

He was quiet for a second. "He had on kind of baggy pants, so I'm not sure."

"Was the hoodie tight or loose?"

"Definitely loose."

She nodded. "That's a big help."

He smiled.

"Could you tell what kind of shoes he had on?"

"I don't think I saw them."

She smiled. "What was the man doing?"

"He was walking toward the kitchen."

"Could you see if he had anything in his hands?"

"Not that I remember."

She smiled again. "How long did you watch the man?"

"Not very long. I got nervous that he was Mrs. Brown's boyfriend or something. I thought he might come up the stairs and see me, so I went back to bed. My stomach was feeling better. I think I fell asleep real soon after that. Susan woke me up yelling… and, well, you know." He looked back down at his lap.

"Ethan, you've helped us tremendously. Thank you so much."

The boy looked at Nick. "That's all?"

Nick said, "We might want to talk to you another day if that's okay."

"Sure. No problem."

When they took Ethan back to the lobby, his mom put her arm around him. "Are you alright, honey?"

He blushed and glanced at Mack. He shrugged his mom's arm off. "I'm not a baby, mom."

Nick said, "Barbara will take your fingerprints and collect DNA samples. Thank you all for coming in."

Walking down the hallway to the bullpen, Nick asked, "How the heck did you know about that video game?

Mack shrugged. "The guy I'm seeing is kind of a geek."

He nodded and said with a straight face, "That's seriously on fleek."

Taken off guard, she burst out laughing. "What the heck does that word even mean?"

"I have no idea. I'm glad I'm not the only old fogey that's not up with current slang."

~~~

As they were walking to the front of the building for the press conference, Chief Davis asked Nick and Mack, "How did Ethan's interview go?"

"Mack handled the kid perfectly," Nick said. "She was able to get everything we needed without asking any leading or suggestive questions."

She hoped that he was warming up to her. "Thank you."

When they walked outside, she saw that along with the local media all of the major broadcasters were represented. Multiple murders were always big news.

Mack and Nick stood behind Davis as he introduced himself. "I will give you a brief summary of what the Skaus Lake Police Department knows to date. We will not be answering any questions today."

A collective moan arose from the crowd.

"But first I'd like to introduce the two investigators that are leading the effort to solve these homicides." Davis introduced Mack and Nick. Then he gave the names of the victims, when and where they were discovered, and a few points on how the investigation was being handled. "That's all we have for today."

The three started back toward the building. The press gathered around them, shouting questions and sticking microphones in their faces. When they reached the front door of the building, Barbara was standing there. "You go on in. I've got this." She held the door open until Mack, Nick and the chief passed through. Then she stepped in front of the entrance, arms crossed.

Mack smiled. She would have like to see someone try to get past Barbara. She was a badass.

CHAPTER 9

Six Years Prior

Mack walked into the apartment that she'd shared with Sean and Samantha. She dropped her handbag and keys on the dining room table as she walked past it. Opening the door to her daughter's room, a sob escaped from deep inside. She lay down on Samantha's 'big girl' bed that they'd bought less than three weeks ago. She remembered the proud look on the little girl's face the first night she'd slept in it. Mack pulled the pillow to her face and inhaled. It still smelled like Samantha. She curled up on the bed, pulling her legs into her chest. Tears dripped into her hair.

It was past midnight when she made her way into the master bedroom. She lay down on the side of the bed that Sean had slept on. "Oh God. I'm so sorry that I didn't go with you. Why didn't I go with you?" Regret ricocheted around inside of her. "I don't want to be here without you two."

Mack was afraid to fall asleep. Afraid that the nightmare would come again. It was always the same. Sean lay on his side in a pool of blood. Samantha was in the carrier on his back. Blood ran down her pink dress. Her body shut down from exhaustion and she fell asleep without meaning to. Suddenly she jerked awake, sweat coating her face. She looked around the room. She was alone, marooned on a private island of despair.

At a quarter to five, she got out of bed and pulled on a pair of jeans and a sweatshirt. Even though it was almost summer, she hadn't been able to get warm since the police had come to her door. She paced from the kitchen, through the dining room, and into the living room waiting for the sun to come up. When she detected light in the sky, she started walking up the street to the Quick Mart. She followed the last steps that her family had taken. She stopped in front of the market. In the weeks following the murders, she'd come here every day and stood in silence, trying to understand. The only thing Mack knew was that when Sean and Samantha had died her universe was also destroyed.

~~~

43

Mack arrived at Haskins Investigations at ten to nine. It was located in a small strip mall close to the Boise River, between a dentist's office and a shredding service.

When she pushed open the door to enter, a bell above announced her arrival. Gus yelled from a room in the back, "In here." Off of the short hall, on the right, she saw a restroom, complete with a shower. Directly opposite that was a kitchenette, with a refrigerator, microwave, and small table and chairs.

She entered his office. It was relatively large, with a couch in one corner. He was talking on the phone, so she wandered around. On one wall there were several photographs of Gus as a young man in a patrol uniform. As it does, time marched on in the pictures. The pictures showed Gus throughout his career. Through the years, he'd lost hair and gained weight. The last picture showed him as a sergeant with five plainclothes detectives.

"That's the Violent Crimes Unit that I led for the four years before I retired," he said, walking up behind her.

She turned to face him. "So, where do we start?"

His eyebrows rose. He reached into his back pocket, pulled out his wallet, and handed Mack two twenties. "We start with you going up the street and getting two orders of biscuits and gravy and two large coffees to go."

"I'm not hungry."

"Didn't ask you that."

He held out the money and wagged it. She jerked it out of his hand and did as she'd been told. As Mack walked the block up Shoreline to a diner, she conducted a conversation with herself. I didn't come here to run errands. Hell, it's not like I have anything else to do. I guess it's better than sitting in the apartment alone.

~~~

Mack returned and set the food on Gus' desk. He opened one of the foam boxes and dug in, sipping coffee between bites. He pushed the second foam box to the other side of his desk. "Try a bite. Tell me what you think. I could go for more pepper myself."

She knew what he was doing, but she decided to humor him. She plopped into the upholstered chair in front of his desk. She set the box on her lap and shoveled a spoonful into her mouth.

He pushed a coffee in front of her.

She swallowed the food, then closed the lid on the to-go box. "It's fine as it is." She took a drink of coffee to wash down the thick gravy.

He continued to eat. "You haven't told me your name."

"Mack Anderson."

"Is Mack short for something?"

"Mackenzie."

"Scottish or Irish?"

"Scottish."

"Do your parents live in Idaho?"

"Look." She set the box of food back on his desk. "Can we cut the chit-chat and get on with this?"

He nodded. "Yes. If that's what you'd like to do." He put his empty foam box in the trash can next to his desk. He pulled a large notepad in front of him. "Date your husband and daughter were killed?"

"May twenty-seventh."

"Address?"

She didn't know the exact address of the Quick Mart. He said her home address was close enough.

Gus picked up the phone on his desk and pressed a speed dial button. "Hey, Sigurd. I need a tower dump from May twentieth through June third." He listened for a second, then repeated Mack's address to the person on the other end of the line. He listened for a few more moments. "I'm sending a young woman to pick it up."

When he placed the handset back in the cradle, she asked, "What's a tower dump?"

"It's how you're going to obtain information on the identity, activity, and location of any phone that connects to a cell tower in that location and within that time span."

"How's that going to help?"

"Whenever a cell phone's used, it sends an electronic signal to the nearest tower. If the phone has GPS, it will send a constant signal. That will, hopefully, allow you to use the cell phone to find the man that killed your husband and daughter."

"Is that legal?"

"Do you care?"

She didn't hesitate. "Not even a little."

He pulled his key ring out of the front pocket of his pants. He selected a key and used it to unlock the bottom drawer of his desk. She could see that the drawer contained a safe. She looked away as he entered the combination. He opened an envelope and counted the money inside of it. He removed a few bills and sealed the envelope. Then he scribbled on a piece of paper and handed both to her. "This is Sigurd's address. Give him the envelope. He'll give you the disc you need."

"I have money," Mack said. " I can pay my own way."

"Fine. Bring me fifteen hundred dollars tomorrow, and we'll be even."

CHAPTER 10

When Grace and the Brown children arrived, Nick again handled the introductions and explained the need for elimination fingerprints and DNA samples. "Since you've been in the house, we're going to need yours also, Grace." He motioned toward the front counter. "If you'll step over here, Barbara can take care of that."

Mack observed the children as they were being fingerprinted and swabbed. Susan Brown was tall and lithe, with lovely facial features. In contrast to her blonde brothers, she had coal black hair, which was in striking opposition to her large pale blue eyes. Mack was reminded of Snow White in the children's fable.

When Barbara finished, Nick said, "Grace, with your permission, we'd like to look through Alan's computer to see if there might be anything of use on it."

"I don't see any reason why not."

"Thank you."

Mack asked Susan, "Would you be alright with Officer Moore and me talking to you first?"

She looked at her brothers. "I'm happy to go first."

Mack asked Grace if she was any objection to Susan being alone when she gave her statement.

Susan said, "I'm okay with talking to you by myself."

Grace said, "The boys and I'll go get ice cream." Grace gave Barbara her cell phone number and asked her to call when Susan was finished.

Mack and Nick ushered Susan down the corridor to the interview room. She agreed to be recorded, so Nick inserted a new tape into the machine and pressed play.

Mack sat in a chair on the same side of the table as Susan.

Nick took a seat on the opposite side of the table. "How are you doing?"

47

"I'm crappy, of course. How do you think I'm doing? That's a stupid question."

He tried to recover. "I'm sorry. I can imagine how bad you must be feeling."

Mack groaned inwardly.

Susan raised her voice. "You have no idea how I feel!" Glancing at Mack, she said, "Neither one of you has any idea how I'm feeling. You have your dad, mom, and brother all die, then you can tell me you know how I'm feeling."

Great, this is going sideways. Mack turned her chair toward Susan. "When I was a little older than you, I lost two people that I loved more than life itself. So, I think I know at least a little about how you're feeling."

Susan took a deep breath and let it out. "I'm sorry for yelling."

Nick said, "It's completely understandable."

Mack smiled. "We'd like to talk to you about Friday night and Saturday morning, if you can do that now."

"I want to help. I'll tell you everything I can. What do you want to know?"

"Why don't you start by telling us what you did Friday."

"Okay. Well, I went to school, as usual. Chrissy and I made plans for her to come over for dinner. Then we'd go to her house. I made spaghetti and garlic bread because that's Chrissy's favorite. Chrissy's a little heavy, so her mom won't let her eat pasta or pizza or stuff like that. That's why we ate at my house. Chrissy came over about six, we ate dinner with everyone, then we walked to her house." Susan paused. "When her mom asked what she'd eaten, Chrissy told her salad and fish. Sad."

Mack nodded.

"Chrissy and I watched the last three Star Wars movies in her room. Then we went to bed." Susan's eyes filled with tears. They slowly rolled down her cheeks.

Nick retrieved a tissue box from a side table and set it in front of Susan. She took one and dabbed her face. "Thanks."

Mack asked, "Can you tell us about Saturday morning?"

Susan took a deep breath. "On the weekends, I work at the bakery on Main Street. So, I got up at seven and walked home. When I opened the front door, I saw mom, Alan, and Jack lying on the floor. I knew right away that they were dead. There was blood everywhere." Tears started to run down her face again. She took another tissue and rubbed her eyes with it. "I was so scared, I wanted to run back to Chrissy's. But I didn't know where Tom and Will were. I was afraid they might be dead, too. I screamed their names and ran up the stairs. They were both in their room asleep. I was so relieved. The boys were confused about why I'd been yelling and why I was crying. I didn't know if the killers were still inside the house, so I closed and locked the door to the boys' room. I told them to get dressed. They kept asking me what was going on. I didn't tell them because I didn't know what to say." She took another deep breath and wiped her eyes. "I told them not to leave their room. I went into the closet so they wouldn't hear and I called the police. Then I went back and stayed with the boys until Officer Moore got there."

Susan looked at Nick. "I didn't know what to do. But you got the three boys out of the house without them seeing the bodies. I can't get that sight out of my head. It was horrible. I'm glad the boys don't have to go through that. Thank you."

"No problem."

Susan turned back to Mack. "Outside, Officer Moore sat the boys down at the patio table and told them that mom, Alan, and Jack were dead. He also explained that he would be taking Ethan home and the rest of us to Grandma's. Tom cried, but I think Will was in shock. When we got to Grandma's, I could tell that she'd been crying. She started making breakfast and telling us where we would sleep and stuff like that. We all walked around like zombies, doing what she told us." Susan paused. "Tom and Will woke up a couple of times last night, crying for mom. I felt so bad for them."

Mack said, "I'm so sorry you went through that. If you're okay with continuing, I'd like to ask you a few more questions."

Susan blew her nose. "Sure, go ahead and ask."

"Are you a senior this year?"

She nodded.

"What grade was Alan in?"

"Ninth."

"Was Chrissy still asleep when you left her house?"

"She woke up when my alarm went off, but she didn't get out of bed. She probably went back to sleep."

"Did Alan have a cell phone?"

"Yes."

"It wasn't in the house or on him. Any idea where it might be?"

She shook her head. "He always had it with him."

"Okay, thanks." Mack paused. "Do you know if Alan had a girlfriend?"

"Not that I know of. But he didn't talk to me about stuff like that."

"Do you know if anyone was upset with Alan?"

"Not that I know of. He was pretty quiet. The only real friend he had was Jack."

"Did you see anyone when you were walking home Saturday morning?"

"No, nobody."

Mack smiled. "Do you have a boyfriend?"

Susan shook her head. "No. I plan to go to college. I don't want the distraction."

"Just a few more questions, then we'll be done."

"Okay." Susan sniffed.

"Besides your mom, you, and your brothers, who else might have a key to your house?"

Susan was quiet for a second. "Grandma has one."

"What about a housekeeper or a neighbor?"

"Two women came in once a week to clean, but mom stayed home when they were there. She didn't want them alone in the house. She was always warning Tom and Will about losing their key and having to replace all of the locks. I don't think mom would have given anyone else a key.

"Do you by any chance know the names of the two housekeepers?"

"No. Sorry."

"Do you know if your mom had a boyfriend?"

"Not that I know of. She never invited a man over. I think she was still sad about dad dying."

"Did your mom mention if she was having problems with anyone?"

"No. She never said anything like that to me. And, I never heard her arguing with anyone."

"Did your mom have a computer?"

"She had a laptop. It's in her room on her desk."

"Do you have a computer?"

Susan nodded. "I have a laptop."

"Do you know where it is?"

"It should be in my room. I used it after I got home from school Friday."

"I asked because it wasn't in the house."

"Oh. Do you think the murderer stole it and Alan's phone?"

"That's a possibility. Your mom's laptop's missing too. But Alan's laptop was in his room. So, it's kind of confusing." Mack looked at Nick. "I don't have any more questions. So unless Officer Moore has any, we're finished here."

Nick said, "I don't have any questions. Thank you, Susan."

"Yes, thank you for all your help," Mack said.

"Let me know if there's anything else you need. I want whoever did this to be caught and punished."

After Susan left, Nick said, "I blew that. Thanks for covering for me by coming up with that story about your loved ones dying. It was a good way to establish a bond with Susan."

"It's not a story."

~~~

Tom and Will Brown both agreed to be interviewed without their Grandmother present, and Grace concurred. Tom volunteered to go first and agreed to have the conversation taped. Mack asked Tom the same type of warm-up questions about school and food.

"What time did Ethan come over to your house Friday night?"

"He came home from school with me. We'd asked our moms the night before if that was okay."

"What did you two do from the time you got home until you ate dinner?"

"We played a video game."

"When did Will go to sleep?"

"He came into the room while Ethan and I were still playing. He went to bed and was asleep right away." Tom shrugged. "He snores."

Mack smiled. "After you went to bed, what happened?

"Next thing I knew, Susan came into our room crying. She told us to get dressed and stay in the room, but she wouldn't tell us what was wrong." Tom's eyes filled with tears. "I knew it was something bad by the way she was acting." He scrubbed at his eyes with the sleeve of his shirt. "Then Officer Moore came and told us."

When they finished asking all of their questions, Mack and Nick walked Tom back to the front lobby. Susan was sitting in a chair next to Will, with both arms around him. He was crying. Grace was patting him on the back and murmuring, "It's okay."

Susan said, "Will doesn't want to talk about it."

"That's not a problem," Mack said. "Listen, Will, don't you worry about it at all. Susan and Tom told us everything we need to know."

Will sniffed his nose. "Okay."

As the Brown children and Grace were all leaving, Susan turned around and mouthed 'thank you' to Mack.

CHAPTER 11

Six Years Prior

Mack got into her car and entered the address Gus had given her into the GPS on her phone. It would take twenty minutes to drive there. After thirty minutes, she was sure that she was lost. By the time she arrived, she didn't have any idea where she was. She pulled onto the dirt lot and parked in front of the dilapidated industrial building. There were no identifying address numbers, but the GPS assured her that this was the right place.

A walkway, surrounded by a chain-link fence with razor wire at the top, led to the only door. Mack took her handbag, locked the car, and walked up to the gate in the fence. A sign said 'Warning. Electric Fence.' Mack looked around. Paranoid much?

Suddenly, a disembodied voice asked, "Who are you?"

She didn't know what direction it had come from. "I'm Mack. Gus sent me."

She heard a buzzing noise. "Come up the walk."

She opened the gate and walked to the front door. It occurred to her that in her former life she would have been scared to death. But now, she didn't give a rat's ass. Mack raised her hand to knock, but before she could, she heard another buzzing noise. The heavy steel door popped open an inch. She stepped inside and saw precisely what the building looked like from the outside. An abandoned warehouse. The massive interior space was a warren of rooms, separated by metal walls.

"Follow my directions," the voice said. "Take the hallway to the left."

She walked to the end of the hall.

"Right to the second hallway, then left, then right at the first hallway."

She walked down the corridors, repeating the directions in her head. She ended up at a dead end. Mack thought that she must have taken a wrong turn somewhere. Suddenly, a hidden door on the right opened inward. She couldn't see what was inside.

"Please, come in."

She stepped through the entrance. The door automatically closed behind her, clicking as it locked. "Wow." Mack was amazed by what she was looking at. The inside was one large open room. A workout area was to the left. A bedroom area was next to it. A complete bathroom was at the far back. A living room area, a small dining area, and a kitchen were to the right. The bathroom was the only area with interior walls. In the middle of the space was a circular array of high tech consoles, video monitors, hard drives, and a lot of other electronic stuff that Mack couldn't identify. All of the equipment was humming, beeping, and flashing.

But the most interesting part of the room was the man standing in front of Mack. He looked like... well... the only thing that came to her mind was... a Viking. He was at least six feet six inches tall. He must have weighed two hundred and fifteen pounds. All of which was pure muscle. His hair was dark blonde, shaved on the sides and back, and longer on top. His beard was bushy and reached several inches below his chin. He had a prominent brow that made him look like he was angry all the time. Mack could see sharp intelligence in his piercing aqua eyes. He was wearing a sleeveless t-shirt, cargo shorts, and flip-flops. Down his arms were tattoos of wings in different shapes, sizes, and shades of red, blue, and black.

"Sorry. I didn't mean to stare," Mack said when she realized that she was doing just that. "You're not what I expected."

"What did you expect?"

"I don't know. Based on the location and this building... I guess a cross between Jeffrey Dahmer and John Wayne Gacy."

The corner of the Viking's mouth turned up. "And, yet, you came inside anyway." The man's accent was as Nordic as he looked. The word 'anyway' sounded like 'anyvay'. He held out his hand. "I'm Sigurd."

She shook his hand. "Mack." She pulled the envelope out of her handbag and handed it to him. "This is from Gus."

He walked over to the center of the room, picked up a disc in a sleeve, and gave it to her.

"Thank you."

"Why did Gus send you to pick this up?"

"Actually, it's for me."

He nodded slightly and led the way back to the door. She saw that it had a handle of some sort on the inside. He held the door open for her. "Goodbye, Mack."

She retraced her steps back to her car. As she pulled out of the dirt lot, she had no idea that Sigurd was already started running her license plate. Within a minute he knew everything about her.

When Mack got back to Gus' office, she held the disc out to him. He looked at it. "That's for you. I have my own work to do. You can use the outer office. I put a set of headphones on the desk."

"What am I listening for?"

"Any reference to a shooting, killing, hit. Any reference to a man and a little girl. Any mention of a nine-millimeter handgun. Also, listen for the words 'nine nina'. Some gang members call a nine millimeter that."

Her brow furrowed. "Is that the kind of gun that Sean and Samantha were killed with?"

"Yes."

"How do you know?"

"I asked a friend of mine at the department to send me a copy of the police report. While you were gone, I read through it. I take it you didn't know."

She shook her head. "They wouldn't tell me anything. Not a single thing."

"I don't want to sound like I'm excusing them, but the detectives may have thought they were protecting you.

Personally, I don't believe that helps loved ones to move forward. But that's just me."

"Do you know anything else about what happened to them?"

"Was there something specific that you want to know?"

Her eyes filled with tears. "I need to know if they suffered. Did Sean know that Samantha was hurt and that he couldn't help her?" The tears started to roll down Mack's face. "Did Samantha call for me? Did she die wondering why her mommy wasn't there to make her feel better?"

Gus came around his desk and patted Mack on the back. "I'll get a copy of the autopsy reports and answer all of your questions as best I can. Okay?"

She nodded. He handed her a clean handkerchief from the front pocket of his jacket. She used it to wipe her face and eyes. She held it out to him.

"You keep it. You need it more than I do."

She sat at the desk in the reception area. She put the headphones on, loaded the disc into the computer's drive, and started listening. She was tired of the endless drone of voices when Gus came out of his office and tapped her on the shoulder. She pressed the pause button.

"I'm heading home for the evening."

She took off the headphones and rubbed her ears. "What time is it?"

"Six-thirty. You can leave that where it is and start again tomorrow."

She could hardly believe that she'd been sitting there for almost seven hours. "Okay." She picked up her handbag from the floor and put on her jacket.

"Here. This is yours." He held out the box of leftover biscuits and gravy. "I put it in the refrigerator after you left this morning. Promise me that you'll eat at least one bite."

She looked at Gus for a few seconds. "Okay. I promise."

"Good. You won't be helping anybody by starving to death."

Mack considered that statement all the way home. She wasn't sure that she wanted to be alive.

CHAPTER 12

Ida and Frank Caldwell came into the police department at four that afternoon. Ida looked like all the moisture had left her body, and she was shrinking inside of herself. Frank's eyes were hollow, reflecting back the pain he was feeling. His face was as taut as a rubber band.

Mack's gut wrenched looking at them. "I'm so sorry for your loss."

Frank said, "Thank you."

"We appreciate you both coming in at this difficult time," Nick said. "We just have a few questions for you."

After the Caldwells agreed to the conversation being recorded, Mack asked, "Have either of you ever been inside the Browns' house?"

Glancing at Frank, Ida shook her head. "No. Jack had his own car, so he drove himself back and forth. He also drove Alan around quite a bit because Alan didn't have a car. Jack wasn't old enough to drive alone at night, though. So, he only drove during the day."

"Did Jack like school?"

Ida dabbed her eyes with a tissue. "Not particularly. He gets... got... good grades, but he wasn't that interested in any of the subjects. I think he was a little bored because everything was so easy for him. He was very smart."

"Did Jack have a girlfriend?"

Ida shook her head. "No. He would have told me."

Mack nodded. "Was Alan his best friend?"

Again, Ida answered. "Alan was really Jack's only friend. He was very shy. He'd a hard time making friends."

"Can you tell us what kind of things Jack was interested in?"

Frank shook his head. "He didn't play any sports. If that's what you mean."

"Was Jack in any clubs at school?"

Ida said, "No. He just wasn't interested."

"What did Alan and Jack do when they were together?"

Ida was quiet for a second. "They mostly watched TV. Jack had his own TV in his room, so they stayed in there when Alan came over to our house."

"What time did Jack go to Alan's house on Friday?"

Ida wiped at her eyes again. "He left the house around quarter to six, I think."

"Do you know if Jack was having any kind of a problem with anyone?"

Frank asked, "Like who?"

"Anyone that you can think of... at school or out of school."

Frank and Ida exchanged looks. Ida shook her head, and Frank said, "Not that we know of. You don't think Jack was the target, do you?"

Mack leaned forward in her chair. "I'm not saying that at all. We're just looking at all possible scenarios and have been asking everyone the same question."

"Okay, I can see that," Frank said. "Please... find the person that did this to our son."

Nick said, "You can be sure that we'll do our best, Frank."

~~~

Nick made Mack a copy of everything he was able to get off of Patricia's cell phone, including contacts, texts, call logs, voice messages, and photographs. He handed her the papers. "You'll notice that my wife's cell number in the call log numerous times. Patricia and Rose were best friends."

She nodded. "Charlie told me. How's your wife doing?"

He ran his hand down his face. "She's pretty upset."

"Charlie also said that your son was in class with Alan and Jack. Did your son know them well?"

"No. Mark said that both boys were quiet and kept to themselves."

She motioned her head toward the list. "Do you see anything out of the ordinary on this?"

"Nothing jumped out at me. Most of the women Patricia talked to are all in a book club that Rose is also in. There are calls to Pastor Beck at the church that Patricia and her kids attended. Of course, there are numerous calls to and from Patricia's mother, Susan, and Alan. The only pictures on the phone are of her kids. I just don't see anything unusual." He paused. "Barbara's taking care of the warrant for the Browns' landline. Maybe there'll be something there."

Nick handed Mack a copy of what he'd found on Alan's laptop. "I didn't have time to look through all the folders, so I made a list of them. Most of the folders are pictures, school work, and other normal fifteen-year-old boy stuff."

She scanned the list. "Thanks for doing that."

"While we were doing interviews today, Charlie looked through Patricia's canceled checks and tracked down the two housekeepers. Turns out, they clean three other houses on the street. He got fingerprints from both of them and from Chrissy Smith. He also interviewed the Browns' five neighbors to find out if any of them heard or saw anything Friday night or Saturday morning. One of the neighbors, Nora Nelson, is out of town, but her husband didn't see anything. He told Charlie that when Nora gets back in town, she'll call if she saw anything." Nick handed Mack a third group of papers. "This is a copy of Charlie's report."

She read aloud. "Mr. Taylor heard a car door slam sometime around five-thirty in the morning. He's not positive about the time because he didn't have his glasses on so he couldn't see the bedside clock very well. Mrs. Lee was awakened four times Saturday morning by her barking dog. Once at three twenty-seven, once at four thirty-two, once at four forty-nine, and again at fourteen past five. She checked her bedside clock each time, so she's sure about the exact time. But she didn't get out of bed and look out the window to see what he was barking at. None of the other neighbors remember hearing anything, including Chrissy Smith's parents." Mack leaned back in her chair and looked at the ceiling. "How are three people brutally murdered without anyone hearing any screaming?"

"Maybe they were held at gunpoint, with the threat of hurting the boys upstairs if they made any noise. Then they were tied up and gagged."

She nodded. "Makes sense."

He sighed. "Well, it's after seven, so I'm going to go home. See you back here tomorrow morning about eight?"

"Sounds good." She smiled. "Good night."

Mack spent the next two hours searching homicide databases for similar cases, with no success. When her cell phone rang, she saw that it was Evan.

"Are you still working?" he asked when she answered.

"I'm just getting ready to call it a day."

"Did you eat any dinner… or lunch, for that matter?"

"We did interviews all day. There wasn't time."

"I worry about you when you're working one of these big cases. You get completely wrapped up in it."

"That's the way it has to be."

"I don't believe that. I think it's the way you choose for it to be."

"Evan, don't start. I'm tired, and I don't want to have to listen to that."

He sighed. "I saw you on TV. Looking at you makes me miss you even more."

"I better go. Talk to you soon."

CHAPTER 13

Six Years Prior

Mack withdrew money from her savings account as soon as the bank opened the next morning. Then she drove to Gus' office.

"Here's the money I owe you." She handed him the overflowing envelope.

He nodded, opened the safe, and sealed the money inside. "Before you get started, would you please walk up to the diner and get the same order as yesterday?"

"Okay. But I'm buying today."

He smiled. "I appreciate that."

She decided to waste less time and drive the block up to the restaurant. She ordered biscuits and gravy, coffee for Gus, and a large vanilla latte for herself.

The woman at the counter asked, "Do you want any eggs with that, sweetie?"

"Sure. Why not. Put them in the same to-go box."

Returning to the office, Mack handed Gus the foam box. "You keep eating like this, and you're going to have a heart attack."

He chuckled dryly. "My wife used to say that same thing to me all the time." He paused. "And still, I outlived her."

~~~

Mack couldn't believe the incredibly ridiculous conversations of some people.

"I love you pookey bear," one woman said in a sickly sweet voice. "Do you love me, pookey bear?"

"Uh. Of course, I do."

"Well, say it, pookey bear."

"The guys are here," the man whispered.

She could picture the poor guy cupping his hand around the bottom of his cell phone, trying not to be heard by his buddies.

"Come on, pookey bear. How am I supposed to know that you love me if you don't tell me, pookey?"

"I love you too."

She heard several men in the background start laughing. *"Oh, isn't that so cute!"* one said. *"How sweet,"* another laughed. *"Kiss, kiss, kiss,"* teased a third.

"I think I'm going to hurl, pookey bear," Mack said.

By four-thirty that afternoon, she had only slogged through a minute amount of the tower dump. At this rate, it would take her three months to listen to the entire thing. She removed the earphones and leaned back in the desk chair. There must be an easier and faster way to get this done. There must be some computer program that can search for keywords in a conversation.

She removed the disk from the computer, put it back in the sleeve and dropped it in her handbag. She went into Gus' office. *"I'm going to call it a day. I'll see you tomorrow."*

"Are you okay?" he asked.

"Just have an errand to run."

He nodded. *"See you tomorrow, then."*

Mack drove back to the bank before it closed and withdrew another fifteen hundred dollars from her savings account. She didn't care if she spent every cent of Sean's life insurance money. She was going to find the man that ended her family's lives.

She used her phone's GPS to find Sigurd's place again. She walked up to the gate. The buzzer immediately sounded, and she slipped inside. She looked around for cameras, but couldn't see any. As she walked to the front door, the razor wire at the top of the fence sliced holes in the afternoon sun.

He remotely unlocked the heavy front door as she approached it. She walked the maze of halls to the hidden door, which also opened on her approach. As she moved inside, the savory smell *of sautéed onions and garlic permeated her senses. Mack inhaled deeply, and a slight smile curled the corners of her mouth. "Hi," she said. "I hope it's okay for me to be here."*

"You're welcome here anytime."

"Thank you."

"How can I help you today?"

She handed him the disc and the envelope of money. "I'm hoping you can figure out a way to search through the tower dump for some keywords. If I have to listen to any more lovey-dovey mush, I'm going to need an insulin injection."

Sigurd tilted his head back and laughed. His face was worn around the edges, but when he laughed, she saw the hardness crumble. He took both items from her and walked over to his circle of equipment. "Pull up a chair. This will take a little while."

She sat in one of the four office chairs and rolled it next to him. He placed the disc in the drive and started typing on the computer keyboard. She watched code stream down the dual monitors faster than her eyes could track.

"What are the words you would like to search for?" he asked.

Mack glanced sideways at him and cleared her throat. "Kill. Shot. Murder. Hit. Take someone out. Gun. Nine millimeter. Nine nina." She spelled the last word for him.

Without pausing, Sigurd continued to type. "Okay. Now we let it run."

CHAPTER 14

First thing Monday morning, Mack and Nick discussed how they should proceed with the case. They agreed that they would spend the morning interviewing Alan's and Jack's teachers, Pastor Beck, and Nick's wife to see if any of them could add some insight into motive and suspects.

The two started at the high school. They figured that before the day began, teachers would be in their classrooms preparing. First, they met with the principal, Tom Martz.

Martz said, "As far as I know we've never had any issues with Alan Brown or Jack Caldwell. Every time I encountered them, they were respectful."

Mack asked, "What about Susan Brown? Any issues with her?"

Martz shook his head. "None that I know of. Sorry I can't be of more help."

With the principal's permission, they obtained a copy of Alan's and Jack's schedules, which turned out to be the same, except for one period. Mack said, "They must have liked each other a lot to spend all day together, then hang out outside of school too."

The boys' teachers were eager to help, but they all said pretty much the same thing. Alan and Jack were quiet, did all of their school work, never caused trouble, and didn't have a problem with anyone at school that they knew of.

Adam Ulrich, the boys' physical education teacher said, "Alan was quite a fast runner, and he had stamina, but he wasn't interested in track or any other sport. I spoke to him a couple of times to no avail. I thought the recognition might be a motivator for him, but he didn't care about that in the slightest." He shook his head. "Alan's sister Susan's the same way. With her long legs, she could be quite a long or high jumper, but again, she isn't interested."

Mack and Nick thanked him and walked to the counselor's office.

Cindy Mire said, "The school's policy is that in the case of a student's death, I'm allowed to divulge any information the student shared with me. But neither Alan nor Jack ever came to see me, so there isn't anything I can tell you."

~~~

As Nick drove, he said, "Rose is going to be royally pissed at me for not letting her know we're coming."

"Blame me. Tell her that I didn't want anyone we speak with today to be forewarned... which is true."

He grimaced. "She's still going to be unhappy with me."

Nick's home was a small bungalow, with a large veranda and well-manicured hedges in front. Mack smiled as they pulled up. "Very nice."

"It isn't grand, but it's home."

Rose was a petite, vivacious blonde. When Nick told her why they were there, she said, "I figured you'd be coming by sometime to talk to me. Would you like something to drink, Mack?" Rose pointed at her husband. "You can get your own."

Nick gave Mack an 'I-told-you-so' look.

She declined the offer and asked, "How did you and Patricia meet?"

"We met shortly after she moved here, at a school open house. I'd never seen her before, so I knew she was new. She looked a little uncomfortable and nervous, so I sat next to her and started chatting. Because our boys were the same age, we had that in common right away." Rose shrugged. "We made plans to meet for coffee the next day. Then she joined my book club. Pretty soon we were spending more and more time together."

"Was Patricia seeing anyone that you know of?"

"If she was, she never said anything to me. I never saw her with anyone, either."

"Was she having any issues with anyone?"

Rose was quiet for a moment, then shook her head. "I never saw her have a cross word with anyone. Patricia was a nice person. I don't know why anyone would want to hurt her."

~~~

Mack and Nick found Pastor Beck in the church office. Mack said, "We'd like to speak to you about Patricia Brown."

Pastor Beck smiled politely. "I'm sorry, but I can't help you. Even death does not absolve me from the duty that confidentiality places on me."

Walking back to where Nick had parked his sedan, Mack said, "That was the first piece of information we've received all morning."

His brow furrowed. "How do you figure?"

"Well, the Pastor told us that Patricia talked to him about something confidential. Let's go see Grace and see if she'll tell us what that something might be. And if it might have anything to do with why Patricia and the boys were murdered."

~~~

When Grace opened the door and saw Mack and Nick, she asked, "Have you found out something?"

He said, "We have some questions for you that might help us with that. Is this a good time?"

"The children are upstairs. I'm going to keep them out of school this week. Come in." After they all took seats in the living room, Grace asked, "How can I help?"

"We just saw Pastor Beck, and he suggested that Patricia had told him something in confidence," Mack said. "We were wondering if you can tell us what Patricia might have discussed with the pastor. Perhaps it was a motive for the murders."

Grace sat in silence for a few seconds. "I'm sorry, but there's nothing I can tell you that might have resulted in Patricia being killed."

The two thanked Grace as she walked them back to the door. Mack was quiet as Nick drove back to the police department.

"Want to share what's on your mind?" he asked.

"Grace said there was nothing that would help with a motive for the murders. She didn't say that Patricia wasn't keeping something secret."

"So, only three people know what the secret is… Patricia, Grace, and the Pastor."

"Grace thinks that only those three people know," Mack said. "That doesn't mean that someone else didn't find out. Someone Grace doesn't know about."

CHAPTER 15

Six Years Prior

Sigurd stood and went into the kitchen. Mack watched as he set two wine glasses, a corkscrew, and a bottle of red wine on the dining table. Then he filled two plates from the pot on the stove and shaved parmesan cheese on top. He set the plates and cutlery on the table also. "Please join me."

She felt trapped and uncomfortable.

"Please," he said. "We might as well do something while we're waiting."

She sat in the chair across from him. "I could smell this the minute I walked in. It smelled wonderful."

"I saw."

She looked up at him. His blue eyes seemed to look into her soul. She drank half of the glass of wine. Her head quickly started to buzz. She realized that she hadn't eaten anything since the one bite of food the evening before. She stuffed her mouth with the pasta in the hopes of clearing her head. She closed her eyes and savored the flavor combination of fresh mushrooms, tomatoes, and zucchini with ziti pasta. "This is delicious. Do you always cook like this for yourself?" She drank the rest of the wine in her glass. She liked the warm feeling that was spreading through her body.

Sigurd filled Mack's wine glass again. "I eat pretty much every meal here." He shrugged. "I got tired of eating sandwiches and frozen pizza, so I started cooking."

She ate more pasta and drank more wine. "Did you teach yourself to cook?"

"My mother was an excellent cook. She was from France. She taught me."

"Was your father Nordic?" Mack gestured to Sigurd's hair and beard, as she finished the second glass of wine.

He smiled his lopsided smile. *"Yes."* *He filled the wine glass again.*

Mack felt more relaxed than she had in many long weeks. She drank and ate some more. Finally, she leaned back in her chair and rubbed her stomach. "If I eat another bite, I'm going to pop."

Sigurd laughed.

She stood to clear the table and wobbled sideways. She knew she'd had too much, but she didn't care. I'm so very sick of feeling sad.

Sigurd reached out and took her arm to steady her. "Leave them. I'll get them tomorrow. Come. Sit on the couch." He led her to the coach and, holding her arms, gently lowered her onto it. She curled her legs under her and leaned back into the cushions.

"Wuut u like more vine?"

She looked up at him. "I know I shouldn't, but I would like some more."

Sigurd scraped the remaining pasta into a covered dish and slid it onto a shelf in the refrigerator. He removed a plate from inside, then selected a bottle of wine from the wine cooler. He set both on the coffee table in front of the couch, along with two fresh wine glasses.

Mack saw that the plate held chocolate dipped strawberries. She smiled. "You sure are a surprise."

"I hope the good kind."

She nodded.

He opened the wine, poured it into the two glasses, and handed one to her. She took a sip. It was smooth, and it slid easily down her throat. He held out the plate of strawberries. She picked up one and bit into it. She washed it down with the wine. The combination of flavors was sublime.

"Tell me how you came by the name Mack."

"My mother's from Scotland. The name Mackenzie is a family name." She shrugged.

"It suits you."

"A lot of people think it's weird."

He smiled. "Well, a lot of people are stupid."

She chuckled. "True." She looked around the room. "So, tell me about all this. Why the need for such security?"

"What I do, and who I do it for, requires secrecy. This provides it and allows me to make a good living doing something that I'm good at, and that I enjoy."

She ate another strawberry and sipped her wine. "How did you learn to do what you do?"

"I think it's something that can't be taught. A person either has it, or they don't. The basics of coding, script, and programming language can be taught. The ability cannot... That probably doesn't make sense."

"It does to me." Mack grinned. "But I'm a little drunk right now."

Sigurd laughed. They sat in companionable silence, eating strawberries and drinking wine.

~~~

Sean and Samantha lay on the concrete floor. Blood soaked the front of Sean's shirt. His vacant eyes stared at nothing. Samantha started crying. "Mommy. Mommy. Where are you, mommy?"

"You're okay. That was the past. You're okay."

The words slowly penetrated Mack's nightmare. She opened her eyes and saw Sigurd. She realized that she must have fallen asleep on the couch. He was sitting on the couch next to her, holding her hand. She sat up, threw her arms around his neck, and started sobbing. "I want it to stop. I want the pain to stop."

"The only way it will stop is if you go through it." He patted her on the back. "Now, go back to sleep. You're safe here."

Mack drifted back to sleep. When she awoke the next morning, she looked around and saw Sigurd at one of his computers. She watched him work for a few minutes. He must have felt her watching because he suddenly looked up.

He smiled. "Good morning."

"Morning."

He stood and went into the kitchen area. "How do you like your coffee?"

"Cream and sugar." She got off the couch and padded in her socks to the kitchen. She saw that he had washed the dishes from the night before. "I'm sorry. I meant to do the dishes."

"You can do them next time. You needed the rest."

"What time is it?"

"Ten-forty."

"Oh my God. I have to call Gus. I told him I'd be in the office early."

"I hope you do not mind. I phoned Gus and told him you were here safe with me." He shrugged. "Your phone kept ringing, and I saw that it was him. I knew he would be worried about you."

She blushed. "Oh... What he must think."

"I told him you brought the disc to me and that we are running a search program. I did not tell him that you came over last night. Besides, he knows me better than that."

She looked down into her coffee cup. "Thank you. And, thank you for last night."

"You are welcome. Now, let's see what that program found."

CHAPTER 16

When Mack and Nick walked into the bullpen, they saw that the numerous items they'd bagged at the Brown house were laid out on eight large folding tables. The tables were placed against the back and side walls of the room. A sign that denoted the rooms the items were collected from hung from the edge of each table. At the front of the bullpen were four large display boards. Copies of the crime scene photographs were adhered to them, again arranged by the rooms in the Browns' house. The four desks in the bullpen were pushed into the center of the room, facing each other.

Charlie looked up at them. "What do you think? Barbara borrowed all the tables and display boards from folks she knows around town. She even badgered people into delivering them."

"This is absolutely amazing," Mack said. "Thank you."

She went to the front lobby and thanked Barbara. "You have no idea how much that will simplify things."

"I'm glad. I'm happy to do anything I can to help find the evil person that killed those three people."

"I do have a question for you."

"Shoot."

"Do you know if Patricia had a boyfriend when she was in high school?"

"Hmmm, let me think a minute." She shook her head. "Not that I can recall. Sorry."

"It was a long shot anyway. I thought maybe Patricia had a spurned lover that might still hold a grudge."

In the bullpen, Mack walked around the room, looking at some of the items from the Browns' house. Then she walked over to the crime scene photographs and took her time studying each one.

She was so focused that she didn't hear Nick walk up behind her. "I'm going to the Browns to pack some of the kids' clothes and other things they might need. I'd appreciate it if you'd come along to pack up Susan's stuff. I don't think she'd appreciate a guy handling her underwear."

"I'd be happy to. I'll drive my vehicle and meet you over there. I have to get some actual dinner tonight before I go back to the bed and breakfast. I can't stand another dinner of nuts."

~~~

When Mack arrived at the Browns' house, Nick was already upstairs packing the boys' things. He said, "I'm using the suitcases that were in the garage. I put one in Susan's room for you."

"Thanks."

When they finished, he said, "Tonight's Rose's book club. I convinced her that she should go. And, Mark's out with his girlfriend. So, if you want company for dinner, I'm free."

"Sure. Eating alone isn't very appealing."

"Great. Follow me. We can drop these suitcases off at Grace's, then head to Bart's. It's one of my favorite places, and, like everything in this town, it's close by. I'll change out of my uniform in the restaurant's bathroom."

Bart's had a good selection of wine and beer and a variety of entrees. Mack ordered a glass of chardonnay and Nick ordered a beer.

After they ordered dinner, he said, "I wanted to apologize for being obnoxious to you when you first arrived. You didn't deserve that. I was angry that Chief Davis asked the state police for help. I felt like it was a slap in my face as the investigating officer in our department."

"I understand. No hard feelings."

"I believed that I could handle the Brown-Caldwell case on my own. But, to be honest, after working with you, I realize that this murder investigation's way over my head."

"I've worked with a lot of officers over the years. It's a pleasure to work with someone that's smart and well trained."

"Thanks. Appreciate you saying that." Nick changed the subject. "So, you mentioned you're seeing someone. Care to share?"

"His name's Evan, and we've only been seeing each other for about three months."

"How did you two meet?"

"We met at a park in Coeur d'Alene," Mack said. "We were both running, and we, literally, ran into each other as we went around a corner."

He laughed. "Seriously?"

She nodded. "Yep. I had a bunch of cuts on my hands and knees. Evan insisted on cleaning them up with water from his water bottle. Before I realized it, he'd convinced me to have dinner with him the next evening. He said it was so that he could properly apologize for knocking me down."

"Nice line."

"I know. I fell for it, though. I actually felt guilty that Evan felt so bad about running into me."

"Have you ever been married?" he asked.

"For a short time. To my high school sweetheart… But it ended." She changed the subject. "How long have you and Rose been married?"

"Thirteen years. We were high school sweethearts too. We've had some rocky times, but we've managed to stay together."

She nodded. "How long have you lived in Skaus Lake?"

"We've been here four years. When the Senior Officer position opened up here, Rose and I agreed it would be a good opportunity. We were living in Boise at the time, and I was working patrol. Rose got to where she worried, every day that I worked patrol. It was taking a toll on her and on our marriage. Mark hadn't started high school, so it seemed like the right move. Mark wasn't happy about leaving Boise and his friends. But he got over it. About the time he met his first girlfriend here." He chuckled.

The waiter brought their food, and they both concentrated on eating. She said, "I didn't realize how hungry I was." As they ate, they chatted about when the autopsy results might be in and when they should release the crime scene back to the family. After they finished eating, they both ordered coffee.

He asked, "What made you decide to become a police officer?"

"That's a long story that's going to have to wait for another time," Mack hedged. "I need to get back to the bed and breakfast so that I can send my daily report to my captain."

CHAPTER 17

Six Years Prior

Sigurd sat in one of the office chairs, pulled a second one up next to him, and motioned for Mack to sit. Then he typed away on the keyboard. "We have two matches to the keywords." He hit a button, and a clear voice came out of the speaker system next to the computer.

"Ernie. It's done. I took Danny out."

"Good. I'll let Uncle David know."

Sigurd looked at Mack. "Do you know who Danny was?"

"Four people were shot. One of them was Daniel Wood. That must be who they're talking about. And, now we know that the killer's first name is Luke. And, his uncle is in charge."

Sigurd nodded. "This is the second match." He struck a key, and the same two voices started talking.

"Ernie. What's up?"

"You fuckin' idiot! You shot three other people. And, one of them was a little girl!"

"Listen. I had to do it like that, man. Danny saw me following him. He ducked into that store. I had to get him there, or he could have got away, man."

"Well, Uncle David's pissed. He wants to see your dumb ass today. So, get the fuck over there now, Luke!"

"Okay, Ernie, okay. I'm goin' man."

When the recording ended, Sigurd looked at Mack and said, "I'll start a search for the three."

"Thank you. Again. For everything," she said. "I should get going."

He walked her to the door and watched her on the monitors until she drove away.

She drove to Gus' office and filled him in on the progress she'd made.

"That's great. Sigurd's one of the best out there."

"I came by to see if you got the autopsies."

"I did."

She inhaled deeply. "Okay. Go ahead. I'm ready."

He moved to the chair next to her and held her hand between both of his. "The shooter used a standard full metal jacket nine-millimeter round. The bullet passed through Sean's aortic cavity, killing him instantly. Because of the penetrative ability of the round, it then entered Samantha's chest cavity. She would have died instantly, also. Neither of them suffered. Neither of them would have known what was happening. Their deaths would have been peaceful."

She tried to be strong, but she couldn't hold back the tears. Wave after wave of grief and sorrow, mixed with relief, battered her. Gus held Mack in his arms until the storm of emotions inside her expended all of its energy.

CHAPTER 18

At the high school, Mack and Nick spoke to the principal, Tom Martz, again. There were twenty-eight sophomores in the school. She wanted to meet with each of them one at a time.

Martz agreed to arrange for the sophomores to come to the library. The students were pulled out of their classes and lunch, four at a time, in alphabetical order.

It took less than five minutes each to speak with the first thirteen students. All thirteen said they didn't know Alan or Jack, except by sight. Their classmates agreed that both Alan and Jack were shy and quiet. None of them saw Alan or Jack hang out with any other students. Some of the girls said that Alan was cute, but he didn't seem interested in any of the girls at school. One classmate said she'd seen Alan and Jack eating at First Avenue Pizzeria once.

The fourteenth student that they spoke with was obviously very nervous. Aaron Paul bounced his knee continually and fidgeted in his seat throughout the entire conversation. Aaron said, "My locker's close to Jack's, but we didn't talk much. You know, we just said 'hi' in the morning and stuff like that." Aaron glanced quickly at Nick, then back to Mack.

She asked, "Was Alan at Jack's locker a lot?"

Aaron nodded. "Yeah."

"Did you two talk at all?"

He shook his head. "Nope."

"Did you see anyone arguing with Jack or Alan ever?"

He shook his head again. "Nope."

"Ok, Aaron, thanks for your time. We appreciate your help."

When Aaron left, Mack asked, "You think he's just a nervous kid or was he nervous because of us?"

Nick shrugged. "Who the hell knows with teenagers."

Three more classmates didn't have anything to add. The next said he'd seen Alan and Jack twice at the Burger King drive-thru.

One of the last students they spoke with was Bethany Malory, whose locker was close to Alan's. In response to Mack's question, she said, "No, I never saw him arguing with anyone."

"Did you ever see him talking to anyone other than Jack?"

"No." She paused, then leaned toward Mack. "To tell you the truth, I thought they were a couple. You know… gay."

"Did you ever see any sign of physical affection between them? Did you see them touch or hug or put their arms around each other?"

She shrugged. "No."

"Do others in the school think Alan and Jack were partners?"

"Oh, for sure."

"Was that a problem for anyone in particular?"

"Maybe Toby Jackson," she said. "He's the football quarterback. The other football players kind of follow him around and parrot what he says. It's pathetic."

"Thanks, Bethany," Mack said. "We appreciate your honesty and willingness to talk to us."

As Mack and Nick were walking back to the front office, they saw Susan in the doorway of a classroom. Mack asked, "Who's that with Susan?"

"That's Victor Albinson, the science teacher here at the high school."

She stopped. "Susan looks uncomfortable to me. Something's going on." She walked up to the two. "Hi, Susan. I'm surprised to see you here. Your grandmother told me that you weren't coming to school this week."

Susan said, "I was just picking up homework so that I won't get too far behind."

Holding out her hand to Victor Albinson, Mack said, "We haven't met. I'm Detective Anderson."

Albinson smiled. "I was telling Susan that if she needs any help with her homework, to give me a call."

Susan quickly said, "I better get going. Nice to see you again."

Mack looked at Albinson but didn't say anything.

He couldn't hold eye contact. "Well, I have class."

After Albinson walked away, she said, "I don't like that guy. There's something off about him."

Nick said, "That's quite a scientific analysis, detective."

Mack chuckled. "Ouch, that hurts both of my feelings."

~~~

Back in Nick's sedan, he asked, "Where to now?"

"Let's go to First Avenue Pizzeria."

When they arrived at the pizzeria, Nick asked to see the manager. Fred Douglas was the owner and manager.

Mack said, "We understand that Alan Brown and Jack Caldwell ate here."

Fred nodded. "Yes. I was so sorry to hear about their deaths. It's such a shame. Those two boys were always polite to the servers, unlike some of the other young men that come in here. And, they were good tippers." He paused. "One of the servers is my daughter, Tina."

"Did you ever see Alan and Jack with anyone else?"

He shook his head. "Not that I recall."

"Ever hear them arguing with anyone on their cell phones?"

"No." He paused. "Sorry I can't be more help, but I'm usually in the back making pizza."

Mack and Nick shook hands with him and thanked him for his time.

When they were back inside the sedan, Mack asked, "You okay with going by to see Pastor Beck again? Put some pressure on?"

Nick grinned. "Fine by me."

The Pastor was not happy to see them. "As I told you yesterday. I cannot tell you what any of the Browns spoke to me about in confidence."

As they walked back to the vehicle, Mack said, "Pastor Beck said 'any of the Browns'. Makes me wonder if someone other than Patricia talked to him. And, if so, about what?"

CHAPTER 19

Six Years Prior

Mack walked into her apartment and found her mother and father sitting on the couch, waiting for her.

"What are you doing here? Are you guys okay?"

Aileen Raines jumped up and hugged Mack. "We were worried about you. We've been calling and texting you all day."

"I'm sorry. I've been busy."

"That's good," Kevin Raines said. "Keeping busy is good. What have you been busy doing?"

She studied her mother and father for a minute and decided she should be honest with them. "I'm searching for the murderer."

"Jesus, Mary, and Joseph!" Aileen exclaimed.

"Mackenzie, that could be dangerous," her father said.

"I'll be fine. Don't worry."

A tear rolled down Aileen's cheek. "I've already lost my granddaughter. I can't lose my daughter too."

"I have to do this. The police have stopped looking… if they ever actually were. I met a private investigator, and he's helping me."

"A private investigator? Can you trust him?" Kevin asked.

"He used to be a police officer. He's a good guy."

"Well, your color's better than it's been," Aileen said. "But please be careful."

"I will be. I promise. Listen. I think you two should go back to Scotland. It's been over three weeks. You can't stay in a hotel forever. I'm doing better. Honest."

"Are you sure?" Aileen asked.

"I want you to go. I'd feel better knowing that you're back home."

"Okay, sweetie," Aileen said. She kissed Mack on the cheek.

"I love you both."

Looking out the living room window, she watched her parents leave. She didn't go to the door and wave goodbye. She couldn't bear to ever do that from this apartment again.

With that thought, Mack knew what she needed to do next. She fished around in her handbag for her cell phone. As she was looking for it, she found the envelope with the fifteen hundred dollars that she'd given to Sigurd last night. On the front, he'd written 'The pleasure of your company is payment enough.'

She found the number for the apartment complex in her contact list and hit the call icon. "Hi. This is Mackenzie Anderson. I'm calling to give you my notice. I'll be moving out at the end of the month."

"Oh. Well. That's only a few days away. We normally require at least a two-week notice. But in this case, I think we can make an exception. We will need your notice in writing, however," the woman on the other end said.

"Thank you. I'll get you that letter today."

She took a shower and changed clothes.

Then she went into the dining room, which was set up as an office/study area and typed her notice letter. She printed and signed it, put it in an envelope, and drove it over to the complex's office. Next, she drove to the nearest moving supply store and bought boxes and tape.

~~~

Mack searched the internet and found a local moving company. She arranged for them to pick up everything in the apartment on Monday morning, and deliver it to the donation center for a battered woman's home in town.

With a new resolve, she started the packing process in Sean's half of their closet. She took his clothes off of the hangers, folded *them, and loaded them into boxes. Shirts, pants, sweatshirts, and jackets. She hesitated as she took Sean's favorite black leather jacket off of the hanger. She'd given it to him for their first anniversary. Holding it up to her nose, she inhaled. It smelled like Sean. Tears filled her eyes. She hung the jacket back in the closet, pushing it to her side.*

Mack took the bedding off of the bed that she and Sean had made love in so many times. She wiped her eyes with a tissue, as she folded and packed the memories away.

She loaded all of his bathroom items into garbage bags and hauled them to the apartment complex's dumpsters.

When she finished in the bathroom, she started on the office/study area. She packed all of the college books that they'd accumulated over the past two years. She would have the moving company take the books to the campus bookstore.

Her cell phone beeped, alerting her that she had a text. She read it. "Have identity of brothers and uncle."

Mack checked the time on her phone and saw that it was five-thirty. She took Sean's jacket out of the closet, put it on, and drove straight to Sigurd's.

CHAPTER 20

A copy of the death certificates, investigator's reports, and autopsy reports for the three victims arrived by courier on Tuesday morning. Mack took out her spiral notepad and quickly read through the death certificates and investigator's reports. Then she laid the three autopsies side by side and carefully compared each section of the three reports.

The autopsies started with the identification of the victims and a general description of the victims clothing and personal effects. Nick was sitting at his desk, across from her. As she read, she relayed the highlights, "No phone on Alan… The victims weren't sexually assaulted."

The next sections of the autopsies detailed external and internal examinations and toxicology tests. The external examinations included measurements of all wounds, and the internal examinations included an assessment of wound tracts Patricia had twelve stab wounds to her chest and abdomen. The surface injuries were one and a half inches wide, with smooth edges. The depth of penetration into the body was between five and three-quarters inches to seven inches, resulting in damage to specific body organs. Alan had the same number and type of stab wounds.

She said, "Whoever the murderer was, he exhibited extreme rage toward Patricia and Alan. Jack Caldwell had one incised wound on the neck that transected the left and right common carotid arteries. The victims were all lying on their backs when they were bludgeoned and stabbed. None of the three victims had any defensive wounds on them. Additionally, there was an absence of both DNA under the victims' fingernails and abrasions on the victims' wrists and ankles where they were bound with the duct tape. The victims didn't struggle."

Toxicology findings showed no directly contributing drug toxicity. "Drugging and poisoning of victims weren't detected."

Patricia's toxicology report showed that she had therapeutic levels of two psychotropic medications. An antidepressant, and an antianxiety agent. Mack stood and walked over to the bag of medications from Patricia's bathroom. She asked, "Do you know a local psychiatrist named Dr. Eli Donaldson?"

Nick shook his head. "Not that I can think of. Why?"

"Both medications Patricia was taking were issued by him."

One latent fingerprint was found on Alan's left shoe. It didn't match any of the victims' fingerprints. She said, "Got a fingerprint we need to run through AFIS."

"Excellent. I'll do it right now." He ran the latent fingerprint through AFIS, the Automated Fingerprint Identification System. The computer database compared the unknown fingerprint against a database of prints. Within minutes he said, "No luck. Didn't get any matches."

"Maybe it's from a sales clerk or store associate. His shoes looked fairly new." Charlie was sitting at his desk, listening to Mack and Nick talk. She asked, "Charlie, can you look through the credit card statements we collected from Patricia's desk and see if there's a charge for Alan's tennis shoes?"

"Glad to."

Mack continued reading the autopsies. "Trace evidence collected from the duct tape on the three victims contained fibers from the victims' clothing and some dust, but no unidentified DNA or fingerprints were present. Trace evidence from the three victims' clothing included unidentified black cotton fibers." She paused. "Could be from the hoodie that Ethan said the man he saw in the house was wearing. Assuming that man was the actual murderer."

Nick said, "Dave didn't find any discarded bloody clothes. So, I guess the murderer isn't stupid enough to just toss them."

"The perp was between five-feet-ten and six-feet-two-inches in height and was right-handed. Weight was between one hundred sixty and two hundred."

He scowled. "Well, that leaves out Charlie. But pretty much every other guy in town fits that description."

"The cause of death was organ failure as a result of incised wounds. The knife found at the Browns' house matched the victims' wounds. The only fingerprints on the murder weapon belonged to Patricia, Susan, and Alan. The time of death was determined to be between three and six that Saturday morning. The manner of death was homicide."

Charlie said, "Most definitely."

The warrant for the Browns' landline was granted, and the phone company supplied a list of calls. Nick studied the list. When Mack finished reading the reports, she asked, "Anything on the landline?"

"Looks like Tom and Will used it to call friends and vice versa. There were a few of the same numbers as on Patricia's cell phone. Nothing to indicate Susan or Alan used the landline for any calls."

She leaned back, thinking. "Where's Alan's cell phone and where are Patricia's and Susan's laptops? Did the murderer take them? If so, is there something on them that the murderer didn't want anyone to see? Or, did he take them to sell them?"

"Alan's phone hasn't been used since the murders, and no pawnbrokers have notified us that they've received any of the items," Nick said. "Guess there's not much else we can do on that front."

When her cell phone rang, she saw that it was the County Medical Examiner's Office. She answered, and Oliver Cooper asked, "How do the autopsies look to you?"

"They're pretty cut and dried. Results are consistent with the medium velocity impact spatter that I saw at the crime scene."

"The Caldwells are pushing us to release their son's body," Oliver said. "Do you have any objection to us releasing the bodies to the mortuaries the families have specified?"

"None that I can think of."

"Great. Talk soon."

When she disconnected, Charlie said, "Found the charge for the shoes. They were bought online two weeks ago."

Nick rubbed his forehead. "We've got nothing to go on so far. Now what?"

"We keep looking," Mack said. "Let's go back to the high school and talk to Alan's and Jack's classmates. See if any of them can give us something."

CHAPTER 21

Six Years Prior

The inside of Sigurd's place smelled heavenly again. Mack inhaled deeply and smiled.

He handed her a glass of white wine and motioned for her to sit on the couch. He sat next to her. "The brothers are Lucas Adler, aged twenty-eight and Ernest Adler, aged thirty-two. The man Luke was actually after was Daniel Wyman, aged twenty-four. The Uncle David that Ernie referred to in the phone conversations we listened to is David Ridley. David is the Adler's uncle. Their father was shot when they were young, and Ridley took them in. Federal agents, the Boise police, and the U.S. Attorneys' Office have been trying to federally indict Ridley for drug trafficking. But, so far, they haven't been able to get enough evidence on him."

"You must be wondering why I'm doing this."

"I knew you would tell me when you're ready."

She sipped wine and told him the entire story, from when Sean and Samantha walked out of the apartment to when she met Gus at the police station.

"I understand how devastating loss like that can be and what it does to the people left behind. My wife and son were killed in a car crash eleven years ago. They were hit by a drunk driver."

"I'm so sorry."

"When they died I started drifting. Going from place to place. I was completely detached from everything and everyone. Then one day I met Gus. Did you know that his wife of forty-four years, their grown daughter, and her two children were killed in a car wreck?"

"No. He never mentioned it to me."

"Gus has been through what I went through and what you are going through now. He had made it to the other side when I met him. He showed me that if I kept traveling down the road, I was

on I would end up dying to the world. You have seen that type of person. They sleep alone in doorways and eat out of dumpsters."

She told him her plan. "I gave notice at my apartment complex. Monday's my last day there. I can't be there with all of Sean's and Samantha's things. I'm giving everything except some of my clothes to charity."

"I walked away from the house we lived in and all of our things. I wish now that I had kept at least one thing of theirs." His brow furrowed. "Where will you live?"

"I thought I'd ask Gus if I could live at his office for a while. There's a bathroom, kitchen of sorts, and a couch. I don't need anything more."

"When the time is right, you'll know what's right. Until then, don't make too many major decisions."

"Okay."

" Now. Let's eat. I'm starving."

"I feel bad about inserting myself into your life like this."

"I want you here. Do you want to be here?"

She nodded her head.

"Good. Then stop thinking and just be. Now, bring your wine glass and come sit at the table and eat."

Sigurd served homemade soup, with a thinly sliced baguette on top. "This is Normandy-style French onion soup," he said.

She realized that she was actually hungry. Having some feeling other than heartache in her body was nice. "Did you grow up in Norway?"

"We split our time between Norway and France."

"What parts?"

"In Norway, we had a home in the northernmost city of Tromsø. In France, we had a home in Paris."

"Wow. Those two can't be more different."

"Yes. But I grew up going back and forth between the two. So, I never thought anything of it."

"So, do you speak Norwegian and French?"

"Ja. Oui. Yes."

Mack chuckled.

"My mother's native language is French. My father's is Norwegian. The language they have in common is English. So, I grew up with all three being spoken in our home." Sigurd grinned. "Neither of my parents speaks the other's native language. When they had a disagreement, I was the only one that could understand everything being said. My father would say things about my mother and vice versa. It was humorous." He paused. "What about you?"

"My mother speaks Scottish Gaelic. But my father doesn't, so the only time she speaks Gaelic is when she's with her side of the family. I learned it as a child, but the only time I get to practice is when I'm in Scotland. I think it would be wonderful to be able to speak three languages."

"Again. For me, it is normal."

"Do you have any siblings?"

"No. I'm an only child. My parents wanted it that way. You?"

"I'm an only child, also. My mom couldn't have any other children. She would have liked a large family. I think that's one of the reasons she wanted to move home to Scotland. She has a lot of relatives there."

He cleared the soup bowls and served a watercress and ricotta torte, warm from the oven.

She ate two pieces. "That was so good. Thank you."

He smiled and started clearing the table.

"Please. Let me. It's the least I can do."

"I'll get dessert," he said.

Mack cleared the table, rinsed the dishes, and loaded them into the dishwasher.

93

Sigurd set two bowls of chocolate mousse, spoons, wine glasses, and a bottle of red wine on the coffee table. He tapped a few keys on one of his keyboards and music started playing.

She sat on the couch. "Oh. Yummy. In my opinion, chocolate should be a food group."

He laughed.

They ate in silence, listening to the instrumental music.

"What's this music?" she asked.

"Gudbrandsdalen. Norwegian Folk Music. My father played the Hardanger fiddle, so this type of music always filled our home."

"I like it. It's... I don't know... happy."

"Yes, it is. It reminds me of my home growing up."

"Do you miss it?"

"I've started to... in the last year or so."

They sat and listened to the lilting music for a while.

She cleaned up the dessert dishes. When she finished, she said, "I better go."

"You are welcome to sleep on the couch again. You won't be able to sleep in your apartment. And, your brain and body need rest." He walked over to a cabinet by his bed and removed a pillow and blanket. He laid both on the couch. "I'm pretty sure I have a toothbrush that you can use." Sigurd went into the bathroom and returned with a new toothbrush and handed it to her. "There's toothpaste in the top drawer."

Mack desperately did not want to go back to the apartment, so she accepted the toothbrush with a small smile.

CHAPTER 22

Mack and Nick parted in the police department parking lot. Nick was heading home. Mack drove straight to the bed and breakfast.

After changing into sweats, she called First Avenue Pizzeria and ordered a small pepperoni pizza and house salad for delivery. She wrote up her daily summary and sent it to her captain. When the pizza arrived, she took it and a glass of Pinot Grigio out onto the patio.

A half-moon cast its light across the peaks and crags of the mountains. A million stars twinkled brightly in the sky.

She sighed as she took her first sip of wine, releasing the tension of the day.

After she finished eating, she sat at the desk and added to her nightly information on the victims and their family and friends. She added additional unanswered questions that she had. To her question of motive, she added 'possible hate crime'.

She liked to have a hard copy of each page that she developed on a case. The questions, the people involved, and the evidence. Often, as she studied them, she would see something she'd missed. *I should have taken my laptop to the police department and printed these off.*

It was nine-fifteen. She hoped it was not too late. She took an unopened bottle of wine and her laptop downstairs in search of Elaine and a printer. Mack found her in the kitchen, prepping tomorrow's breakfast.

Seeing the wine bottle in Mack's hand, Elaine said, "I hope you're here to share that."

Mack held up the laptop. "I was hoping I could trade you wine for the use of a printer."

"Of course," she said, "As long as you'll help me drink the wine."

Elaine showed her where the printer was. After Mack printed everything she needed, she went back to the kitchen. Elaine opened the wine and poured two glasses. They took the wine out to the back enclosed patio, where a fire was crackling. Mack and Elaine settled into two overstuffed chairs in front of it.

Elaine sighed. "Oh, that feels good."

"Do you have many guests right now?"

"I have one unfilled room out of seven," she said. "That's fairly normal for this time of year."

"How long have you had the bed and breakfast?"

"A little over twelve years. I opened it when my husband died. I needed to do something other than sitting around and being sad. This place has been perfect for me. I love meeting different people from different places. I even have repeat customers that I've become good friends with. I don't have children of my own, so it's been nice for me to watch their children grow up over the years."

Mack nodded. "That sounds nice." She paused. "Do you have other siblings besides Barbara?"

"No, it's just the two of us," she said. "You know, Barbara's been working at the police department for over forty years. She lives for that place."

"One of the officers told me that the love of Barbara's life was killed in Vietnam. That must have been devastating for her."

Elaine filled up their wine glasses. "His name was Pete Elgin. He was eighteen, and he enlisted in the Marine Corps. Pete and Barbara were planning to get married when he got back. Of course, that never happened. I didn't think Barbara would ever come out of the blackness." She took a large drink of wine. "When she did stop being depressed, she switched to being angry."

"Was she angry at Pete for enlisting?"

Elaine leaned at Mack. "No. She directed all her anger at Al Franke. Al was Pete's history teacher, and he's the one that convinced Pete to enlist. Al told Pete about all the benefits Pete would have when he got home. Pete wanted those benefits for the family he and Barbara planned on having. Al also told Pete that since the war was winding down, he probably wouldn't see any action."

"Was Al Franke related to Grace Franke?"

"He was her husband," she said. "And Barbara directed her anger at Grace as well."

Mack noticed that Elaine was beginning to slur her words a little. "Why was Barbara angry at Grace?"

"Well, Barbara said that if she didn't get to be happily married, then Al's wife shouldn't get to be happy either. It was completely illogical, but Barbara didn't see it that way. To make things worse, Grace was pregnant with Patricia at the time. All Barbara could see was how the Frankes were living the life she never would have. She hated them with a passion."

"It must have been hard for you too, seeing your sister suffer like that."

"It tore me up. Especially since I didn't know how to help her." She shrugged. "As they say. Time heals all."

Mack stood. "Well, I'm sorry to say it, but I better get back to work. Thank you for letting me use your printer."

When she was back in her room, she added 'Barbara Miller's hatred toward the Franke family' to her motive page.

CHAPTER 23

Six Years Prior

Mack slowly walked to the door of Samantha's room. She left it until last because she knew it would be the hardest room to pack. Stepping inside, tears immediately filled her eyes.

As she packed the little clothes, the tears rolled down her face. She kept Samantha's favorite pair of pink booties with hearts on them. When she first got the booties, she hadn't wanted to take them off. She'd even worn them to bed that first night.

Mack sat on the floor in the room and thought of the birthdays that her daughter would never see. She would never have a first kiss, or get married, or know the joy of having her own child. As she sat there, sadness was replaced by anger. Her anger grew and grew. With a new resolve, she packed Samantha's booties in tissue paper, then put them into the one small rolling suitcase that she would take with her.

She selected the clothes she would take with her and packed the rest in boxes. She kept three pairs of jeans, two long-sleeved shirts, two short-sleeved t-shirts, and two zip-up sweatshirts. She kept one pair of sandals, her hiking boots, and one large handbag. The only jacket she kept was Sean's.

In the bathroom, she packed a small travel bag with the basics of her toiletries. The rest went into the garbage.

She walked around the apartment wondering what her future would be like. She locked the front door behind her and put the suitcase on the back seat of the car.

~~~

Using her phone, Mack searched the internet for the address she was looking for. When she arrived, she took a deep breath and went inside.

The man at the counter asked, "How can I help you today, young lady?"

"I'm looking for a handgun. I've never owned one before, so I'd like to hear your recommendation."

"Are you going to use it for personal protection?"

"Yes." She didn't tell him her real intention.

"I recommend a Glock 19 Gen 4. It has a modular grip for smaller hands, a dual recoil spring for less kick, and a fifteen round mag. It's light and small."

"Okay. I'll take it."

The man raised his eyebrows. He pulled the handgun out of the display case and placed it and two boxes of ammo on the counter. "You know how to use one of these?"

She shook her head. "No idea."

"We have classes. Group and personal."

"Thanks. I'll keep that in mind."

The man gave her the forms she needed to fill out. While she did that he totaled up the gun and ammo.

Mack paid him. She stored the handgun and ammo inside the suitcase in her car. Then she drove to Sigurd's.

CHAPTER 24

After Mack's daily run the next morning, she showered and went down to the breakfast room.

Elaine came over to her table and served her coffee. She laughed. "I think I drank too much wine last night. My head was a little sore when I woke up. But I certainly enjoyed talking to you. The evenings are when I get lonely around here."

After eating, Mack drove to the crime scene before going to the police department. She needed to release the crime scene so that the Brown children could have access to the rest of their belongings. But she wanted one more look first.

She took a pair of latex gloves out of her pants pocket and put them on. She went inside the Browns' house and sat on the couch for a few minutes. She closed her eyes and tried to picture the murder playing out. Then she got up and started going through each room again. She looked for possible hiding places and difficult access areas that she and Nick may have overlooked in their first search.

In the bedrooms, she pulled dressers, nightstands, and desks out from the walls and looked at the back of them for something that might have been hidden. She removed all the drawers and looked at the backs and bottoms. Then she did the same with every item of furniture downstairs. She found absolutely nothing.

After she finished, she looked around the house and wondered who would ever live in it again. It was undoubtedly a beautiful house. But it felt tainted by ugliness now.

~~~

When Mack walked into the bullpen at the police department, Nick said, "There you are. I was just going to call to make sure you were alright."

She smiled. "Thanks. I appreciate the concern. I went back to the crime scene, to make sure we hadn't missed something."

"Find anything?"

She shook her head. "Nothing. We can release it."

"I'll call a cleaning service. Then I'll let Grace know that they can get in."

"That's nice of you."

"I have my moments."

"Moment," Mack said with a straight face.

"Huh?"

"One. Singular. Moment… not moments."

"Oh. You're hilarious." Nick grinned. "Seriously though, Grace doesn't need anything else on her plate right now. She set up the memorial service and burial for Friday morning at ten." Nick rubbed his hand down his face. "Jeez, burying her only daughter and a grandson. I can't imagine."

"Do you know when Jack's memorial is?"

"Friday at one o'clock. The high school canceled classes that day so all the teachers and students can attend."

"I thought I'd go to the services." She shrugged. "See who's hanging around. You going?"

"Yes. With Rose."

"We need to talk." She motioned with her head. "Outside."

In the back parking lot, Nick asked, "What's with all the cloak and dagger stuff?"

Mack told him about her conversation with Elaine the night before.

He rubbed his forehead. "No way. No way Barbara could be a murderer."

"Look, I don't want to believe it either. But we have to add her to the suspect list. We need to talk to her and find out if she by any chance has an alibi for early Saturday morning." She paused. "If you want, I can talk to her by myself. You don't have to be there."

He shook his head. "Damn. No, I should be there."

~~~

Barbara was confused about why she was in the interview room.

Nick set up the tape recorder. "We need to record this."

Barbara looked back and forth between the two. "What the hell's going on?"

"I understand that when Pete Elgin was killed in Vietnam, you blamed Al Franke," Mack said. "You were angry that the Franke family was alive and happy and having a daughter, while you lost the person you loved."

"Are you friggin kidding me? You actually think I waited forty years, then killed Patricia and Alan because they were part of the Franke family?"

"Barbara, you've worked for the police for forty years. You know we have to ask. Can you please tell us where you were this past Saturday morning before seven?"

"I was at home asleep. I went to bed at nine-thirty. And before you ask. No. Nobody else was there. So, I don't have an alibi." Barbara looked at Nick. "You know me. You know I didn't murder anyone. I couldn't."

"I'm sorry," he said. "But you know we can't ignore this."

"So, until you find the real murderer, I'm a suspect?"

Mack said, "We have to look at all possibilities."

Barbara sneered at Mack as she left the interview room. "This is such bullshit."

Chief Davis came stomping into the bullpen a few minutes later. "What the hell are you thinking?! I convinced Barbara not to quit just now, but she has good reason to be angry!"

Mack stood from her desk chair. "Captain. This is the unbiased investigation you wanted, and... frankly, need."

Davis bowed his head and took a deep breath. "You're right. I know you are, but I don't like it one bit."

102

CHAPTER 25

Six Years Prior

"Mommy? Mommy? Where are you, mommy?" Mack jerked awake and sat straight up. She was confused for a second about where she was. Sigurd was sitting on the edge of the couch.

"Same nightmare?"

She nodded. *"A version of the same one every night. I'm sorry I woke you."*

"You want to tell me about it?"

"Samantha's always calling for me. Asking where I am." Tears ran down her face. *"Why didn't I go with them? Sean wanted me to, but I said no. If I'd gone, Samantha wouldn't have died without me."*

He put one arm around her shoulders. She rested her head on his chest. *"It's called survivor's guilt. We have all felt it. But here is the bare fact. If you had gone with them, then you would be dead, too."*

"I know I'm not supposed to think this, but I don't want to be alive if they're not."

"It's perfectly natural to feel that way. Again, all of us survivors think that at one time or another. But you are alive. That is another fact. And someday, you'll figure out a purpose for that life. I promise you. Now, go back to sleep. I'll stay here until you fall asleep."

Mack savored the safe feeling that enveloped her as she drifted off to sleep. When she woke the next morning, Sigurd was still asleep. He was lying on his back. He'd kicked off all of the covers. She saw that he didn't have a shirt on.

He turned his head and looked at her. *"Good morning. Coffee?"*

"Please."

He rolled out of bed and walked into the bathroom. She tried to covertly watch him go. She'd never seen his back before. Two *large blue wings stretched from one shoulder to the other. In the middle of the wings was a red heart.*

After he finished in the bathroom, she took a turn. When she came out, she folded up her bedding and put it back in the cabinet. He handed her a large mug. He pushed the cream and sugar toward her. They took their coffee to the couch.

"Now that you know the identity of the murderer, what are you going to do?"

"I'm not sure. I can't exactly walk into the police department and say that I know who the guy is. I guess I could watch him and try to catch him doing something else illegal. If I had enough evidence, I could go to the police with it." She shrugged. "What do you think?"

"We can track him through his cell phone. I'll get the trace started."

"I need to finish packing the apartment. I want to finish today so that I don't have to spend any more time there than absolutely necessary."

"Do you want help?"

"Thank you. But this is something I need to do myself."

"Okay. Come back tonight. I would feel much better if you were here, instead of at Gus' office. Plus, I enjoy the company, and there's no sense in you being alone right now."

"I'd like that. Thank you." Mack put her shoes on, gathered her things, and left.

Sigurd watched her on the monitors until she drove out of sight.

CHAPTER 26

After Davis left the bullpen, Mack said, "I want to go back to the high school and talk to that nervous kid, Aaron Paul. And to the quarterback, Toby Jackson. You up for it?"

Nick nodded. "Better than sitting here and having Barbara glare at me."

They drove in silence to the high school. The principal didn't seem pleased to see them again. "I thought you'd interviewed all of the students?"

Nick said, "We need to follow up with two students." He gave the receptionist the two names. She looked up their schedules on her computer, jotted it down on a piece of paper, and handed it to Martz.

The principal escorted them to Aaron Paul's class. He knocked on the door and stepped inside. "Please excuse the intrusion. Aaron, come with me."

Mack thought that the kid was going to wet his pants as he walked out of class and saw them. Martz led the three to the library.

"We wanted to talk to you again because you seemed very nervous yesterday," Mack said. "We thought you might have something else to tell us."

"Like... like what?"

"Anything you might have been afraid to tell us before."

"No... No." He picked at the hair on his arm. "There isn't anything."

"Is there a reason why you're so nervous?"

"I... I get nervous around police." He looked at Nick. "My brother was arrested at the last place we lived. So, I get nervous."

Mack asked, "What's your brother's name?"

"Ricky."

"What did Ricky get arrested for?"

"Uh. He was speeding. He got pulled over, and he had some pot on him." Aaron shrugged. "He got a year and a hundred hours of community service."

"Are you sure that's all?" she asked. "That's why you're so nervous? Because of your brother? Nothing else?"

He shook his head. "No. Nothing else."

She sat back in her chair. "You can go back to class. Thanks for speaking with us again."

After Aaron walked out of the room, Mack said, "When we get back to the department, let's check out his story about his brother."

Martz pulled the quarterback, Toby Jackson, out of class next and brought him to the library.

Toby smirked and slumped into a chair. "What can I do for you?"

Mack said, "It's come to our attention that you thought Alan Brown and Jack Caldwell were gay. And that you had a problem with that."

He sat up and squinted his eyes. "Who told you that?"

"That's not relevant," she said. "Did you think that Alan and Jack were gay?"

He sneered. "Yeah. So what? That's not a crime, is it?"

"Of course not. It's routine for us to follow up like this." She paused. "Did you have a problem with them being gay?"

He tilted his chin up. "Yeah, I had a problem with them. It's not natural."

"Did you ever tell Alan or Jack how you felt?"

He sat back in his seat and crossed his arms over his chest. "No. And I didn't have anything to do with those two queers getting killed." He sat forward and smiled. "I can prove it, too. I was with my girlfriend at her house all night. Her parents were out of town."

"What's your girlfriend's name?"

"Abby Garrett. She's in our class. Ask her. She'll tell you."

"We will. Thanks for talking with us again."

Mack and Nick went back to the front office and told the principal that they needed to see Abby Garrett. They walked to her class, and Martz called her out into the hall.

"We just need to ask you a quick question," Mack said. "Were you with Toby Friday night and Saturday morning?"

Abby looked at the floor. "Yeah. He came over and spent the night Friday because my parents were out of town." She looked up. "You won't tell them, will you?"

Mack shook her head. "Don't worry. We don't need to tell them."

Abby sighed loudly. "Thanks."

"What time did Toby leave your house on Saturday?"

"He left around noon."

"Were you with him the whole time? He never left your house?"

"We were in bed together the whole night and all morning."

"Thank you, Abby," Nick said. "We appreciate your time."

Walking back to the sedan, Mack said, "I may not like Toby, but at least we can eliminate him as a suspect."

~~~

When they arrived at the police department, Chief Davis was waiting for them. He tapped his foot. "I got a call from Toby Jackson's parents. They said that if you want to talk to their son again, you're not to do it without his attorney present." Davis handed Mack a slip of paper. "Here's the attorney's name and number."

She flopped down onto her desk chair. "Ah, spreading good cheer everywhere." She sat back and looked at the ceiling.

Pushing with her feet, she started slowly turning the chair in circles.

Nick typed on the computer keyboard for a minute. "Aaron Paul's story about his brother's arrest checks out. So, maybe that's really why he's so nervous around us."

She stopped turning and shook her head. "I think there's something he's not telling us."

"Any idea what?"

She started the chair turning again. "Not a clue."

He raised his eyebrows. "And here I thought you were supposed to be this great detective."

As she came around to face him, she said, "You got anything better, Mr. Senior Officer?"

He chuckled. "Well… on that note, I'm going home. Where there are people that love me. See you tomorrow." He left by the back door.

Mack said, "I used to have people at home that loved me."

CHAPTER 27

Six Years Prior

Sigurd took Mack's suitcase from her. "How was packing?"

"It was rough. But I made it through." She looked at the suitcase. "Everything I have in the world's in there."

"Not everything. You have your parents, and Gus, and me."

She nodded. "I'm thankful for all of you."

He set the suitcase next to the couch. "I'm going to finish dinner. Want to help?"

"What can I do?"

"I thought I would make Fårikål, which is the national dish of Norway and my father's favorite."

She chopped cabbage, peeled potatoes, and watched Sigurd. He was utterly confident as he worked in the kitchen. She was sure that he'd be confident of himself anywhere.

After the two finished eating and did the dishes, they sat on the couch and sipped Grappa.

"Luke Adler's phone is nowhere to be found," he said. "The last time it was used was the call from his brother. The one we listened to."

"Any theories?"

"If I had to guess, I would say that his uncle made arrangements for him to disappear." Sigurd shrugged. "That is what I would have done."

"How the hell do I find him?"

"His brother's phone is still active. They might keep in touch. We can keep listening to his conversations. Also, Ernie might go to see his brother."

"So, I need to follow Ernie."

Sigurd looked into Mack's eyes.

"What?"

"Do you want to tell me what you're planning?"

She sighed and told him about the handgun that she'd bought.

"I've been where you are. And I know how you feel. The drunk driver that killed my wife and daughter got twelve months for involuntary manslaughter. Two people were killed, and his punishment was twelve whole months. I planned to go back to New York after he got out and kill him. Meeting Gus is the reason I didn't. And, why I'm not in prison or dead right now."

"How's that?"

"Gus showed me that if I wanted to be free, all I needed to do was let go."

"I can't let go. Hatred of that man is the only thing keeping me going right now."

"These men are dangerous. If you're going to do this, then I'm going with you."

She shook her head. "Absolutely not. I'm not going to involve you any more than I have already. Or take up any more of your time. You have a business to run."

"You're not even slightly qualified to be out there on your own. I'm going with you. End of discussion. Tomorrow, I'll teach you how to use that gun you bought."

Mack hated to admit it, but she was relieved. "Thank you." She signed. "I feel like I keep saying that to you. And, saying it so inadequately expresses my appreciation for all that you've done for me."

"I am just happy to know you. Sorrow is a razor that cuts the heart to shreds. I have laughed more since meeting you than I have in years. So, I thank you."

CHAPTER 28

When Mack arrived at the bed and breakfast later that evening, she found Elaine waiting for her at the front door. "Did you intentionally get me a little drunk last night so that you could get information about my sister out of me?"

"I'm sorry. I assure you that was not my intention."

"Well. Nevertheless. That's what happened." She paused. "You can stay here tonight, but I want you to check out tomorrow morning after breakfast. You're not welcome here anymore."

Mack nodded. "I understand."

Upstairs in her room, she set her Glock on the bedside table. Then she emptied the rest of the wine into a paper cup and took it out onto the balcony. Sitting on a patio chair, she looked at the beautiful snowcapped peaks. *I hate that I've alienated two seemingly wonderful women. I just don't believe that Barbara could kill anyone. But hell, I've been wrong about people before.* Mack's cell phone rang. She looked at the screen and saw that it was Evan. She groaned. *I'm not up for conversation right now.*

"Hi. Are you okay? You sound down," he said when she answered.

"I'll be looking for a new place to stay tomorrow morning." She explained the generalities of what had happened.

"You know you did the right thing."

"I know." She sighed. "I'll be fine."

"What are you doing until you go to sleep? I hope you'll take a mental break and not work."

"I owe the Browns and Caldwells more than that."

"I figured." He paused. "Talk to you soon."

For the next two and a half hours, Mack typed up her daily summary and looked through the pages she'd printed the night before. She was surprised when there was a knock on the door. Mack grabbed her Glock, hid it behind her leg, and opened the door. "Evan? What are you doing here? I told you I don't have time for you to visit."

His arms were loaded with two insulated bags and a wine bag. He set the bags on the glass coffee table in the lounge area. Then he started unpacking the insulated bags, which Mack saw contained food from one of her favorite restaurants in Coeur d'Alene. "I know you didn't eat tonight," Evan said. "And, I know you're going to be in Skaus Lake awhile, so I brought you more wine."

"I'm working. I don't have time for this."

"I know. But I couldn't stand thinking of you here, alone and down. It's only for an hour or so. Come on, let's eat. I'm famished."

She sighed. "You're pushing. You know I don't like it when you push."

"I'm not trying to push. I only wanted to help you out. You can't fault a guy for that, can you?" He opened a bottle of wine and poured it into the two glasses he'd brought.

"You're exasperating. Somehow you talk me into things I don't want to do. And, I feel guilty if I don't do them." She shook her head. "No wonder you're one of the youngest CEOs."

The two ate hummus on pita bread, shrimp artichoke dip on baguettes, and jumbo prawn cocktail. As they ate, Mack observed the first man she'd dated since Sean. Evan wouldn't be called classically handsome, but when he walked into a room, every woman within viewing distance seemed to be drawn in by his presence. There'd been several occasions when some random woman boldly flirted with him even though she'd been standing right by his side. And, he seemed to enjoy it. Maybe that was why she wasn't sure that she completely trusted him. Whatever the reason, she couldn't make herself take the next step in their relationship. Sean was the only man she'd ever been with and thinking of being intimate with Evan felt wrong.

When they finished eating, as if he'd read Mack's thoughts, Evan said, "I want to take our relationship to the next level."

"I'm sorry." She looked into her glass of wine. "I don't think I'll ever be able to give you what you want."

He looked out the window. "I see."

"You're a great guy. Just not the right guy for me. I'm sorry."

He smiled sadly and stood to leave. "I understand… I hope you find that guy someday. You've been alone a long time."

~~~

The next morning Mack carried her things downstairs and checked out. She didn't stay for breakfast, opting to eat somewhere where the hostess didn't glare at her.

She drove to a downtown diner that was doing a good business. She figured it couldn't be too bad if the locals ate there. At the waitresses' suggestion, she opted for the biscuits and gravy, which were a specialty of the restaurant. Comfort food sounded perfect right then. As she ate, she was reminded of when she'd first met Gus.

When Mack was almost finished, she called Nick to let him know that she was going to look for another place to stay before coming into the police department.

"I have a friend that has several rental properties here in town," he said. "Stay where you are, and I'll give him a call."

"Thanks, I appreciate that." Mack drank coffee while she waited.

"One of his properties is currently empty," he said when he called back a few minutes later. "Since my buddy doesn't live here in Skaus Lake, it won't matter if the entire town becomes a suspect, nobody will evict you. And, since it was sitting empty, he'll rent it to you for the same price as the bed and breakfast. How does that sound?"

"Perfect. Thank you so much."

"No worries." He chuckled. "I'm only doing this so that you'll owe me a favor."

She smiled. "I should have known you'd have ulterior motives."

"Write down this address. The rental agent will meet you there in a few minutes."

"You're a good guy. A pain in the ass, but a good guy. See you soon."

Mack drove to the address Nick had given her. The rental agent was waiting on the sidewalk. The house was a delightful one bedroom cottage that faced the lake. It had a steep, overhanging roof with gables. The outside was tan stucco. The roof, front door, and trim details were all painted dark brown. A small porch covered part of a courtyard area that was enclosed by a low stone wall. A bay window jutted out from the front of the house, next to the courtyard. The sidewalk led to an iron gate in the wall surrounding the courtyard.

She stepped through the front door into a comfortably furnished living room. The cottage had an open floor plan with vaulted wood beamed ceilings. Every room was painted the same shade of pale blue, which matched the color of the lake. The master suite was to the left of the combination living and dining room. A laundry room and half bath were to the right. The furnishings mimicked the color of the beach surrounding the lake. Pops of dark blue and brown were added with decorative pillows and accent pieces.

The rental agent asked, "What do you think?"

"It's lovely. I'll take it."

CHAPTER 29

Six Years Prior

The movers arrived promptly at nine Monday morning. Mack stood in the kitchen as they loaded the past two years of her life into the moving truck. She gave them the donation address for Women in Distress and paid them.

After they left, she walked through each room of the apartment one last time. At the front door, she turned and whispered, "Goodbye." She took the keys to the office and drove away for the last time. Mack knew that she was leaving a part of herself behind.

When she got back to Sigurd's place, he was ready to go. He had on jeans, a t-shirt, zip up hoodie, and tactical boots. The clothes covered up his tattoos, which Mack thought was a pity.

"Grab your gun and ammo." He walked over to his clothes wardrobe and opened the double doors. He shoved the clothes to one side and pushed on the back panel. It swung into another room.

She looked inside. "What is that?"

He shrugged. "You never know. Better safe than sorry." He bent over and stepped through. "Come on."

She climbed through the wardrobe into what looked like a garage. A silver Ford F-150 truck was backed into the room. They loaded into the truck. Sigurd pushed the button on a fob on his key ring. The wall in front of them opened like a garage door. After they'd driven through the opening, the panel closed automatically. Mack turned around and saw that it was invisible from the outside.

He drove out of town, then off-road for a couple of miles. He seemed to know exactly where he was going, so she didn't ask. When they parked, he took four target stands out of the back of the truck. He paced off distances and set up the stands. Then he attached a paper bullseye target on each one.

Sigurd walked back to the truck. He explained to Mack how to safely handle, transport, and store her Glock. Then he showed her the different parts of the gun, how to correctly load and unload it, and how to sight on a target. He had her repeat every detail until she memorized them. Then he handed her a pair of hearing protectors and inserted his own pair into his ears.

"Now you are going to practice shooting. The first target is six yards away, the next ten yards, then fifteen yards, and lastly twenty-five yards. You have fifteen rounds. I want you to shoot four at the first three targets and three at the last one."

Sigurd demonstrated how to stand. "This is called the fighting stance. It was developed by military Special Forces and is the only one you need to learn. You stand square to the target, with your feet at shoulder width and your firing side foot slightly behind your support side foot." He stood behind her and adjusted her legs. "Good. Now, flex your knees to absorb recoil, lean slightly forward, and extend your arms straight out. Keep your head level to maintain balance. Good. Now, align the sights, take a deep breath, let it out, and slowly squeeze the trigger."

Mack aligned, breathed, and squeezed. She completely missed the target.

"That is okay." He stood behind her, placed his hands on hers, and showed her how to properly sight in on the target. "Now squeeze the trigger. Do not jerk it. Just squeeze."

She squeezed and hit the target. "I did it!"

"Good. Now do it three more times."

She fired, pausing several seconds between each shot.

"Now, I want you to fire at the other targets. Only faster. Try not to think so much. Just aim and squeeze."

After she emptied the first magazine, he helped her with corrections. She reloaded and repeated the process again and again until she'd used both boxes of ammo.

"You are not going to win any contests, but you could hit a man if you needed to," he said. "Which, I sincerely hope you do not."

The sun was setting as Sigurd drove back to his place. Mack rolled her shoulders and flexed her wrists.

"Sore?"

"A little. But I'll be fine."

~~~

After dinner, sipping Sambuca, Mack asked, "How did you learn all that gun stuff you showed me today?"

"I was a police officer with the Norwegian civilian police agency for six years before moving to the States."

Her eyes widened. "So, tell me more."

"I was a member of a specialist agency within the police. The National Criminal Investigation Service. It is known as Kripos. I was a computer expert." He shrugged. "That is how I learned some of the things that I do now."

"Why did you get out?"

"We were the center for international police cooperation. We worked with Interpol and Europol. We were like rat catchers. We caught people that were sub-human. Over time I realized that fate favors the bad as often as the good. When I got married, and we had our son, a jolt of fear would strike me every day. I did not want to start our car one day and end up as a handful of dust. So, I quit, and we moved to the U.S." He paused. "I came to the states to keep my family safe, and instead it got them killed."

She reached out and took his hand in hers. They were both buried in the memories of their lost loved ones. He rubbed his thumb over the back of her hand. She closed her eyes and savored the feeling of that small human contact.

~~~

The next morning Mack and Sigurd bought more ammo for her handgun. Then they drove to the same target practice spot.

She practiced shooting for two hours. Then she held her Glock out to him. "Want to shoot some?"

117

"I brought my own handgun. I will do some practicing with it. It has been a while since I have been out here." He walked back to the truck and retrieved his handgun from under the passenger's front seat.

As Sigurd loaded his gun, Mack asked, "What kind of gun is that?"

"A Heckler & Koch P30 semi-automatic. This is what I used when I was with the Norwegian police. I am comfortable with it, so that is what I bought for personal use."

He put new targets on the stands, took aim, and fired off all fifteen rounds in quick succession. He retrieved the targets and stands.

She held out her hand. "Can I see?" She looked at the paper targets, then at Sigurd. "Every shot is a bullseye."

He shrugged and grinned. "I was a pretty good marksman in the day. I guess it is like riding a bike."

"I sure am glad you're on my side."

CHAPTER 30

Mack listened to the recording of the 911 call. "Please help. Help us!" Susan cried.

Dave was on duty that morning. "What's your emergency?"

"My mom and Alan are dead. And... And Jack. Someone killed them. I don't know if they're still in the house." She started sobbed.

"Where are you?"

"At home."

"What's your address?"

She gave him the address. "Hurry. Please hurry."

"An officer's on his way. Where are you in the house?"

"Upstairs in my brother's bedroom."

"Is the bedroom door locked?"

"Yes."

"Good. Can you hear anyone in the house?"

"No. I don't hear anything."

"Okay. Stay in the bedroom. And stay on the line with me until the officer arrives. It'll only be a few minutes more. What's your name?"

"Susan... Susan Brown."

Mack leaned back in her chair and closed her eyes. She felt tired just listening to Susan's fear and anguish.

Nick asked, "You okay?"

"No matter how many times I listen to one of these, it never gets easier."

He shrugged. "Maybe that's not such a bad thing."

She gave him a small smile and sighed. She started looking at each item they'd found in Patricia's handbag. Two dollars and ninety-seven cents in change, two fives, one ten, and three twenties. A driver's license. A medical ID card. Car insurance card. A debit card. Two credit cards. Checkbook. Sunglasses. Lipstick. Tissue packet. Fingernail file. Notepad. A set of keys with a car and house key. Patricia had either recently cleaned out her handbag, or she had kept it very neat. Either way, there wasn't anything of value to the investigation in it.

Mack carefully looked at each item collected at the Browns' house. She started with the downstairs rooms. "Nothing. Absolutely nothing," she murmured.

Barbara came into the bullpen. "We got a call from Nora Nelson. She's the Browns' neighbor that was out of town when Charlie interviewed them. She saw two men Saturday morning." Barbara glared at Mack. "Maybe now you'll have real suspects, not some figment of your wild imagination."

Mack pinched the bridge of her nose. "You have no idea how much I hope that's true."

~~~

Emmett and Nora Nelson lived in the fourth house north of the lake, between the Kings and the Smiths. The Smiths' home was at the top of the hill, which was also the end of the street.

"Please come in," Nora said after introductions. "I'm sorry for not contacting you until today, but I've been out of town visiting my mother." She was in her mid- to late-fifties, with brown eyes and graying, shoulder length, brown hair. She indicated the couch in the living room. "Have a seat." She sat in the chair opposite. "I had a nine o'clock flight out of Seattle, so I left the house at five-thirty Saturday morning. As I was driving down our street, I passed two men walking up it. I didn't recognize them, so I slowed down and took a good look as I drove by." She paused. "I don't know if it means anything or not, but I thought I should mention it."

"Thank you," Nick said. "We appreciate any information you can give us."

Mack said, "At five-thirty it would still have been dark outside. You said you took a good look at the two men?"

120

"Yes. Well. They were walking on the same side of the street that I was driving on. The headlights were on bright, so I saw them pretty clearly."

Mack gave her a small smile. "Great. Can you describe the two men?"

Nora paused for a few moments. "They were both white. One was a couple of inches shorter than the other. One had short black hair. The other…"

Mack interrupted. "Could you describe each man separately, one at a time, please."

"Of course. Okay. Let me see. One had short black hair. It was combed straight back, and it was shiny. Like it was wet, or there was some sort of hair gel on it. He had a black mustache. He had on a light blue t-shirt under a gray fleece jacket. The jacket was zipped up part way. He had on faded blue jeans and light brown shoes of some sort." She paused and waited for Mack to finish taking notes. "The other man was the taller one. He had shoulder length brown hair. It was parted in the middle, and he had glasses on. He was wearing a black pull-on sweatshirt, faded blue jeans, and white tennis shoes."

"Can you describe the first man's mustache?" Mack asked, "Was it thin or wide, bushy or long on the sides?"

"There was nothing outstanding about it that I can remember."

"You said the second man had glasses on. Can you describe them? Were they round, square, oval, rectangular, large, small?"

"They were rectangular in shape and were a dark color… maybe black or brown."

"You said one of the men was taller than the other. Do you have an idea of how tall they were? Would you say they were tall or short or medium height in general?"

"They didn't strike me at the time as being tall or short. So, I'd say they were medium height. But I can't be sure."

"What about weight? Could you tell if they were thin or heavy?"

"They weren't thin or heavy. They had regular, medium builds. I'm sure of that."

"Did they have any distinguishing marks that you could see? Like tattoos or scars?"

Nora closed her eyes for a few moments. "Not that I can recall."

"Did you see if either man wore any jewelry? Earrings. Rings on their fingers. Necklaces. Bracelets?"

"I didn't notice anything of that sort, but I could have missed something." She paused. "I probably only saw them for maybe thirty seconds or so."

"Would you be willing to work with a police sketch artist to develop a facial composite of the two men?"

"I'll be happy to do anything I can to help. The Browns were good neighbors. The children were always quiet and polite. And Patricia was a nice woman."

"Thank you," Mack said. "We'll give you a call to set that up."

They all stood. Nick said, "Thank you for your help. We appreciate it."

The two left the house and walked back to the sedan. Sitting inside, Nick asked, "Well, what do you think?"

"I'm not sure. It could have been the murderers. Or, it could have been two random guys. Although, I'm not sure why they would have been walking on this street that early in the morning."

"You think you can get the state police to approve the sketch artist coming here?"

"I'll go through official channels first. If that fails, I'll call the detective that's the sketch artist. She'll come on her own time if she has to. She's dedicated. And she cares. Especially when children are involved."

CHAPTER 31

Six Years Prior

Sigurd didn't say anything as he drove. Mack thought they were going back to his place, but he drove to a small camera store in a sketchy part of town. He and the owner apparently knew each other. They greeted by hugging and slapping each other on the back.

"Sigurd. My friend. It's been too long."

"Roland, this is Mack. Mack, this is my old friend, Roland Larsen."

He took her hand and kissed it. "Any friend of Sigurd's is a friend of mine."

"Thank you."

Sigurd glared at Roland, blue eyes flashing like emeralds. "We need a Canon L-1, a pole camera with a thermal video head, and a GPS tracker."

Roland dropped her hand and chuckled. He went into a back room and came out with the three items in boxes. He scribbled prices on a notepad, tore off the sheet, and handed it to Sigurd.

Sigurd pulled his wallet out of his back pocket, counted out several hundred dollar bills, and handed them to Roland. He shook his friend's hand. "Thank you. We appreciate it."

"Anytime, my friend." Roland walked them to the door. After Mack stepped outside, he said to Sigurd, "I'm happy to see you're taking an interest in something other than computers." He looked at her and grinned.

Sigurd shook his head. "It is not like that. She is a very young woman that is alone and in need of help."

"Uh huh. Okay. You keep telling yourself that. But I haven't seen that look in your eyes in years."

"Kukskalle," Sigurd said in Norwegian. In English, the word loosely translated into 'dickhead'.

CHAPTER 32

"It's only been five days since I got your evidence and you're already calling me." Tony Gare said after Mack identified herself.

"You're the man. I know you've had plenty of time to get it done."

"Yours isn't the only case I have, you know. And it hasn't been designated a priority one."

"You and I both know that the Brown-Caldwell case should be a priority one. We have three bodies, two of which are fifteen-year-old boys. You and I also know that you can designate it a priority one. So, why haven't you?"

"Come on. Quit busting my balls."

"Tony. There are four children that would like to know that it's safe to go to sleep at night. I can't tell them that until I catch the murderer. And, I can't catch the bad guy without evidence."

"Jeez. You sure know how to make a guy feel bad." He paused. "Okay, okay. I'll start it this morning and get it to you as soon as I can."

~~~

At the cemetery that afternoon, Mack saw that about thirty people were gathered for the Browns' graveside service.

Pastor Beck was the officiant. He started the service, saying, "We gather together today to commit Patricia and Alan Brown to their final resting places. We gather to comfort each other in our grief and to honor the life that Patricia and Alan led."

She stayed in the back of the gathering, observing the people in attendance. Grace, Susan, Tom, and Will sat on folding chairs in the front. Nick, Rose, and Mark stood behind them. Ethan's and Jack's parents stood close to the front.

She saw that only three of Alan's and Jack's classmates came. *Guess they didn't want to ruin their day off of school by coming to their classmates' burial service.* She shook her head. In this day and age, young people think the TV show 'The Insider' is a news program. So, what could she expect?

Most of Alan's teachers and Principal Martz were present. Chief Davis, his wife, Barbara, and the Nelsons were also there. Mack didn't recognize anyone else.

The pastor continued. "For centuries, we have used the ringing of a bell to mark the passing of the beloved. Patricia and Alan, with the ringing of this bell, we release you now to the next part of your journey."

After the memorial ended, Nick walked over to Mack. She asked, "Is there anyone here that you're surprised to see?"

He studied the attendees that were now lining up to pay their respects to Grace and the Brown children. He shook his head. "No. Nobody stands out to me."

She placed her hands on her hips and motioned with her head. "Victor Albinson."

He looked where she indicated. Victor Albinson was rubbing Susan's arms. His face was very close to hers. Susan stood as stiff as a mannequin.

Suddenly, Mack was moving toward them at a brisk pace.

"That a girl," Nick said. "I'm right behind you."

"Mr. Albinson. Teachers should not be touching students," she growled when she reached his side.

Albinson jerked back and dropped his hands to his sides. He looked at Mack. "I was telling Susan how sorry I am for her loss."

"Well, I suggest you do that without your hands and while standing a respectful distance away." Her hazel eyes flashed.

Susan stepped to Mack's side and took hold of her arm.

"I was just leaving anyway," Albinson said.

Nick said, "Good."

"Are you okay?" Mack asked after Albinson walked away.

125

Susan nodded. "I better go find my brothers." She walked away.

Nick said, "Now I agree with you. There's something off about that guy."

~~~

Nick didn't see any unusual attendees at Jack Caldwell's service either. There weren't as many people present as at the Browns' service.

One glaring absence to Mack was Victor Albinson. She said, "Albinson didn't show here. So, was the only reason he went to the Browns' service to see Susan?"

"That thought disgusts me and really pisses me off at the same time."

She grinned. "You know, I think I'm beginning to like you."

CHAPTER 33

Six Years Prior

"Where do we start?" Mack asked Sigurd early the next morning.

"We are going to set up the pole camera at Ernie Adler's house to monitor who comes and goes. We use the GPS tracker to monitor where he frequents throughout the day and night. And, we keep monitoring his phone calls. After a week, we should have enough information to know what we do next." He took two baseball caps out of his wardrobe and handed one to her. "Put your hair up and put this on. If anyone looks at us, duck your head a little. The cap will hide your face."

She nodded, went into the bathroom, and emerged with her hair hidden under the cap. He tugged the bill down a little.

They loaded the equipment into the front seat of Sigurd's truck. They both stored their handguns under the seat.

He used his phone's GPS to find Adler's house. The homes in the neighborhood were small, and they all looked very similar. She saw that one of the houses across the street had windows covered with plywood. Cars were parked on the front yards of many of the homes.

He slowed the truck a few doors before they reached the address. "We can only drive by once. We don't want to attract any attention." He drove by the house, looking for a good place to set up the pole camera. He took a left, made a U-turn, and parked in front of a vacant lot. He took the pole camera off the back seat, changed settings, and held it close to his left leg. They walked back to Adler's house.

In front of the next door neighbor's house, he said, "We are out in the open here. I do not like it. You keep watch. If anyone comes, warn me in plenty of time to get out."

She nodded.

He walked between the two houses. She watched from the corner of her eye. He crouched behind an overgrown bush and started attaching the camera to a more significant limb in the center of it.

Suddenly, the front door of the neighbor's house opened, and an old woman came out. She started walking toward Mack. "Can I help you?" the old woman asked.

Mack closed the distance between them. "I'm supposed to meet my girlfriend, but I think I may be at the wrong address." She flicked a look at Sigurd. He was clearly visible from where they were standing, so she slowly shifted her body until the old woman's back was to Sigurd. "Do you know Mary Halsted by any chance?" She had no idea where that name came from. It just popped into her mind.

The old lady was quiet for a few seconds. "I don't think so. What's her address?"

"Well, that's the problem. I left the address at home and Mary isn't answering her phone." She stalled, trying to give Sigurd some more time. "Oh, how rude of me. I didn't get your name."

"I'm Francis Baker."

"Hi, Francis. I'm Hanna." Mack looked and saw that Sigurd had attached the camera pole to the large bush with brackets. He was adjusting the position of the camera head. "I'll check again and see if I can get Mary." She pulled her phone out of her back pocket and pretended to scroll through the contacts. She punched the screen a couple of times and held the phone up to her ear. "Oh, Mary. Finally. I've been trying and trying to call you. I'm lost. What's the address again?"

Sigurd walked out from between the two houses. He tipped his hat as he walked past the two women.

"Oh. Okay. Got it," Mack said to her pretend friend. "I'll be there in a few minutes. Bye, Mary." She pushed on the phone screen again and smiled at Francis. "Thank you for your help. I have the address now." Walking away, she turned and waved at Francis.

Sigurd was waiting for her in the truck. "Everything okay?" she asked.

"All set… Hannah."

She chuckled. "I just learned something about myself."

"What's that?"

"I'm a helluva good liar when I need to be."

"Well, I am glad of it. For a minute there, I thought I was going to be spending the night in jail." He pulled a laptop from the back seat and set it up on the center console. He tapped on the keyboard for a minute. "We are good to go. We can wirelessly observe Adler from a safe distance. As soon as he leaves, we will follow him. First chance we get, I will attach the GPS to his car." He started the truck. "I need to find out how far we can get before we lose reception." He drove south on the street, then turned and drove a while, then turned again. They were going in a circle around Adler's house. "I have what I need." He sped up and drove to a local convenience store. "Coffee?"

"Yes, please. Largest they have."

"Lock the doors."

Sigurd returned a few minutes later and handed Mack a foam cup. He drove back the way they'd come and stopped at a park. He adjusted the computer and settled back in his seat. "Now, the long and boring process of waiting occurs."

She finished her coffee. There was no movement at Adler's house. She fidgeted. "Tell me some more about Kripos. What kind of cases did you work on?"

"Kripos assisted police districts with technical and tactical investigations of serious crimes. And, we were responsible for working organized crime." He paused. "Hold up. Adler is on the move." He turned the computer so that she could see. He started the truck, keeping an eye on the computer screen. They watched as Adler got into his car and drive off.

Sigurd slammed the truck into gear and sped around a few corners until they could see Adler's car. Sigurd pulled over and closed the laptop. "We are going to stay far enough behind so that he does not get suspicious." When Adler got to the intersection, Sigurd pulled into the street and sped up to the corner. Adler turned right. Sigurd waited for two cars to pass by, then turned right. "With the two cars between us, we have cover. Keep an eye on Adler's car."

"He has his signal on," she said. "He's turning right."

"Okay." He slowed and watched Adler turn into the parking lot of a restaurant. A car behind them honked. Sigurd turned into the lot and parked at the back of the building. He got the GPS ready. "Okay. You are on lookout again."

They got out of the truck. Mack followed Sigurd to the corner of the building.

He said, "Stay here."

She watched as he walked behind the vehicles in the parking lot. At the back of Adler's Buick, Sigurd dropped his keys. When he bent down to retrieve them, he reached forward and placed the GPS under the car's trunk. He stood back up and walked to the front door of the restaurant. He patted his pockets like he'd forgotten his wallet. Then he turned around and walked back to the truck.

Inside, Sigurd typed on the laptop. "One more stop." He drove a few minutes to an RV dealership. He drove around the outside of the large fenced lot, looking up through the side window.

"What are you looking for?" Mack asked.

"That." He pointed at a small dish about ten feet off of the ground. He stopped next to the pole the dish was attached to and left the engine running. He opened the laptop and started typing. Then he pointed what looked like a remote control at the gray box below the dish.

She had no idea what he was doing, but whatever it was, it didn't take long.

"Okay. Now we can go home."

"What was all that?" she asked as he drove away.

130

"Without getting too technical, I tied our video camera into their centralized video hub. I will tie into the network when we get to my place. That way, we can watch our video camera from there." Sigurd smiled his crooked smile. *"Much more convenient."*

CHAPTER 34

Mack drove straight to the police department after Jack's service. Nick had gone home to be with Rose. She logged onto her computer, chiding herself for not checking Victor Albinson out before this.

She found Albinson's car registration and his Skaus Lake home purchase information. She didn't find any arrests, court warrants, summons, or unpaid traffic tickets. Next, she looked at his federal tax records. He didn't have any outstanding taxes. She continued looking at his tax records. Suddenly, she said, "Well, crap!" She took out her cell phone and punched in Nick's number.

When he answered, he asked, "What's up?"

"There's absolutely no trace of Victor Albinson before his move to Skaus Lake five years ago."

Nick arrived at the police department less than fifteen minutes after Mack phoned him. "So, who is he really?"

"A new suspect," she said. "Albinson's obviously obsessed with Susan. What if he went to her house that Saturday morning? He might have had plans for the two of them. When he found out that she wasn't there, he went into a rage. Maybe the reason he's using a fake ID is that he's messed with minors before."

"How are going to find out who he really is?"

She sat back in her chair and looked at the ceiling. "We need a search and seize warrant for his house, car, and cell phone. I think Principal Martz will consent to our request to search Albinson's workspace, so we don't need one for it. Martz can also give us a copy of Albinson's high school job application. There may be something in it that could point us to his true identity."

"You start writing the warrant request up. I'll give the chief a call and give him a heads up. Then I'll call Judge Cooley's office and let them know our request is coming and urgent."

An hour and a half later, the principal met them at the high school.

Mack said, "We need you to keep this to yourself until we arrest Albinson."

Martz sat on his desk chair and shook his head. "This is terrible. I don't know how this happened. Albinson had a nice cover letter and an intriguing resume. I interviewed him myself. He responded thoroughly and competently to all my questions."

"Don't beat yourself up too much," she said. "Albinson's slick."

Martz provided Mack and Nick with a copy of Albinson's job application paperwork, as well as his teaching portfolio. Then he walked them to Albinson's classroom.

Nick sat in front of Albinson's computer. "Password protected." He looked at Martz. "Do you know the password?"

The principal shook his head. "No. Each teacher sets the password on their computer."

Mack and Nick looked through everything on top of the desk. They searched through all the drawers. They pulled them out and looked at the sides and bottoms. They looked at the bottom of the desk chair and under the desk. Then they started searching the room. They looked through the storage closets and the equipment in them. After an hour, they hadn't found anything incriminating. They also didn't find the password for the computer.

Suddenly, Mack said, "Susan."

"What about her?" Nick asked.

"No." She air quoted with her fingers. "Try 'Susan' as the password."

Nick sat and typed it in. "That's it."

Martz paced and murmured, "Oh, my Lord."

Mack looked over Nick's shoulder as he searched the folders and files stored on Albinson's computer. Nothing but science related items. Then they looked at his browsing history. Again, there was nothing incriminating.

CHAPTER 35

Six Years Prior

Mack and Sigurd spent the rest of the week watching the video feed from Ernie Adler's house. He didn't have any visitors, and there was no sign of his brother, Luke. There was also no sign of anything illegal or suspicious.

Sigurd said, "Adler probably keeps his guns, drugs, and money in a stash house that is guarded by some trusted member of their affiliation. Let's see where he frequents most." The GPS that Sigurd had placed on Adler's car showed that he visited the neighborhood pub most evenings, returning home around midnight each night. During the day, he spent most of his time at home or at David Ridley's office complex. The data showed one other address that Adler frequented. "The only way to know if his brother is there is to stake it out."

"I'll do it."

He rubbed his forehead. "On one condition. You are to do nothing but watch and take photos of anyone that comes in and out. Agreed?"

"What if I see Luke?"

"You do absolutely nothing. If you see him, we will discuss how to proceed."

She didn't respond.

"Agreed?"

She nodded. "Okay."

~~~

The next morning after breakfast, Sigurd loaded a field pack for Mack. He put a two-way radio, binoculars, camera, sandwiches, and a large thermos of coffee into it.

She added her Glock and ammo, loaded it into her car, and drove to the address. She and Sigurd had looked at the location's street view on Google Earth before she left. He showed her where to park and set up. She was far enough away from the building so as not to be obvious, but close enough to take pictures.

She was hopeful of seeing Luke the first few hours, but as the day dragged on, her hopes and mood lagged. She checked in with Sigurd every hour, as agreed. "There doesn't seem to be anyone around the area at all. Just abandoned old warehouse buildings."

At five-thirty that evening, he contacted her on the radio and told her to call it a day. She drove back to his place. When she walked in the door, she saw that Gus was there, drinking a glass of wine with Sigurd.

Mack hugged him. "I'm happy to see you."

"Sigurd's been filling me in on what the two of you have been up to."

Sigurd handed her a glass of wine. "Dinner is ready. Let's eat."

As they ate, they told Gus more about the search for Luke Adler.

Gus asked Mack, "If you find him, what will you do?"

She shook her head. "I don't know."

"Have you seriously considered what you want to happen?"

She sipped her wine. "I want Adler to pay for what he did."

"Does that mean you want him to spend the rest of his life in prison? Or, that you want him dead?"

"I'm not sure."

Gus patted her on the shoulder. "Well, I'm sure you'll make the right decision when the time comes."

CHAPTER 36

As soon as Mack and Nick stepped inside the door of the police department, Chief Davis came out of his office, waving the Albinson warrant. "Got it. I walked Judge Cooley through the requests myself. Charlie's at Albinson's place, keeping an eye out. I also called the county sheriff's office. They're sending an officer here to take him to lock-up after we process him."

Nick said, "Thanks much."

Davis slapped him on the back. "Go get the SOB."

The two hustled back to Nick's sedan. He hummed some unidentifiable tune the entire six-minute drive to Albinson's residence.

"You excited or nervous?"

He glanced at her. "Both, I guess."

Charlie was parked just before the turn onto Albinson's street. Nick stopped next to the driver's side window. "Let's do this."

Both vehicles quietly pulled up in front of Albinson's house, which was a plain A-frame. His car was in the driveway. The three walked up the sidewalk to the front door. Nick handed Mack the warrants. "You sniffed him out. You do the honors."

She knocked loudly. When he answered, she said, "Victor Albinson, you're under arrest for identification fraud." She handed him the warrant. "This is a warrant to search these premises, your car, and your cell phone." She held out her hand. Albinson pulled his cell phone out of his pocket and handed it to her. As Nick cuffed Albinson, Mack read him the Miranda warnings. "You have the right to remain silent. Anything that you say can and will be used against you in a court of law. You have the right to an attorney. If you cannot afford an attorney, one will be appointed for you free of charge."

"The only thing I have to say is that I want a lawyer."

She said, "You can call one from the police department after you've been booked."

Nick nodded at Charlie. "Would you please take Mr. Albinson to the police department for photographing and fingerprinting? Detective Anderson and I will be there as soon as we're finished here."

"Be glad to." Charlie took Albinson's arm and led him out the door.

Mack closed the front door and looked around the inside of Albinson's house. The front living area consisted of closed-in boxy rooms. At the back of the house, there were two bedrooms and a bathroom off of a long hall. She was relieved to see that it looked reasonably clean.

As she snapped photographs, Nick walked through the house, quickly looking in the bedrooms and bathroom.

They started their search in the living room, then moved to the kitchen, then to the dining room. After, they moved to the back of the house and searched the bathroom, as well as Albinson's bedroom. They didn't find anything to indicate who Albinson actually was or why he was using a false identity.

Albinson was using the second bedroom as a personal office. The top of his desk held appointment cards for doctors' visits, a few bills, a box of tissues, a laptop, and a small printer. Nick bagged the laptop and carried it out to his sedan. Mack noted it on their inventory sheet. There was a shredder sitting next to the desk. They bagged the paper inside it. They also bagged all of Albinson's bills, and his bank and credit card statements. As they had at his school office area, they took the drawers out of the desk and searched all potential hiding places. Then they moved on to the rest of the room.

Mack was looking through the books stored on a short bookshelf, when Nick exclaimed, "Mother fucker!"

She looked up. "What?"

Nick had opened the closet doors. He was standing in front of the closet, looking inside. "You'd better come see this."

She walked to his side. The walls of the closet were plastered with pictures of Susan. "This guy has a serious problem."

"He's going to have a new problem... me!" Nick started ripping the photographs off of the walls.

She placed her hand on his arm. "Hold up."

"Why?"

"Take a good look at the pictures. All of these were taken at the high school."

He rubbed his forehead. "Damn it."

"He doesn't need permission to take photos in a public place. According to the Idaho code, we can't charge him with harassment or stalking. He hasn't caused any bodily injury to Susan or threatened her. We might not like it, and it might be sick, but it's not illegal. And, the warrant only covers items that are related to the identity fraud charge."

"So, we just leave these here?"

She was silent for a few seconds. Then she grinned. "I can't identify all of the people in these photographs. Can you?"

His brow furrowed. "No."

"We may need to use these photographs to identify the people in them. We may need to speak with those people, in case they can provide a lead as to Albinson's real identity."

A smile spread across Nick's face.

~~~

When the two walked through the police department's back door, Charlie jumped up. He handed Nick a piece of paper with Albinson's face on it. "Meet Joseph Cox, formerly of the state of New York. Six years ago, he served ninety days for first-degree harassment of a female high school student of his. Probably a little hard to get a teaching job with that on his record."

Mack and Nick smiled at each other. She said, "Well, let's make it even harder."

They went down the hallway and into the interview room. Albinson said, "I've been sitting here for hours, and I still haven't been allowed to call my lawyer."

Mack said, "I told you that you can call your attorney after you're booked."

Nick stood by the door, arms crossed over his chest, smiling at Albinson.

She turned on the tape player and identified herself and Nick. She noted the date, time, and location. "Please state your name, address, date of birth, and Social Security number for the record."

When Albinson finished his answers, Mack said, "Thank you. That completes the booking process."

"What? That's it?!" Albinson looked back and forth between Mack and Nick. "I've been sitting here all this time, and that's all you have to ask me?!"

"Officer Moore will bring you a phone so that you can call your attorney now. An officer of the county sheriff's office will then transfer you to their detention center. Your attorney can meet you there."

Mack stood and removed the tape. "See you real soon, Joseph Cox."

CHAPTER 37

Six Years Prior

The next two days of stake out were as unfruitful as the first was. One or two cars drove by on the street, but there was no activity in the warehouse. Mack spent the mind-numbingly tedious hours thinking about what Gus had said the night before. She tried to picture herself meeting Luke Adler in an alley. Would she pull her Glock out of her handbag and shoot him or would she let him walk away? She still didn't know the answer.

"This is your two o'clock check-in," she said irritably into the radio on day four.

"Thank you."

"I have no idea why I'm doing this every hour. There isn't another soul within sight."

"You are doing it for me. I need to know you are safe."

"Okay. I owe you that. At a minimum."

"Talk to you at three."

After a few minutes, Mack poured herself a cup of coffee and leaned back in her seat. Taking a sip, she loudly sighed. She'd just finished the coffee when the glass of her driver's side window came raining in on her. She screamed and dropped the coffee cup. She threw her hands up to shield her head.

A large man reached inside and grabbed her arm. She could feel the glass scrape her side as she was pulled through the window. At first, she was unable to get her feet under her on the gravel road. When she did, she looked up at the man. She didn't recognize him. He dragged her down the hill and into the warehouse. He pushed her onto the floor in the middle of the room. The rough concrete scraped her hands and knees. She quickly jumped up to her feet and pushed her hair out of her face. She looked into the eyes of David Ridley. Ernie Adler stood next to him with his hands on his hips.

"Who are you?" Ridley asked.

Mack didn't answer.

Ridley nodded his head. The big man stepped over and punched her in the stomach. She buckled and fell to her knees. She wrapped her arms around her and drew in a ragged breath.

Ridley said, "Get her up." The big man grabbed Mack's forearm and pulled her to her feet. "Who are you?" Ridley asked again.

"Becky Parsons."

Ridley's eyes narrowed. "Okay, Becky Parsons. Why are you staking out my warehouse?"

She tried to think of something to say, but her mind was blank.

Ridley nodded, and the large man backhanded her across the face. Her head snapped to the side, and she fell onto the floor. She tried not to cry, but tears streamed down her face.

"Up," Ridley demanded.

The man again grabbed Mack's forearm and dragged her to her feet. She staggered. She could taste blood.

"Why are you staking out my warehouse?"

Mack sobbed.

Ridley nodded at Adler. He walked behind Mack and grabbed both of her elbows, pulling them backward and pinning her to him. She whimpered.

"Why are you staking out my warehouse?"

No good lie came to Mack's mind, so she told the truth. "I'm looking for Luke Adler."

Ridley was clearly surprised by that. He looked questioningly at Ernie Adler. Adler shrugged. "Why are you looking for Luke?"

"He's my boyfriend. I haven't heard from him in a couple of days. I thought he might be here."

"How come I've never heard Luke talk about you?" Adler asked.

"I don't know." Mack turned her head and wiped her bloody mouth on her shirt. "Maybe because we've only been dating a short while."

Ridley asked, "How do you know about this place?"

"Luke told me he sometimes comes here. We drove by once, and he pointed it out to me."

Ridley took a step toward her. "Well, you've been wasting your time. Luke left the country, and he's not coming back." He looked between Adler and the big man. "Get rid of her." He turned and walked out of the warehouse.

Adler let go of her arms. The other man slapped her across the face. She stumbled sideways and fell onto the floor.

Adler said, "You can go. I've got this." He smirked. "I'm going to have a little alone time with the lovely lady before I get rid of her."

His words permeated Mack's haze of pain. She tried to push herself to her feet, but she fell back. Mack couldn't see the large man anymore.

"It's just you and me now," Adler said.

She sat up. She pushed herself away from him with her arms.

He grinned. He walked over to Mack, then knelt beside her. He grabbed the front of her blouse and ripped the buttons off.

"No! Don't touch me!" She slapped and kicked at him.

He captured her hands. Then he straddled her legs, pinning them beneath him. She screamed and bucked.

He laughed. "Go ahead and scream, nobody's going to hear you. And, I like a fighter." With his free hand, he jerked her bra down to her waist. He started fondling her breast.

She bucked again. "No! Stop!" Adler twisted her nipple and laughed. She screamed and began sobbing.

He grabbed his crotch. "I'm ready for you." He unbuttoned and unzipped her jeans and pushed them to her knees. He tore

143

her panties off and threw them to the side. Then he undid his own pants.

Mack turned her head to the side and squeezed her eyes shut. She sobbed. Tears ran into her hairline. Suddenly, Adler was no longer on top of her. Mack sat up. She jerked her pants up, then pulled the front of her shirt closed with one hand.

Mack looked around. She saw that Sigurd had picked Adler up and thrown him against a wall. Adler was sitting on the floor. He shook his head. As he stood, he drew a pistol from a hidden ankle holster. Sigurd charged and grabbed the gun. It discharged into the ceiling. Sigurd punched Adler in the face with one hand and twisted the gun with the other. The two men struggled, and the gun went off again. Adler slumped to the floor. Blood trickled down his temple. His eyes stared vacantly ahead.

Sigurd rushed to Mack's side. She threw her arms around his neck and cried. He hugged her tightly. "You are safe now." He took off his shirt and draped it over her shoulders. "Let's get out of here." He helped her to her feet. "I will come back later and take care of this."

"Wait." Mack stepped over to Adler's body and kicked him in the ribs. "Asshole. Who's laughing now?"

Sigurd slid an arm around Mack's shoulders and guided her to his truck. He helped her climb inside. He buckled her seat belt, then quickly moved to the driver's side. He started the truck and pulled out of the parking lot.

She asked, "How did you know?"

"You did not check in at three." He took her hand. "What happened?"

Mack told him about the large man and Ridley.

"I should never have let you go there. I am so sorry."

"It's not your fault. I was going to do it with or without you. You couldn't have stopped me."

~~~

144

Mack scrubbed her skin with soap until it was pink. Then she washed her hair twice. When she emerged from the bathroom, Sigurd handed her a glass of scotch over ice. She drank the contents without taking a breath.

He filled her glass again. "Sit on the couch and let me take a look at you." He treated the cut on Mack's mouth and the one next to her eyebrow. He rolled up the bottom of her t-shirt. A bruise had already formed on her rib cage. He gently probed it. "You're going to be sore for a week or so. But no bones are broken." When he finished, he pulled her shirt back down.

She drained the second glass of scotch. He took the glass from her and set it on the coffee table. Then he picked her up and carried her to the bed. He laid her on the comforter.

Tears ran down her face. "Will you hold me, please?"

Sigurd lay down next to Mack and cradled her in his arms. "Sleep now."

CHAPTER 38

On her daily run Saturday morning, Mack could feel the three pieces of pizza she'd eaten the night before. *I need to eat healthier. Right, like that's going to happen.* Mack tried to ignore her stomach and instead, looked at the beautiful tapestry of land and water. The lake was surrounded by a thick green cloak of pine and fir trees. She didn't understand why people ran with earbuds blasting music. She loved the peace and quiet of nature. At the end of her three miles, she held her face up to the sun and took a deep breath of the crystal clean air. *I love that smell.*

Mack walked the rest of the way back to the cottage. She stopped in front of it and smiled. *Sure am glad Nick found this place.* She opened the front gate and walked into the courtyard. As she was attempting to get the key into the lock on the front door, she heard a faint noise behind her. She looked around the courtyard and saw a small kitten hunkering in the corner. She crouched down and held out her hand. "Kitty, are you okay?"

The kitten meowed and ran over to her. It started purring and rubbing itself on her. The kitten was pale orange with darker stripes and ears that were too big for its head.

She stood back up and unlocked the door. "Ok. Go on." She gently pushed the kitten away with her foot. She opened the door, and the kitten sprinted inside. "Hey! What are you doing? You don't live here."

The kitten put its tail in the air and walked around the house, checking out each room.

"Is it to your satisfaction, missy, mister. Which are you?" She picked up the kitten and checked. "Mister."

The kitten purred and rubbed his head on her chest. She snuggled it for a few seconds. "Okay, buster, I have to get coffee, take a shower, and get to work." The kitten meowed.

She set it on the kitchen floor and made coffee. As she poured cream into the cup, the kitten started meowing in earnest. "Are you hungry? Well, I know milk isn't good for you. It'll give you gas. And neither one of us wants that, do we? I do have some tuna. I bet you'd like that."

She took a foil pack of tuna out of the pantry and emptied it into a bowl. She filled up another bowl with water and put both on the kitchen floor. "Here you go. Now listen, buster, don't get used to this."

She drank coffee while the kitten ate. When she went to take a shower, the kitten followed her. He continued to be her constant shadow as she got ready for work. When she left, she picked up the kitten and put it outside in the courtyard. "Go home."

~~~

At the police department, Mack introduced Nick to Gale Parker, the state police's sketch artist. She was a big boned, tall woman. She had brown eyes and shoulder length brown hair that framed her pleasant face.

He shook her hand. "We appreciate you coming up here on your day off."

"No problem. I'm happy to help. Besides, as payment, I made Mack promise that she'd introduce me to a good guy. Although, now that she and Evan aren't dating, I guess it won't be a rich friend of his."

Nick looked questioningly at Mack. "I didn't realize you two broke up." He paused. "I'm sorry to hear that."

"Don't be." She shrugged. "He wasn't the guy for me. Enough of that. Let's get this going." She cleared off her desk and helped Gale set up.

When Nora arrived, Nick escorted her to the bullpen. After introductions, Gale got started by explaining the process. One man at a time, she first asked questions about the shape of his face, color of his skin, eyebrow color and thickness, and size of ears. Next, it was time for visual aids. Nora went through a book and picked out which nose looked the most like the one she remembered. Which mouth looked the most similar. Which eyes. Lips. Then, Gale started sketching, piecing together a complete face from Nora's descriptions. Once Gale had a basic sketch,

Nora gave her feedback. Finally, they had two facial sketches that were very close to the men that Nora had seen. The process took about four hours to complete.

Mack picked up one of the sketches and studied it. "This guy looks familiar to me, but I can't figure out where I've seen him."

Nora stood. "I better get home."

Gale gathered her things. She walked with the other three to the front door.

Mack and Nick thanked Nora. "Please, let me know if you need anything else."

"I better get on the road," Gale said. "I'm not looking forward to the drive back."

Mack walked Gale to her car and gave her a hug. "Thanks again."

"Don't thank me. Just introduce me to a good guy." She waved as she drove off.

Mack found Nick in the bullpen looking at the sketches. "They're not portraits, and they don't look like a picture out of a magazine," she said. "But, hopefully, they'll help us find out who these two guys are."

CHAPTER 39

Six Years Prior

Mack woke up early the following morning to find Sigurd gone. He'd left a note on his pillow that said, "Be back soon. Help yourself to coffee."

She tried to sit up, but pain shot through her right side. She rolled onto her left side and pushed herself off of the bed. She shuffled to the kitchen and poured herself a cup of coffee. She drank and paced around the perimeter of the building.

Sigurd came back about an hour later. "Good morning. How are you feeling?"

"I was a little anxious when I woke up and found you gone."

He walked over to Mack and kissed her on the forehead. "We need to talk." She frowned. He poured himself some coffee. They both took their cups to the couch and sat.

"Ernie Adler's body and vehicle will never be found," he said. "There is no trace that he was killed in the warehouse or that we were ever there."

"Ridley told me that Luke Adler's out of the country and not coming back. I'm not going to be able to find him, am I?"

He shook his head. "If I cannot find him, I doubt anyone can. His uncle did a good job of making him disappear. But that is the last thing you should be worried about right now."

"Why is that?"

"As you found out yesterday, Ridley is a dangerous man. He is going to assume that you had something to do with his nephew's disappearance. So, you need to leave town. I have made arrangements for a private plane to fly us to Edinburg tomorrow. From there, a car will drive you the twenty miles to your parents' home."

Mack didn't speak for a full minute. Finally, she asked, "Can we say goodbye to Gus?"

~~~

Gus came to Sigurd's at six o'clock that night. After dinner, the three talked until it was time for him to leave.

Mack handed him the keys to her car and the carrying case with her Glock inside. "Sell these. I owe you a lot more than you'll get for them."

Gus patted her on the back. "They'll be waiting for you when you come back." Mack started to protest, but he held up his hand to silence her. He kissed her on the cheek and shook hands with Sigurd. "This isn't goodbye. We'll see each other again. Until then, take care of yourselves."

"Come on," Sigurd said after Gus drove away. "Let's get some sleep. We have a long day tomorrow. The car is picking us up at five in the morning to take us to the airport."

Mack lay down on his bed. When he lay down next to her, she curled into his side and draped her arm across his chest. After a few minutes, she said, "You aren't going to Scotland with me, are you?"

He shook his head. "I will drop you in Edinburg, then go on to Denmark. I told you that I have been thinking about going back home. My father has been ill. I want to spend time with him before it is too late. I would regret that forever. And, I do not want to live with any more haunting regrets."

"I understand. I'm just going to miss you."

~~~

Mack and Sigurd spent most of the eleven-hour flight talking about their families.

She told him about her numerous aunts, uncles, and cousins in Scotland. "I'll be glad to be around them again. It's been years since I've seen them. They're a big, loud, happy group."

"It will be good for you to be around family at this time. You have not grieved yet, and you need to do that."

"I don't want to do it without you. I'm afraid I won't survive it."

He took her hands in his. "You are a strong woman. Stronger than you think. You need to do this without me. Otherwise, you will always think that you can't survive on your own."

She nodded. She held onto his hand for the rest of the flight.

When they landed in Edinburg, he walked her to the waiting car. He held her face in his hands. "You can call me anytime. I will always be there for you."

She threw her arms around his neck and hugged him tightly. She whispered in his ear. "I'll never be able to thank you for all you've done for me."

He hugged her. After a minute he stepped back and kissed her on the forehead.

Mack waited until Sigurd's plane was out of sight before she started to cry.

CHAPTER 40

When Mack walked out of the police department later that evening, she found Susan sitting on the back doorstep. "Are you okay?"

Susan jumped up. "I... I don't know why I'm here."

"Does Grace know where you are?"

"I told her I was going for a drive and I'd be back later. She's too sad to really care anyway."

"I haven't eaten since this morning, and I'm starving. I thought I'd get pizza. Want to join me?"

"I'm not really hungry."

"Okay. Well, I'm going to First Avenue Pizzeria. Come by, if you want to talk."

Mack walked to her sedan. When she got inside, she saw that Susan was walking to her car. As she drove, she wondered what had prompted Susan's visit. When she arrived, she ordered a salad for two, a large cheese pizza, a glass of wine for herself, and a coke. The pizza was delivered just as Susan walked in. Mack put a slice of pizza on a plate and slid it across the table.

Susan sat and started to eat. After they both ate two slices and some salad, she said, "I didn't know who else to talk to. Nobody else understands."

"Want to tell me what happened to make you say that?"

"Chrissy called me tonight and asked if I wanted to go to a party with her." Susan paused. "Seriously? I buried my mother and brother yesterday, and she wants to know if I want to party? I guess she thinks I should be over it by now. It's been a week. Seven whole days." She looked into Mack's eyes. "Did people treat you like that too?"

Mack was quiet for a few seconds. "I've found that, in general, there are two ways that people react to those of us that are grieving. A lot of people... good people, caring people... feel awkward about what to say when someone dies. So, they avoid saying anything at all." Mack shrugged. "In case they might say the wrong thing." She paused "Then there are those that say way too much. Someone inevitably says, 'You're strong. You'll get through this.' Someone else says, 'There are no accidents, and someday all this will make sense to you.' And, my favorite, 'There's a silver lining to every cloud."

"Oh my God. You're so right. I never thought about it like that. I was just annoyed by everyone."

"Maybe if you explain to Chrissy how you feel, she might surprise you. She's never experienced a loss like yours. Give her a chance."

Susan nodded. "Okay."

"I wanted to let you know that we arrested Victor Albinson yesterday."

"For the murders?"

Mack shook her head. "No. His name's actually Joseph Cox. He was a high school teacher in New York and was convicted of harassing one of his female students. He served time for it. He used a false ID here to get a job."

"So, I'm not the only student he had a thing for." Susan leaned back in her chair. "He was so creepy. You know? He never really did anything. He was just so icky."

"I know what you mean. Well, he won't be bothering you anymore."

"Good."

"Can I ask you something?"

Susan nodded.

"Were Alan and Jack gay? Some of their classmates thought they were."

"I don't know for sure. I wasn't lying when I said that Alan didn't talk to me about stuff like that. I had my suspicions, but I never saw them do anything to make me sure. And, I didn't ask. That was their business." She frowned. "Do you think that someone killed them because of that?"

153

"We're not sure."

"Do you have any suspects? You must have something by now."

"Right now, Albinson is our primary suspect for the murders. He may have been trying to get to you. And, since you weren't home he became furious."

"Oh, God. I might be the reason they're dead?"

Mack shook her head. "You're not responsible. If he is the murderer, it's not because of you. It was his decision. It's not your fault."

Susan nodded. "Okay." She took a drink of her coke. "There's something I didn't tell you when we talked at the police department."

"If you want to, you can tell me now."

"Alan and Jack smoked. They bought it from a guy in their class."

"Aaron Paul?"

Susan sat forward. "How did you know that?"

Mack grinned. "I am a detective, you know."

~~~

Mack sat in her sedan outside the pizzeria and called Nick. She told him what Susan had said. "We don't have any hard evidence against Aaron for drug dealing. But, as I see it, he could be another potential suspect for the murders. What if Alan and Jack owed Aaron money for the pot and he came to the house to collect it. It's weak. But we need to look at him."

"Great. We have three potential suspects with motives and two unidentified suspects. But we don't have a shred of evidence against any of them."

She felt happy as she drove up to the cottage a few minutes later. Parking in front, she sat in her car and looked at the house. She suddenly realized that she'd never felt that way coming back to her townhouse in Coeur d'Alene.

When she opened the front gate, the kitten came running from a corner of the courtyard. He stared up at her, meowing and circling her legs.

"Okay, you can come in for the night. It's going to get cold, and I don't want to be responsible for you freezing out here." She opened the door, and the kitten sprinted inside, tail in the air.

She fed him some more tuna. Then she poured herself a glass of wine from one of the bottles that Evan had brought her. She felt a little guilty for drinking it, but she knew that Evan would be even more upset if she tried to give it back to him. Sitting in the corner of the couch, she tucked her legs under her and sipped wine.

When the kitten finished eating, he jumped into her lap and curled into a ball. She rubbed his ears. He started purring.

She closed her eyes and leaned her head back on the couch, listening to the rhythmic sound. No visions of bloody bodies came into her mind. No haunted faces of family members insinuated themselves either. She didn't realize what had happened for a couple of blissful minutes. Then she sat up and looked down at the kitten. "Where did you come from? Are you some kind of magical beast?" She finished her glass of wine, then went into the bathroom to wash her face and brush her teeth.

The kitten sat on the bathroom floor and watched every move Mack made. His greenish yellow eyes glinted when they caught light from above.

When she changed into a nightgown and got into bed, the kitten jumped up onto it. He curled into a ball on her chest. She petted him. He started purring again. They both quickly fell asleep.

~~~

Sean and Samantha lay on the floor of the convenience store. Their eyes were vacant and blood pooled underneath them. Mack was viewing the scene from high above. Suddenly, the gunman turned toward her and stared into her eyes. There was no mask covering his face. She was looking into the face of the man in the police sketch. The one that looked familiar to her.

155

Mack sat up in bed. "Oh my God. I found him."

The kitten stretched and meowed sleepily.

She turned on the light and looked at her phone. One o'clock in the morning. She did the calculation in her head. Nine in the morning in Norway. If that was still where he was. Almost a year had passed since they'd last spoken. She searched the contacts in her phone and hesitated only a second before she pushed the call button.

"I think I found Luke Adler," she said when Sigurd answered.

"How can I help?"

"I… I don't know. I don't even know why I called you."

"I am glad you did."

"Me too. It's been too long." Mack realized how happy she was to hear Sigurd's voice.

"I agree."

She swallowed and tried to blink away the tears that filled her eyes.

"Congratulations on your promotion to detective," he said after a few seconds of silence.

"How did you know?"

"I have been keeping track of you, of course. Did you think I would forget about you?"

"I guess I did."

"That is never going to happen."

She smiled. "I'm glad." She wiped her eyes on the hem of her pajama top. "How have you been?" She took a deep breath to steady her voice.

"I have been well."

"How's your father?"

Sigurd hesitated. "He died last spring."

"I'm so sorry."

"Do not be. It was time. He was suffering. I spent a few good years with him. I am glad for that."

"What have you been up to?" she asked. "Anything exciting happening in your life?"

"I have been working and spending time with family. What about you? Are you seeing anyone?"

"I dated a guy for a few months, but we broke up. I couldn't make myself feel enough for him. I'm not quite sure why."

"When it is the right man, you will know it. There will not be any hesitation."

"You said you've been working. I just realized that I don't actually know what you do. We never talked about that."

"We find missing and exploited people. It is like being a detective. Except, we hopefully find them before they die. It is gratifying."

"I thought you worked alone. I didn't realize you work with someone else."

"I work with one other man. He is a specialist also. We formed a partnership after I left Kripos. I needed to bring on another person, but it needed to be someone that I trust completely."

"I've always been amazed at how you can find someone by just using a computer. How do you do that?"

"How can I explain it?" He paused. "There are millions of people on this planet. Each person leaves footprints in lines of code. I follow their footprints."

The two talked for over two hours. Mack felt like they'd never been apart. She wondered why she'd gone so long without talking to Sigurd. She suddenly realized that she felt abandoned by him when he left her in Scotland. But she knew now that he was right. If he'd stayed with her, he would have been her crutch.

Sigurd interrupted Mack's thoughts. "You said that you think you found Luke Adler. I take it you are not sure it is him."

"Well, as you know, his face was covered when he shot Sean and Samantha. The only picture I've ever seen of him was the one you showed me when you identified him. And, all I have of the man that lives here is a sketch from a witness."

"Can you get an actual picture of the man in Skaus Lake?"

"So far I don't have one. But I'm not giving up."

"What are you going to do if you do find Adler?"

"After all these years, I still don't know the answer to that question."

"Well, like Gus told you, you will know what to do when the time comes."

"I wish you were here to help me."

CHAPTER 41

Mack drove to the police department after her daily run, a shower, coffee, bowl of cereal, and some packaged tuna for the kitten. She went to the front desk and said hi to Bob. He was on dispatch duty.

Bob smiled. "You sure are dedicated. Being here on a Sunday."

"I owe it to the victims. They deserve justice, and they can't get it for themselves."

Bob stood. He shuffled his feet. "I was wondering if you'd like to get a drink with me sometime?"

"Oh. Thank you for the offer. I appreciate it. But I just ended a relationship. I'm not ready to date yet."

He looked down at the floor. "No problem. I just thought I'd take a chance."

Mack hurried down the hall to her desk. She sat on her chair. *Okay. Back to work.* She leaned back and looked up at the ceiling. *Toby has an alibi. That leaves three suspects with motives. Barbara was angry at the Franke family, and Cox was obsessed with Susan. Neither of them has an alibi. Aaron Paul was selling them pot. Maybe they owed him money.* She stood. She walked to the front of the room and studied the crime scene photographs. *Extreme anger.*

She pulled her desk chair up to the conference table that held the bagged items from Alan's room and his person. She carefully examined each item. There just wasn't anything there. She picked up Alan's laptop and rolled back to her desk. She searched through his emails. There was nothing to or from Aaron. She did a word search and didn't find anything either. Next, she went on Alan's Facebook, Instagram, and Twitter accounts and started looking through his posts, likes, and comments. Surprisingly, Alan posted very little. He also had a small number of friends for a guy in high school. She couldn't find any mean or nasty comments from anyone to him or vice versa.

Mack looked through the few things from Tom's and Will's room. Then she looked through the items from Susan's room and the two bathrooms. She took her time. Nothing struck her as being relevant.

She stood. She reached her arms over her head, then bent at the waist and touched the floor. She placed both hands on her back and bent backward.

Sitting back down in her desk chair, she rolled over to the table with Patricia's items on it. She looked through the things in Patricia's handbag again. Then she began looking through each item from Patricia's desk. She started with the credit card statements. *Amazon, grocery store, restaurants, gas station, drug store, clothes stores, doctors, dentists*. Next, she read the checking account statements. *Cell phone, electricity, water, trash removal, house taxes, car insurance, credit card bill, landscaping maintenance, federal and state taxes*. She made a few notes, including the name and number of a plumbing company that Patricia used a couple of times.

Mack looked at the other items from Patricia's desk. There were user instruction booklets for a cell phone, camera, and laptop. There was paperwork for the purchase of the Browns' house and county tax statements. There were receipts for doctors, dentists, and prescriptions. Both cars were paid for and had clean titles. There was a copy of Patricia and Greg Browns' marriage certificate. She jotted down the date that they were married in Seattle. She also made a note of the birthdates of the four Brown children. Susan was born in a hospital in Seattle. Will, Tom, and Alan were born in the same hospital in Alaska. Mack read the birth certificates. "Well, crap."

~~~

"Do you need to speak to Ethan again?" Joe Williams asked Nick and Mack when he answered the front door of their house.

"Actually, we need to ask you and your wife a few questions," Mack said. "May we come in?"

"Of course." He escorted them to the living room. "Please have a seat."

160

Mack and Nick sat on the couch. Joe sat in an armchair next to the fireplace. He called for Alice.

She came into the room and sat in the chair next to her husband. "What's this about?"

Mack leaned forward. "Joe, it's come to our attention that you're actually Susan Brown's biological father."

His eyes widened. "What? No, I'm not. Who told you that?"

"Patricia listed you as the father on Susan's birth certificate." Mack handed him a copy. "Not Greg Brown. Patricia and Greg were married eighteen months after Susan was born."

He read the paper. "Oh my God. She never told me."

Mack asked, "So, you didn't know that Patricia was pregnant?"

He shook his head. "No. We dated for a little over seven months during our senior year of high school. I was crazy about her. A week after we graduated she told me that she had no desire to stay in this town. She said she didn't love me and she wasn't interested in the two of us continuing our relationship."

Mack looked at his wife's face. "You don't look surprised, Alice. You knew, didn't you?"

Alice looked down at her hands in her lap. "Yes."

Joe turned toward her. "What?!"

"She told me. Did you forget that we were best friends in high school? She made me promise not to tell anyone, and I kept my word." Alice shifted to the edge of the chair. "I didn't know that I'd fall in love with you two years later."

"All this time and you never told me?" Joe shook his head. "How could you?"

"Mom, dad... what's going on?" Ethan asked. He'd come into the room without anyone noticing.

"Everything's fine, son," Joe said. "Please go back upstairs. Your mom and I will come up to talk to you after the officers leave."

Ethan left the room. He glanced back at his parents as he climbed the stairs.

Mack leaned toward Alice. "When Patricia moved back to town with Joe's child, were you upset?"

"Of course I was. My husband's first girlfriend comes back with his love child. I asked her why she'd moved back here. She said she and the children needed to be close to Grace after her husband died. She said she had no intention of telling Joe or Susan."

Mack asked, "Can you both account for your whereabouts last Saturday morning between two and six?"

"We were both here at home, asleep… together," Joe said.

"Is that correct, Alice? You and Joe were both here that morning?"

"You don't seriously think that one of us would kill Patricia and those two boys, do you? That's ridiculous. Our son was there!"

Joe stood. "I'd like you to go now. If you have any other questions for us, we will answer those with our attorney present."

Nick stood. "Thank you for your time." Joe escorted them out. When they got to Nick's sedan, he asked, "Are you buying their stories?"

"Both of them had motive. Alice was upset that Patricia was back. And, even though Joe says he didn't know, he may have found out somehow. Maybe he wanted to be a part of Susan's life, and Patricia didn't want that. Or, maybe Joe was angry that Patricia hadn't told him." Mack rubbed her forehead. "When Joe and Alice were at the police department, they said they've both been inside the Browns' house. Their fingerprints will be in it. Looks like we have two more suspects."

CHAPTER 42

Mack and Nick sat in Chief Davis' office and updated him on the potential suspects they had so far. Then they gave him a copy of the sketches of the two men seen the morning of the murders.

"I'm glad Barbara isn't the only person on your list." Davis rubbed the back of his neck. "I'm getting pressure from the Mayor and others in town to show some progress. The sketches are perfect for that. We can have another press conference and ask the public to help us identify these men. We'll make it clear that they're not suspects, just someone we want to talk to."

Mack sat forward in her chair. "Chief, if we do that we'll get crazies coming out of the woodwork. And, if those two men are the murderers, they'll be tipped off."

"I realize that. But this will give the public something to concentrate on other than the fact that we haven't arrested anyone yet."

As the two walked back to the bullpen, she said, "I frigging hate politics."

~~~

The press conference was called for two that afternoon so that the sketches could be on the evening news. Again Mack and Nick stood behind Davis.

"As you are all aware, three people were murdered last Saturday morning. We're asking for the public's help in identifying these two men." The chief held up the composite sketches. "A witness saw them walking close to the scene of the murders. The two men are not suspects. They may have seen something that could help with our investigation. Anyone with information on the identity of the two men is asked to call the Skaus Lake Police Department. Thank you."

Again, as Davis, Mack, and Nick walked back inside the police department, reporters pelted them with questions. The three ignored them.

The chief assigned Barbara and Charlie to answer the phone calls when they started coming in. They would screen out the non-relevant ones and give Mack and Nick call-back information for any that actually had potential.

Nick said, "Let the fun and games begin."

After the press conference, Mack phoned the plumbing company that Patricia used. Mack identified herself and asked to speak to the manager. She was told that the owner was Fred Coates. When he answered, she said, "We'd like to speak with the employee of yours that worked at the Brown house. We're trying to eliminate known fingerprints from those collected at the crime scene."

"Give me a minute, and I'll check my database to see who that was."

She could hear him typing on the computer keyboard. Then, there were a few seconds of silence.

"That employee no longer works here."

"What's his name?"

"Brody Lugo." Coates spelled it for her.

"Can you tell me why he left your employ?"

He cleared his throat. "He was fired."

"Why?"

He sighed loudly. "I received a complaint from a client. She claimed that Brody went through her underwear drawer. She didn't have any proof. Things were disheveled, but nothing was missing. Brody denied it. I kept him on because I thought the woman must have been mistaken. But another client said she saw him peeping through her window the same night he worked at her house. So, I fired him."

"Were charges pressed?"

"No. The woman didn't want to go through all that. She just didn't want Brody to ever come back."

"Who were the clients that complained?"

164

He cleared his throat again. "The first complaint was from Gloria Higgins. The second was from Patricia Brown."

"What?! And it never occurred to you to let the police know this?!"

"I didn't want word to get out that someone like that had worked for me. It would be bad for business."

"Well, business could get a lot worse. I could charge you with obstruction of justice."

"Please. Don't do that. I'm sorry."

"Address for Lugo." Mack wrote down the address, then slammed the phone down. "Moron!"

Nick frowned. "What's up?"

Mack filled him in as she searched for Lugo in the crime database.

"Jesus. What the hell? Three people are dead!"

After a few seconds, she shook her head. "No record. Let's stop by Lugo's apartment and have a little chat."

Dave came into the bullpen and said to Mack. "You've got a call from the county prosecutor's office. I'll forward it."

When the phone rang, she picked up the phone on her desk. "Detective Anderson."

Deputy Prosecutor Ivan Archer said, "Mack, how are you?"

"I'm fine. Why are you calling?"

Ivan chuckled. "Right to the point, as usual." He paused. "I wanted you to know that we've reached a plea agreement with Cox. He'll plead guilty to ID fraud. He'll serve ninety days in lockup, followed by two years of probation."

"Wow. Way to punish him."

"It's a good deal. None of us will have to waste time in court on a misdemeanor."

"It's not a good deal for the two high school girls that he had the hots for. Should I send you a copy of the photos he took of his latest victim?"

"You get me the proof he's actually guilty of stalking or harassment, and I'll put him away for a long time. Until then, this is the best I can do."

She rubbed her temple. "I understand. I don't like it, but I understand. Thanks for letting me know, Ivan."

"We'd appreciate it if you and Nick would attend the arraignment."

"We wouldn't miss it." She hung up, then told Nick about the plea deal.

"Damn it." He shook his head. "Well, at least he won't be able to harass any young girls for a while. We did good there, I guess."

~~~

Brody Lugo opened the door of his apartment. He was big and fleshy, with a sheen of grease on his face. He looked at Nick's uniform. "What do ya' want?"

Mack held out her badge. "I'm Detective Anderson, and this is Officer Moore. We have a few questions for you."

Lugo blocked the doorway. "About what?"

She said, "I'm sure you've heard about the three murders at the Brown's home. We understand that you did some plumbing work for Patricia. We're interested in clearing innocent people who've been in the house. We need your fingerprints for elimination purposes. If you're willing, we could come in and get them right now. That way you wouldn't have to come down to the police department."

Lugo hesitated for a moment. "I guess that's okay." He stepped aside.

Nick glanced at Mack. "I'll get my kit out of the car."

The inside of Lugo's apartment smelled like body odor, dirty socks, and fried food. Every flat surface was piled with used paper plates and fast food wrappers. Mack shivered. *Gross.*

Lugo looked her up and down. "It's been awhile since I've had someone as good lookin' as you in my apartment, pretty lady."

"Detective."

"Huh?"

"I prefer that you refer to me as detective, not pretty lady."

Nick walked inside in time to hear what Mack had said. The look on his face was enough to cause Lugo to take a step backward. "Sit down," Nick growled. "We can get this done in a few minutes."

Mack perched on the edge of a dirty chair that was across from where Lugo sat. "Did you hear about the murders on the news?"

"Yeah."

"I bet you were surprised when you heard that it happened at a house where you'd worked."

"Yeah."

"After Patricia Brown got you fired though, I imagine you weren't too sad that she was dead."

"Nah." Lugo watched Nick take his little finger and roll it in black ink, then roll it on a fingerprint card.

"I bet you were pissed at her."

"I was. That stupid bitch."

She leaned forward. "Were you angry enough to kill her?"

"Huh?" Lugo looked up her. "No. I didn' kill nobody."

"How about you tell us where you were last Saturday, between two and six in the morning." She shrugged. "That way we can eliminate you as a suspect."

"I… I don't know. Let me think. Yeah. Yeah, I know. I went to Tiny's Bar that night. I stayed until they closed."

"What time was that?"

"Two. Candy came back to my place with me."

"Candy?" Nick said, in an 'are you serious' tone of voice.

"What's Candy's last name and phone number?"

"I don't know."

"Which one don't you know?"

"Neither. She's always at Tiny's when I go there. I buy her a few drinks close to closing time, then sometimes she comes back here with me. We don't talk much. If you know what I mean."

Nick said to Mack, "Why do people keep assuming we're celibate idiots?"

Lugo's brow furrowed. "Huh?"

She asked, "What time did Candy leave here on Saturday?"

"Let's see. We slept until about one that afternoon. So, somewhere about then, I guess."

"I'm all finished," Nick said. "I need your birth date, height, and weight." He pointed at the empty fields on the card. "Here. See?"

Lugo gave Nick the information.

"Great," Mack said. "Thanks for your time, Brody." Walking back to the sedan, she said, "Please tell me you have hand sanitizer in your car."

CHAPTER 43

As it was Monday and Nick's wife had her book club, Mack and he went to dinner at a sports bar that had great burgers. He changed out of his uniform in the men's room again. She scrubbed her hands with lots of soap in the women's restroom. They ordered burgers, fries, and a pitcher of beer.

He ran his hand down his face. "Damn it. I feel like we could stand on Main Street, throw a dart, and hit someone with a motive for the murders."

"Compared to some of the other murders I've investigated, this case is complicated."

"Do you think that Patricia was talking to Pastor Beck about Susan's birth father?"

"I don't know what else it could have been. If one of the Brown children was talking to him like he insinuated, what could that have been about? Was it Alan, because he was gay? Or, maybe Susan actually knew about her birth father. Too many unanswered questions." She paused. "Let's try talking to Grace again. We also need to go back to the high school and confront Aaron Paul. And, we need to verify Lugo's alibi with Candy."

"Okay. Enough about work. Let's talk about something else." He tented his hands on the table. "Last time we ate dinner, you said the reason you became a police officer was a long story. We have time tonight. Tell me the story."

She finished her beer and poured another. "You tell me why you became one. Then I'll tell you why I did."

"My story isn't very interesting," he said. "My dad was a policeman, and I always wanted to be one. After high school, I got an associate's degree in criminal justice. The day I turned twenty-one, I applied for the academy and was accepted." He took a drink of his beer. "Okay, now you."

Mack hadn't eaten lunch, and the beer was going straight to her head. "My sophomore year in college, my husband and two-year-old daughter went to a convenience store to get milk. A masked gunman came in and killed them both."

"Oh God. I'm so sorry."

She took another drink of beer and swiped at her eyes with a napkin. "I went to the police department every single day to see if they had any leads." She sighed. "After about two weeks, the detective handling the murders started acting like I was annoying him by being there. The third week he told me that I was wasting my time and his." She shook her head. "It was like a switch flipped inside me. I went from severely depressed to incredibly angry. I called that detective every four letter word I knew, and I put my hands on him. It wasn't pretty. Looking back, I'm kind of surprised that he didn't arrest me." She shrugged. "Or put me in a psychiatric hospital.

The next fall, I went back to college and changed to a double major in criminology and criminal justice. When I wasn't in class, I volunteered at a friend's private investigator's office. Which was also where I lived for those two years of college. After graduation, I went back to Coeur d'Alene and applied with the state police. I continued to work for the private investigator on the weekends.

After the academy, I worked patrol for six months. When a position for an officer in an investigative unit opened up, I asked to be assigned to it. I worked with that unit for eighteen months. I was vocal about wanting to become a detective. I took the detective's test, then applied for the first position that came open after that." She shrugged. "As they say, the rest is history."

"Wow." He rubbed his forehead. "That must have been rough."

"Don't. Don't start feeling sorry for me. I hate when people give me that 'poor thing' look. Shit happens. All the time. People do horrible things to each other. All the time."

~~~

When Mack got back to the cottage that night, the kitten greeted her at the front door. "Still here?" she asked as she opened the door and let him in. The kitten ran straight to the kitchen and started meowing.

Mack fed him and put out a bowl of water again. She poured herself a small glass of wine and took it to the couch with her printouts of people and questions she'd developed. She read each page and set it upside down on the end table. No flashes of genius hit.

The kitten finished eating and jumped into her lap.

She rubbed his ears. "If you're planning to stick around, we're going to have to get you a litter box. That way you won't have to be outside in the cold during the day. We also need some food other than tuna." She sipped wine and listened to the kitten purr. She felt the tension seep out of her body. "How do you do that? Okay. We need a name for you. I can't keep calling you cat or buster. Hmmm. Let me think. Draoidh is Scottish Gaelic for an enigma. And, you certainly seem to be that. I think I'll call you Drao. What do you think?"

The kitten meowed.

Mack fell asleep on the couch, curled up with Drao. The sun shining in her eyes woke her the next morning.

Drao meowed, then yawned and stretched to his full length.

Mack picked him up and kissed the top of his head. "It's a bad idea for me to get attached to you. Getting attached only leads to getting hurt. Bad idea."

CHAPTER 44

When Mack walked in the back door of the police department, she could hear the phones in the reception area ringing.

Nick looked up at her from his desk and shook his head. "It's been like that since six this morning."

She silently cursed Chief Davis. "Let's get out of here and go see Grace and Aaron Paul before Cox's arraignment at eleven."

"Excellent idea. Let's do it."

They decided to go to Grace's house first. When she answered the door, Mack asked, "May we come in?"

Grace stepped aside and motioned for them to enter. She led them into the kitchen. "Please sit. Can I get you some coffee?"

Mack nodded. "Yes, please."

"Sure, Nick said. "Thanks."

Grace poured a cup of coffee for the three of them. She set a sugar bowl and cream in the center of the table. She helped herself to both. "Are you here to tell me that you've arrested the man that killed my daughter and grandson?"

"I wish we could tell you that," Mack said. "We have several suspects. But we need your help."

"With what?"

Mack sipped her coffee. "We found Susan's birth certificate in Patricia's things. We know that Joe Williams is Susan's biological father."

"Oh. I see."

"Does Susan know?" Mack asked.

"No. And, you can't tell her. Patricia didn't want Susan to ever know. Greg Brown was the only father Susan has ever known. And Greg adored Susan, even though she wasn't his biological child. On top of everything else, this news would devastate Susan."

Mack nodded. "I understand. If it doesn't have anything to do with the murders, there isn't any reason why Susan should have to find out."

"Why would it have anything to do with the murders?"

"We're just checking all possibilities." Mack took a drink of coffee. "We need to know if that was what Patricia talked to Pastor Beck about. Or, is there something else we should know about."

"Patricia told me that she'd talked to the pastor about Susan's paternity. I think Patricia hoped that she and Alice Williams would be friends again when she moved home. But Alice wasn't happy that Patricia was back in town. Patricia was upset about that."

"Did Patricia mention any of the children talking to Pastor Beck?"

Grace shook her head. "She never said anything like that to me. Alan helped Pastor Beck on Saturdays. But I don't know if there was anything Alan talked to him about. Or if Susan did."

"How long had Alan been helping Pastor Beck?"

"Oh, ever since they moved here."

"Okay," Mack said. "Thank you, Grace."

"Thanks for the coffee," Nick said as Grace walked them to the door.

~~~

"I think I should talk to Aaron alone," Mack said when they parked in front of the high school. "He might be more willing to talk without someone in uniform present."

Nick nodded. "You're right. I'll wait here."

Martz didn't seem surprised to see her. And, he didn't complain when she asked to see Aaron Paul again. He checked Aaron's schedule and walked her to the classroom. Then the three of them went to the library.

"Thank you, Mr. Martz," Mack said.

Nodding, he left.

Aaron's right leg again hopped up and down in fast motion.

"Aaron, it's come to my attention that you're selling drugs here at the high school." She held up her hand to stop his denial. "I don't care about that. I only care about the murders. That's why I'm here. I understand that you sold pot to Alan and Jack."

"No. No, I didn't."

"Come on Aaron. I know you sold them pot."

"No. I'm telling the truth. I didn't."

She leaned toward him. "Help me out here. I'm wondering if they might have owed money to someone for drugs."

"They didn't owe me any money. Honest."

"I'd like to believe you, Aaron, I would. I'd also like to eliminate you from my list of suspects for the murders."

"What? No. No. I didn't have anything to do with the murders. I didn't!"

"Where were you Friday night and Saturday morning?"

"I was at home. My mom works nights, and she came home about six-thirty that morning."

She leaned back and sighed. "So, nobody can vouch for where you were Saturday morning before six-thirty?"

"No. I played a video game and watched a movie. Then I went to bed. I didn't see anyone else that night."

"Okay. You can go back to class."

Mack shook her head at Nick as she walked to the sedan. "Aaron said he wasn't selling pot to Alan and Jack. And, he doesn't have an alibi."

"Damn. I was hoping we could eliminate at least one suspect from our list."

~~~

At Cox's arraignment, Judge Cooley advised him of the charges against him and asked how he pled to those charges. Cox pled guilty. The prosecutor explained that an agreement was reached regarding sentencing. Mack fumed internally as the judge accepted the plea and the sentence. Nick tapped his right foot during the entire proceeding, so Mack figured he was upset too.

Everyone stood as the judge left the room. Mack and Nick watched Cox being led out of the courtroom. Cox kept his eyes on her from the second he left the defendant's table. When he was directly in front of her, he smiled eerily. Then he slowly ran his tongue over his lips.

Nick took a step toward Cox. Mack placed her hand on his forearm. "Don't give him the satisfaction."

CHAPTER 45

Mack and Nick sat at their desks and looked at the pile of phone messages between them.

She picked up the messages and counted them. "Eleven for you and twelve for me." She handed him his half.

"Yippee," he mumbled.

They both picked up the phone on their desk and started returning calls.

"Mrs. Stuart? This is Detective Anderson. You said that you think one of the men that we're trying to locate is your neighbor?" She listened for a minute. "I see. So, your neighbor's twenty years older than the man in the photograph. Well, thank you so much for calling."

She called the next number and identified herself again. Again, she listened for a few minutes. "So, the man with the dark hair looks like your nephew? Can you give me your nephew's address, please?" She started writing down the address but stopped. "He lives in Tampa, Florida. Okay. Thank you for the information. If we need anything else, we'll give you a call."

She rubbed her forehead. "Oh my God." She continued to make follow-up calls to the people that thought knew the two men in the police sketches.

When they both finished, Nick asked, "You got any actual leads on the identity of the two men? I have one. Out of eleven. I thought Barbara and Dave were supposed to be screening these damn calls."

"I have two potentials." Mack grinned. "Oh, and this one's actually for you. Let me read it to you. "Ms. Jeanne Grandsen begged the dispatcher to give her Officer Moore's phone number. She said he was very good looking. And, she knew they had a connection because Officer Moore looked right at her during the press conference." She tipped her head to the side. "You going to call Ms. Crazy back, good lookin'?"

"Ha, ha. You're a riot."

She chuckled. "Let's go visit our three potentials."

Nick drove to the address of the first contact. Mrs. Olivia Belton was eighty-five, with milky brown eyes and snow white hair. When the two followed her into the living room of her house, they saw coffee and chocolate cake on a tray. Mrs. Belton had set out a silver coffee set, porcelain cups and saucers, and linen napkins. Mack and Nick glanced at each other.

Mack sat on the pink floral French provincial settee. Nick looked uncomfortable as he sat on one of the small antique cane-backed armchairs in the room.

"I hardly ever have company anymore," Mrs. Belton said. "Since my Ben died, I'm here all alone."

Mack said, "This looks lovely. Chocolate's my favorite kind of cake."

"Oh, I'm so glad. Let me get you a large piece."

"Thank you. I'd love some coffee too."

Mrs. Belton smiled. "Of course, dear. Here you are. Can I get you some, Officer Moore?"

"No thank you."

Mack cleared her throat to get his attention, then gave him a look that would have petrified Medusa.

"Well, if it's not too much trouble, I'd love some."

She looked around the room. "You have a lovely home. How long have you lived here?"

"Oh, thank you, dear. I've lived here since Ben and I got married, sixty-two years ago."

She swallowed a bite of the cake. "Were you born here in town?"

"Yes. Ben and I went to school together from first grade on." She smiled. "We never dated anyone else. There was only one person for both of us."

Nick set his cup on the coffee table. "You said on the phone that you think the two men in the police sketches work at a store downtown. But you couldn't remember the name of the store."

"Yes. Well, I found a receipt, and it's the Cedar Street Market. My granddaughter takes me shopping there every other week, you see."

~~~

On the way to the second address, Mack was quiet for a while.

Nick glanced over at her. "What are you thinking so hard about?"

"I can't believe that lovely woman has family here in town, and they don't go to see her very often. It makes me sick to think of all the elderly people who are blatantly shunned. It's like they're invisible. They're often regarded as feeble-minded and lacking the ability to contribute to society." She paused. "I think that by the time they reach that age they have a lot of wisdom to impart to younger people. If we would only listen."

He nodded. "Amen to that."

She mentally shook herself out of her reverie. "Who's next?"

"Next on the list is Jacob Nemeth. He said the guy with the black hair and mustache is his niece's boyfriend." Nick parked on the street in front of Nemeth's house. They walked up the driveway to the sidewalk that led to the front door. The yard was covered with white river rock. Nick knocked on the door.

A thin man in his sixties opened it. He stepped outside and closed the front door.

Mack asked, "Are you Mr. Nemeth?"

"That's me."

She introduced herself and Nick.

Nemeth glanced at the door. "My wife doesn't know I called you. It's actually her niece's boyfriend that I called about." He handed Nick a small piece of paper. "I've written down my wife's niece's name and address and her boyfriend's name. I don't know what his address is. I've only met him once. Sorry, I can't be more help." He glanced back at the door again. "You better go before my wife sees you."

"Thank you for the information," Nick said. "We appreciate you calling." They walked back to the sedan and got in. He read the paper. "The niece's boyfriend's name is Chris Purvis."

~~~

The last person they met with was Noah Paxton. He lived in a large, gated apartment complex, which was close to downtown. Every building in the complex was painted the same shade of beige, but the landscaping added some color. Mack and Nick looked at the numbering system on the outside of the buildings and found the one for Paxton. They walked up the concrete steps to the second floor and knocked on the third door.

Paxton opened the door. He looked to be in his early thirties. He had stringy brown hair that hung over his ears. Like Nemeth, Paxton stepped outside. He nervously glanced around. "The two guys aren't wanted for anything, right?"

"That's right," Mack said. "We just want to talk to them. Hoping they saw something that might be pertinent to the murders."

He stuck his hands in his pockets. "The guy with the black hair is named Chris Purvis. The other guy's name is Floyd Rupp. My girlfriend works with Chris' girlfriend, so we've been at parties together. Chris and Floyd work at that market downtown."

Mack asked, "Cedar Street Market?"

"That's the one." Paxton looked down. "I don't want them to know it was me that told you who they are."

"Don't worry," Mack said. "We'll keep your name out of it."

179

CHAPTER 46

Mack and Nick walked through the automatic double doors at the front of Cedar Street Market and started to look around. They spotted Floyd Rupp on aisle twelve, squatting as he restocked shampoo on the bottom shelf.

Rupp looked up. He stood and looked at them for a few seconds.

Mack mumbled, "Don't do it."

Purvis started running down the aisle, away from them. He turned left when he reached the end.

Nick yelled, "Stop! Police!"

As Mack ran left, she motioned for Nick to follow Purvis. When she reached the last aisle, she saw the door leading outside close. Nick was closer to it than she was. She pointed. "Back!" She sprinted toward the front door. She yelled at customers as she approached them. "Out of the way! Police!" She flew out of the front door in time to see Rupp running through the parking lot. She ran after him. She saw Nick running toward her. "Car!"

Nick sprinted to his sedan and got in. He turned on the lights and siren. Mack continued to run across the parking lot.

Rupp fumbled with the door of his car. Seeing Nick's car speeding toward him, he turned and started running toward a bank of trees on the edge of the parking lot.

Mack was gaining on him. "Stop! Police!" Rupp glanced over his left shoulder at her as he ran. Just before he reached the trees, she dove and tackled him.

He grunted loudly as he hit the blacktop. "Fuck!"

She grabbed his right arm, then his left. She bent them behind his back and cuffed him.

Nick squealed to a stop and jumped out of his sedan. He hauled Rupp to his feet. "Yep, you're definitely fucked."

Mack bent over and placed her hands on her knees. "Read him his rights." She drew in large breaths of air.

"I didn't do nothin', man!" Rupp yelled as Nick recited the Miranda warnings.

When he finished, she asked, "Do you understand these rights?" She grabbed Rupp by the arm and hauled him to Nick's sedan.

"I didn't do nothin'!"

"I asked you a question."

"Yeah, yeah. I understand. What are you arresting me for?"

"Evading the police, for starters. I'd like to arrest you for being an idiot, but unfortunately, that's not against the law."

~~~

Nick and Mack ushered Rupp to the front of the police department, where they photographed and fingerprinted him. Then Nick took him to the interview room. Nick used the key to release the cuff from Rupp's left wrist. He secured it to a metal ring soldered to the side of the table. He put a fresh tape in the machine and informed Rupp that he was being recorded.

While Nick was doing that, Mack ran Rupp's fingerprints through AFIS. She got one hit. Nine years ago, he was convicted of third-degree burglary in Boise. He'd been sentenced to one year in jail, plus three years of probation. She ran Chris Purvis' name. She didn't get any hits. She walked in the door of the interview room.

Nick leaned on the wall in his usual place, arms crossed in front of his chest.

Rupp was looking down at the table. He glanced up at her. She sat across from him. "Floyd, we have a witness that places you and Chris Purvis on Skyline Road at five-thirty the Saturday before last. Why were you there?"

"We was just takin' a walk."

"At five-thirty in the morning? Where were you walking to?"

"Uh… we was walkin' to the top of the hill."

"What were you going to do when you got to the top of the hill?"

"Uh… turn around and go back down."

"Why did you pick Skyline Road to take this walk at five-thirty in the morning?"

"A guy told us it was real nice. So we was checkin' it out."

"Checking it out for what?"

"Just to see what it looked like."

She leaned her forearms on the table. "Okay, Floyd. Help me out here. I'm confused. You say that you were going to walk to the end of Skyline Road, turn around, and walk back. Just checking it out to see what it looked like. Why? Were you looking for something in particular?"

"Naw, we was just lookin' to see what was there."

"When you were walking up and down Skyline Road, did you see anyone else around?"

"We seen one lady drivin' down the road, but that was it. We didn't see nobody else."

"Floyd, I know you served time for burglary nine years ago. Is that why you were looking at the houses on Skyline Road?"

He looked down at the table. "We was just lookin'."

She sat back in her chair. "I don't think you're telling us everything. You know that you aren't doing yourself any favors by not telling us the whole truth. So, we're going to give you some time to think about your answers. When we come back, I sure hope you'll help yourself out." Mack stood and motioned for Nick to step outside.

He followed her out the door and closed it.

She said, "Let's let him sit while we go see if his buddy Chris Purvis is at home."

The two drove to Purvis' home address, but he wasn't there. They decided to visit his girlfriend. Her apartment was on the first floor of a two-building complex that looked more like a motel.

Nick pounded on the door. "Police. Open up."

A young woman, wearing an oversized t-shirt that said 'Seattle Seahawks' on the front, opened the door. When she saw Nick, her face turned pale. "Can I help you?"

Mack asked, "Diana Lewis?"

"Yes."

Mack held up her badge. "I'm Detective Anderson, and this is Officer Moore. We're looking for Chris Purvis. We understand that he's your boyfriend."

"We dated. I don't know that I'd call him my boyfriend."

"Do you know where he is?"

Diana shook her head. "No. He told me he needed some time alone and that he would be gone for a couple of weeks."

"When was that?"

"Uh… Monday, I think." She nodded. "Yeah, Monday."

"Did he say where he was going?"

"No."

Mack took notes. "Have you spoken to Chris since then?"

"No. He told me that he'd be out of cell phone range."

"We need his cell number."

"Sure." Diana lifted up one side of her t-shirt and pulled her cell phone out of the back pocket of a pair of work-out shorts. She scrolled through her contacts and handed the phone to Mack. "Here it is."

Mack made a note of the number and handed the phone back. "Thank you." She pulled a card out of the front pocket of her shirt and handed it to Diana. "If Chris contacts you, we need to know. You can get me at that number anytime."

183

Diana looked at the card. "Okay. I'll let you know if I hear from him."

Mack thought, *Crap. If Chris Purvis is Luke Adler, he's done another runner.*

~~~

The two walked back into the interview room "Hey, man, it's not fair that you guys just left me in here for so long.

Mack sat down opposite Rupp. "Fairness is definitely overrated." She leaned forward. "Well, have you thought about what you need to tell us to save yourself?"

"I don't know what you want me to say."

"I'm not playing cat and mouse with you anymore, Floyd. Let me ask you this. Why did we find your fingerprints inside the Browns' home?"

Nick flicked his eyes to Mack, then back.

"No way, man. I wasn't ever in that house."

"My theory is that you were looking to get back into your old profession. You and Purvis were casing Skyline Road. You choose the Browns' house. When you went in, you got caught. Purvis didn't want any witnesses, so he killed the three victims. You're an accessory to murder."

"No way. No way man. We didn't break into nobody's house that morning. I admit it, we was casin' the neighborhood. If it panned out, we was gonna' come back another day. I swear. That's the truth. Honest. You gotta' believe me. You can ask Chris. He'll tell you the same thing."

"Your buddy Chris is in the wind. He left you high and dry. We can't charge you with thinking about committing a crime."

Nick moved to the table and placed both of his hands flat on it. He leaned close to Rupp's face. "Believe me, we're going to be watching you closely. Everywhere you go, someone from this department's going to be there. So, you better not even think about committing a crime here again."

She stood. She left the room. Nick following her, closing the door behind himself. In the hallway, she said, "I think he's telling the truth. I don't think they're our guys."

"Well, then who the hell is?"

~~~

Mack stopped at the pet store on the way home and picked up a litter box and litter, cat food and bowls, and some toys that she found in one of the isles. As soon as she opened the front gate of the cottage's courtyard, Drao sprinted to the front door. He meowed loudly, circling her legs. "Okay, okay, patience please."

She opened the front door and headed to the kitchen. She unpacked the bags from the pet store. "Look what I got you. Real food. The pet store guy said hard food's better for your teeth. This one is for kittens. I hope you like it." She set the two bowls on the floor, where she wouldn't be kicking them. She filled one with the food and the other with water. Drao gobbled up the little round morsels of food.

"Where should we put the litter box? I guess in my bathroom. Makes sense, since it's the room to do that kind of stuff in." She walked into her bathroom and set up the litter box according to the directions. She pushed it into the space next to the toilet. Drao trotted in. Mack picked him up and set him in the litter box. "Do you have any idea what this is for?"

Drao meowed and jumped out.

"Okay, buddy, you're going to have to figure that out. This is a rental."

CHAPTER 47

Mack slept fitfully because her hip was sore from tackling Rupp. Every time she rolled onto her right side, she woke up. When the alarm went off the next morning, she was still asleep. Drao was curled up next to her chest, making it toasty warm. She'd happily had a nightmare-free night. She rolled onto her left side and pushed herself into a sitting position on the bed. The kitten yawned and stretched.

She went into her bathroom. Drao followed. She picked him up and set him in the litter box. He dug a hole, did his business, and covered it up. "Good job! You're a smart little guy."

She shuffled in stocking feet to the kitchen to make coffee. She stood in front of the machine until the carafe was an inch full. Then she pulled it out and poured coffee into a large ceramic cup. After sticking the carafe back, she pulled the refrigerator door open and filled a zip-lock bag with ice. She shrugged into her coat. She took the coffee and ice pack to the front patio. She sat in one of the wicker chairs and placed the bag of ice on her side. She sipped coffee and soaked in the peacefulness of the view.

The serenity of nature was one of the reasons that she loved living in Idaho. Whenever there were chaos and ugliness at work, she only needed to look outside to feel better.

Her husband loved the outdoors, too. When Sean and Mack first started dating in high school, they would hike in the Bitterroot Range near Coeur d'Alene every weekend possible. After they were married and moved to Boise to go to college, they continued to hike in the surrounding foothills. When Samantha was born, they bought a child carrier. Sean used it to pack Samantha around with them. Mack hadn't been hiking since Sean and Samantha were killed. *Maybe someday.*

~~~

When Mack walked in the back door of the police department, Nick held up a package. "Courier delivered the evidence analysis earlier. I've been waiting for you to open it."

"Do it. Let's see what we've got."

He ripped the package open. "Ten days! This usually takes thirty." Suddenly, he looked at her. "You had something to do with this, didn't you?"

She shrugged. "I made one call. That's it."

"That must have been some phone call." He grinned and handed the package to her. "Read it out loud."

Mack skipped the case summary and procedures sections and went straight to the findings section. "There's one unidentified fingerprint... from the edge of the kitchen counter. The rest belong to the Brown family, Grace, Jack, the Williams, Chrissy, and the two housekeepers. No unidentified DNA."

"That's a little disappointing." Nick ran his hand down his face. "Actually, that's a lot disappointing. I was hoping we'd find the fingerprints of one of our suspects. That would have been way too easy though, I guess."

"People don't get arrested for committing a murder, they get arrested for not planning one properly."

"I don't know about you, but Cox is still number one on my list."

Mack took up her thinking pose, leaning back in her chair and looked at the ceiling. "Toby Jackson has a strong alibi. Chris Purvis and Floyd Rupp have each other for an alibi, even though we still haven't found Purvis. But you and I both think that Rupp was telling the truth. Joe and Alice Williams say they were together. Their alibi may be suspect. They could be protecting each other. If Lugo's alibi pans out, that leaves Barbara, Aaron Paul, and Cox without alibis. And, neither of us believes Barbara could be a murderer. I'm with you. I still think Cox is our primary suspect. And, as we know, repeat offenders often increase the severity of the crimes they commit." She sat up and looked at Nick. "How do you feel about paying Cox a visit in prison tomorrow?"

"I like that idea." He grinned. "That way Cox will know that he's still on our radar. Give him something to think about while he's doing nothing all day. I'll call and arrange for a visit."

Since they had time before they went to Tiny's to speak with Candy, Nick looked at the items collected from the Browns' house. Mack figured that a fresh set of eyes would be good. Maybe he would see something that she'd missed.

While he did that, she looked through the folders on Alan's laptop. From what she could see, he was very organized. He had one folder for each class he was taking. In the English Literature folder, she found two subfolders, one with a reading list of short stories, poetry, and novels. The second subfolder held a variety of essays that Alan wrote. She looked through Chemistry, Algebra, and French III folders. The last was a History folder, which contained the most subfolders. Sources, maps, timelines, projects, assignments, and independent research. Mack groaned. *Oh, crap.* She was not a fan of the subject of History. She slogged through the first two subfolders, but couldn't take any more. She stood and stretched her arms above her head. She walked to the small coffee mess that was set up in the front of the bullpen. She poured herself a cup of coffee and added sugar and creamer. *I'm going to need all the stimulants I can get to stay awake.*

"You got anything?" Nick asked.

"Crossed eyes. You?"

He chuckled. "I don't see anything."

She headed back to her desk and the computer. She made it through the next three folders without falling asleep. When she opened the subfolder marked independent study, she said, "What the heck?"

"What is it?" Nick came over to her desk.

"Take a look."

"What's all that?"

"Well, it's sure not history."

Inside the subfolder was page after page about sexual abuse. He pulled up his chair, and she started scrolling through each page. One page contained the definition of sexual abuse. Another had abuse statistics. Alan had highlighted three sentences. 'One in ten children is sexually abused before their eighteenth birthday. Thirty percent of children are abused by family members. As many as sixty percent are abused by people the family trusts.' There was information on the effects of sexual abuse, with one highlighted section. 'Sexually abused children who keep it a secret or who tell and are not believed are at greater risk than the general population for psychological, emotional, and social problems, often lasting into adulthood.' Lastly, there was one highlighted section on the abuser. 'People who abuse children look and act like everyone else. In fact, they often go out of their way to appear trustworthy.'

Mack said, "Grace told us that Alan volunteered with Pastor Beck."

"You think he was abusing Alan?"

"That would explain why Alan was so quiet at school, yet, he would volunteer with Pastor Beck. Alan would have been about thirteen when he starting helping at the church."

"That thought makes me sick to my stomach."

"I think a visit to Pastor Beck's in order."

Mack could tell Nick was fuming as he drove. "Stay calm," she told him. "We don't actually know that the pastor did anything."

"Okay. You're right." He took a deep breath and blew it out.

When they walked through the church's office door, they could see that Pastor Beck was behind his desk. Nick didn't wait for an invitation.

"Hey!" the receptionist said, as he stormed by.

Mack held up her badge. "Hold the pastor's calls." She walked inside and closed the door to his office.

"What's this about?" The pastor looked between the two.

Mack patted Nick's back and motioned him toward one of the chairs in front of the pastor's desk. She sat in the other chair and said, "We know about Susan Brown's paternity and that Patricia spoke to you about that."

"I'm sorry, but I still can't discuss it."

"We also know about Alan Brown's sexual abuse."

Beck paused for a couple of moments. "Oh, I see."

Nick said, "You see?!"

She placed a restraining hand on his arm. "Why don't you tell us about the abuse? As you know, confession's good for the soul."

"I can't do that."

"Can't or won't?" Nick asked.

"Officers, I'd like you to leave now."

Mack held up her index finger. "Just one more question. Where were you the Saturday morning that the murders occurred?"

"I was in bed, asleep. Alone." He stood. "Goodbye, Officers."

~~~

Mack and Nick decided to go talk with Candy before they went back to the police department. Tiny's was a short, wide building, with a bar to the left of the front door, a dance floor to the right, and bathrooms at the back. A small stage for a band was set up at the front of the establishment.

The two stood in the doorway for a moment, letting their eyes adjust to the dim lighting. The place was doing a robust happy-hour business. Little by little the noisy bar quieted, as people noticed Nick's uniform. Soon, everyone in the bar was looking at them.

Mack walked up to the bartender. "We're looking for Candy."

He pointed. "That's her. The blonde in the short skirt."

Candy had bleached, platinum blonde hair, piled high on top of her head in a mess that looked to Mack like a bird's nest. She was at least forty pounds overweight, five of which may have been make-up.

Mack motioned with her head, and Nick followed. When they walked up to Candy, the guy on the stool next to her stood and left. Mack held up her badge.

"What can I do for you officers?" She gave Nick the once-over. She smiled lasciviously at him.

Mack said, "We need to ask you about Brody Lugo."

"What about him?"

"Did you go home with him the Saturday morning before last, after the bar here closed?"

"I did. Brody may not be much to look at, but he has hidden talents. If you know what I mean." She gave Nick another lewd smile.

Nick's eyes flashed, and he opened his mouth to speak. Before he could say anything, Mack stopped him by grabbing his arm.

"What time did you leave his place that Saturday?"

"I don't know. I guess it was about one-thirty that afternoon. Something like that."

"Okay. That's all we needed to know. Thank you."

"Officer handsome," Candy said to Nick. "Come on back sometime and buy me a drink."

"Don't say a damn thing," he growled at Mack as they walked back to his sedan.

She chuckled. "Kill-joy."

~~~

When Mack opened the cottage's front door, Drao was waiting for her. He circled around her and meowed until she picked him up. "Hello, you little fur ball. How was your day?" She set him on the floor, went into the bedroom, and changed into her favorite warm pajamas. She put on a pair of thick socks

191

and padded to the kitchen. Drao following her every move. She had stopped on the way home and bought herself a large turkey and provolone cheese sandwich. She poured herself a glass of wine and took it and the sandwich out to the patio.

Drao followed her out and jumped into her lap when she sat down.

She set the wine and sandwich on the side table and rubbed Drao's ears. He immediately started purring.

When Mack finished inhaling the sandwich, she sat back, sipped wine, and enjoyed the peacefulness of the incredible scenery. She finished the glass of wine and stood. "Alright my little furry friend, we better get to bed. Tomorrow's bound to be another long day."

CHAPTER 48

Nick arranged to meet with Cox at eleven-thirty on Thursday morning. He was serving his sentence at the Idaho Correctional Institution in Orofino. The facility's designed to house around five hundred male, medium custody offenders. The drive to Orofino from Skaus Lake took four hours.

Nick parked in the lot. "You been here before?"

"A couple of times. You?"

"This is my first."

They both left their service weapons and cell phones in the trunk of the sedan, as required for visitation.

One of the guards at the entrance checked a list and found they were approved for entry. "Do you know where to go?" he asked.

"I do," Mack said. "Thank you."

Sitting at one of the metal tables in the visitation room, they waited for Cox to be escorted from his cell.

When he arrived and saw who his visitors were, he smiled. He sat at the table and smiled. "Why officers, how nice of you to come for a visit. I was afraid we wouldn't get to say goodbye."

"Oh, don't you worry about that," Nick said. "I'm sure you'll be seeing a lot of us in the future."

"Now, why would that be?"

Mack said, "We know that you murdered Patricia and Alan Brown and Jack Caldwell. You went to the Browns' house Saturday morning for Susan, but you didn't count on her being at Chrissy's house. You were so angry that you murdered three people."

Cox's laugh was mirthless. "That's quite a theory, detective. But you're going to have a hard time proving it, aren't you?"

Nick leaned toward him. "Oh, we're going to prove it. You can count on it."

Cox smiled. "Well, I wish you good luck with that. Now, if you'll excuse me, I want to get back to this fascinating book I was reading. It's about a young woman that was the victim of a brutal rape and is now the obsession of a serial stalker. Riveting." He laughed as he stood up and walked away.

Mack and Nick didn't say anything as they walked back to the sedan. They retrieved their things from the trunk. After they climbed into the car and closed the doors, he pounded the palm of his hands on the steering wheel. "Damn piece of shit! I want to slam my fist into that guy's smirking face!"

She closed her eyes and took a deep breath. "Okay. Well, that made me even more determined to prove that he's guilty of the murders."

Nick drove back to Skaus Lake faster than he'd driven to Orofino. Mack knew he was fueled by fury. They got back to the police department just before five.

"I need a drink... or two, before I go home," he said. "You interested?"

"Definitely."

"Let's meet at the sports bar where we had dinner. I'll go inside and change clothes first."

"See you in a few," she said, walking toward her car.

When Nick arrived at the bar, he saw that Mack was sitting at a table with two shots in front of her. He sat down across from her and pointed at the glasses. "What is it?"

"A fine Scots whiskey."

He picked his shot up and held it out to her for a toast. She picked up her glass and held it out too. He said, "To the best female partner I've ever worked with." They clinked glasses and drank the shots in one swallow.

"Am I the only female partner you've ever had?"

"Yep."

She laughed. "Well, I guess it's the thought that counts."

He raised his hand for the waiter and ordered another round.

"I need food too." She ordered the burger loaded with bacon and blue cheese.

Nick ordered the same thing, then called Rose. He told her he wouldn't be home for dinner. "Love you too." He disconnected.

The waiter brought the second round of shots and, mustering the best Scottish brogue she could, Mack gave the next toast. "May the best you've ever seen be the worst you'll ever see. May ye keep hale and hearty till ye're auld enough tae die. May ye be just as happy as I wish ye tae be."

He swallowed the shot. "I'm starting to feel better."

She chuckled. "I'm feeling light-headed."

The burgers and fries arrived, and they both dug in. Neither of them had eaten lunch.

"Are both of your parents Scottish?" Nick asked between bites.

"My mother was actually born and raised in the Scottish Highlands, in a small town named Dollar. My father was born and raised in Coeur d'Alene. He was backpacking across Scotland the summer after he graduated from high school. My parents always said that they took one look at each other and fell in love. So, my dad stopped his travels there in Dollar. They spent the rest of the summer together, got married, and moved back to Idaho. They've been madly in love for forty-six years."

"Do they live in Coeur d'Alene?"

"No, they moved to Scotland when I graduated from high school. My mother was homesick, and since their only child was happily married, they thought it was a good time to go back. They live in Dollar. I try to get there to visit them every couple of years. I love it there. It's amazingly beautiful, and the people are some of the nicest I've ever encountered."

"So. No brothers or sisters?"

She shook her head. "No. What about you? Do you have siblings?"

195

"One brother. He's a cop, too. He still lives in Boise, where my folks are. Rose's parents live there, too. We go for a visit at least once a month."

"It's nice that they're so close. I miss my parents."

"No aunts or uncles or cousins?"

"My father was an only child, but my mom has three older brothers. They're married and have children and grandchildren. They all live in Scotland. So, I have lots of relatives there."

When they both finished their meal, he said, "I'm amazed at how much food you can pack away. How do you eat like that and stay so slim?"

"I run three miles pretty much every morning."

"Ah, that also explains how you were able to catch Rupp. Have you always been a runner?"

"No. I didn't start running until I got accepted to the police academy. I figured I better get in shape or I'd fail the physical exam. I kept running after I graduated from the academy, mainly because I didn't want to be outrun by perps."

Nick chuckled. "Well, I better get home. Thanks for this. I needed it."

Mack smiled. "My pleasure."

CHAPTER 49

Rupp was arraigned Friday morning at nine. His public defender and the county prosecutor had expedited plea negotiations. Rupp agreed to plead guilty to the misdemeanor of obstruction of justice. He would be fined a thousand dollars and serve one year of probation. He hadn't been evading arrest, so Mack and Nick had agreed with the county prosecutor that restitution and monitoring would be the best course of action.

"Do you need us to attend the arraignment?" Mack asked the prosecutor when she called him.

"You're not needed there. This is a fairly minor offense, and I know you have much bigger fish to fry."

"Okay. Let us know if you need anything else."

Around noon, Barbara walked into the bullpen with a smug smile on her face. "Maybe now you'll believe me when I say I'm not the murderer."

"Okay, what's going on?" Nick asked.

"A guy just walked in. He says he's the murderer."

He stood so fast that his chair toppled over backward. He and Mack rushed up the corridor to the front lobby.

"My name's Marvin Jergins," the man said when he saw them. "I killed those three people."

Jergins looked to be in his mid-sixties. He had shoulder length, gray, unkempt hair and pale brown eyes that seemed dead in his sunken face. His shoulders slumped forward, seemingly too weak to hold the weight of the dirty, knee length, tan wool coat he was wearing. He wore khaki pants and a light gray t-shirt under the coat. His shoes were made of tan leather and were so worn that Mack could see the imprint of his toes at the ends. Neither of the shoes had laces, and he wasn't wearing socks. His fingernails were long and filthy. She could smell the body odor from where she was standing.

Mack read him his rights and Nick fingerprinted and photographed him. She went back to her desk to run Jergins fingerprints through AFIS.

Nick led Jergins into the interview room and cuffed him to the table. He left him there and went to Mack's desk. "Anything?"

"He's been picked up for loitering and petty theft. Nothing even remotely close to murder."

Nick rubbed his forehead. "Let's go see what the guy has to say." In the interview room, he explained the conversation was being recorded. He took a seat across from Jergins. He identified himself, Mack, the date, time, and location. "Mr. Jergins, are you giving this statement freely?"

"I am."

"Are you under any duress from Detective Anderson or me?"

"No, I am not. I came into the police department of my own free will."

Mack asked, "Mr. Jergins, would you please repeat what you said to Officer Moore and me in the front lobby of this police department."

"I murdered those three people."

She placed her hands flat on the table. "What three people are you referring to?"

"That mother, her son, and the son's friend."

She rapidly fired questions at him. "When did this occur?"

"It was early the Saturday before last. About four in the morning."

"And, where did this occur?"

"In the living room of their house."

"Do you know the address of the house?"

"No. I just know where it is. It's on the north side of the lake, a couple of houses up from the lake.

"How did you get inside the house?"

198

"The back door was unlocked. I just walked in."

"And, how did you kill the three victims?

"I stabbed the mother and son, and I slit the other boy's throat."

She leaned in. "How many times did you stab the mother and son?"

"I don't know. I didn't count. A lot of times."

"What did you use to kill them?

"A big knife that I found in the kitchen."

"How were you able to kill all three of the victims without them screaming or putting up a fight?"

"I had a gun. I told them to be quiet and lay down on the floor. I tied them up, then I killed them."

"What did you tie them up with?"

"Some tape I found in the garage."

Mack's brow furrowed. "If you had a gun, why didn't you shoot them instead of stabbing them?"

"Shooting them would have been too noisy."

"What were you wearing when you killed them?"

"Jeans and a sweatshirt. I buried the clothes under a tree in the forest, along with the gun."

"Where exactly in the forest?"

"I don't know. I just kept walking until I was far enough away from the house."

"Why did you kill them?"

"I was going to rob the house, but they heard me. I had to kill them so they couldn't identify me."

Mack sat up straighter in her chair. "But you're here today, confessing. Why would you kill them, then confess?"

"I just couldn't take the guilt. It weighed on me. I needed to get rid of the guilt."

"Did you take anything from the house?

"No. I just left after I killed them."

"How did you get to the house?"

"I walked. I walked into the trees, then down the road toward the lake. When I left, I walked up the road, then back into the forest."

"It was cold that morning," she said. "Didn't you have your coat on?"

"I left it outside by the back door. I didn't want to get it bloody. I had these clothes in a bag," Jergins said, indicating the clothes he had on. "I left them outside too. I changed into these when I buried the bloody clothes."

"Where did you go after you buried your clothes in the forest?"

"I walked back into town. I went to a restaurant and ate breakfast."

"What restaurant was that?"

"I don't remember the name. I just walked until I was hungry. I stopped at the first place I saw after that."

"Where do you live?"

"Sometimes I stay at the homeless shelters in whatever town I'm in. Sometimes I just sleep under the stars."

Where did you stay that Friday and Saturday night?"

"I slept in the Catholic Church both nights. They don't lock the doors, and it's warm inside."

"Did anyone see you at the Church?"

"No."

She sighed. "Okay. Sit tight. We'll be back."

Mack and Nick went back to the bullpen and sat at their desks.

"Well?" he asked.

"I don't believe he did it. We've said all along that the murderer exhibited extreme anger toward the victims. This guy isn't exhibiting any emotion at all. Also, he said he didn't take anything from the house. But we know that two laptops and a cell phone were taken. It doesn't feel right."

"Well, damn. Why would the guy confess?"

"Same reason most false confessions occur. The person's craving attention and believes he can gain notoriety by confessing. Or he's suffering from a serious mental condition."

"He has a pretty good story."

"All the details he gave us have been in the news. Anyone could make up the rest of the story. He can't tell us where the bloody clothes and gun are buried. He can't tell us where exactly he ate that morning. None of it can be corroborated."

Nick rubbed his forehead. "Well, what do we do?"

"Let's take another crack at him. See if his story changes. Can you get Charlie to start searching to see if Jergins was ever in a mental facility?"

Nick nodded. "I'll call and get him here."

"Okay, let's go back in there. You take the lead questioning Jergins this time."

Mack and Nick spent the next two hours interviewing Jergins, but his story didn't change. They finally called the county sheriff's office and had him taken to a holding cell.

~~~

Charlie spent the time finding out everything he could on Jergins. When Mack and Nick got back to the bullpen, Charlie briefed them on what he'd found. "Jergins was born in Seattle in 1947. He enlisted in the Army when he was eighteen. He fought in the Cambodian Campaign from 1966 to 1970. He was one of nine men in his company that left Cambodia alive in June of 1979. The rest were either killed, or wounded and evacuated."

"That's rough," she said. "Being a survivor can weigh on a person."

Charlie said, "After the Army, it seems that he became a drifter."

Nick's eyebrows rose. "Almost forty-five years. That's a long time to not have a home."

"I can't find any record of Jergins having been in a mental hospital."

Chief Davis came into the bullpen. He moved faster than Mack had ever seen him do. "Barbara told me. This is fantastic. Our murderer confessed."

Mack and Nick looked at each other.

"I believe it's a false confession." She shook her head. "He's not the murderer."

"The hell you say." The chief turned to Nick. "What do you think?"

"I agree with Mack."

"Son of a bitch." Davis looked back and forth between the two. "Well, you two better come up with someone better real soon, or we're arresting Jergins. Nobody will buy that we let the guy that confessed to the murders go, just because we didn't believe he did it."

CHAPTER 50

Mack was mentally exhausted as she walked up the sidewalk to the front door of the cottage that evening. Her briefcase was loaded with copies of transcriptions of every interview, reports taken from the Browns' neighbors, call logs from Patricia's cell phone and everything else that they'd gathered on the Brown-Caldwell case. She planned to stay at the cottage all day Saturday and review everything they had so far. Tomorrow was Nick's mother's sixtieth birthday, and his family was throwing a grand surprise party for her. She'd insisted that he go.

She poured a glass of wine and took it out onto the patio. She sat in one of the chairs. Drao jumped into her lap and started purring. A nighthawk flitted after bugs in the evening light. She watched it bank left, then quickly turn right, then left again.

A truck drove slowly down the street. It made a U-turn and stopped across from Mack's cottage. She stood and tried to see who was in the truck. She held her hand over her eyes to shade them from the glare of the sun.

A man got out of the truck and closed the door.

Mack's heart did a flip-flop, and her breathing quickened. His hair and beard were shorter, but she would have recognized Sigurd anywhere. She walked through the gate and onto the sidewalk. She kept walking toward him as he walked toward her. They met in the middle of the street. She threw her arms around his neck and, tiptoeing, hugged him fiercely.

He put his arms around her waist and held her tight. He rested his cheek on the top of her head.

She closed her eyes and savored the feel of him. She didn't know how long they stood there, but a horn honking shocked them both. They drew apart and waved at the driver.

She took his hand and led him into the courtyard. She closed the gate and looked into his eyes. "Hi."

He smiled. "Hi."

"Come in." Mack felt a little shy as he followed her into the cottage.

Drao rubbed himself all over Sigurd's legs. He picked the kitten up. "Hello, little one." Drao meowed and started purring.

"Please, have a seat. I'll get some wine."

Sigurd nodded and sat on the couch.

Mack quickly put some cheese and crackers on a tray. She poured two glasses of wine and added them to the tray. As she set it on the coffee table, she was aware of his eyes following her. She sat on the couch. She picked up both glasses and handed one to him. "I'm so glad you're here."

"Talking to you on the phone made me realize how much I wanted to see you in person. And, you said that you wished I was here. So, here I am."

"How did you find me?"

His blue eyes twinkled, and one side of his mouth curled up in that lopsided grin that Mack remembered.

She chuckled. "That was a stupid question."

He laughed. "When did you get this little guy?" He petted Drao, who was curled up on his lap.

"He just showed up and wouldn't leave."

"Does he have a name?"

"Drao. Short for Draoidh. It means enigma."

"So, is he?"

She nodded. "I think he might be." She looked up from the kitten to find Sigurd's eyes boring into hers. Mack's breath caught in her chest. They both leaned toward each other. She felt like a magnet was drawing her slowly forward.

He placed his hand on the side of her face and gently kissed her lips. She returned the kiss, which quickly turned passionate. He took the glass of wine from her hand and placed both his and hers on the coffee table.

She stood and held her hand out to him. She led him into the bedroom, where they stood facing each other. She wrapped her arms around his neck and pulled his head down for a kiss.

They continued to kiss as Sigurd slowly undid the buttons on Mack's shirt. He slid it over her shoulders and down her arms. Then he reached around her back, unhooked her bra, and removed it.

She tugged his shirt out of his pants and up his chest. He reached behind his shoulders and pulled the t-shirt over his head, dropping it on the floor. She placed both of her palms on his chest, marveling at the taut muscles under his skin. She moved her hands down and unbuttoned the top button of his jeans. Then she unzipped them.

He sucked in his breath and quickly relieved Mack of her pants, sliding them down her legs. When they were both naked, he picked up her and carried her to the bed. The made love slowly.

Mack laid her head on Sigurd's shoulder. He wrapped his arm around her. After a few minutes, she looked up at him. "I'm starving."

"Stay right there." He walked into the living room naked and brought back the tray of cheese and wine. He handed a glass to her and sat on the bed.

She ate a slice of cheese. "How long are you here for?"

"I do not know for sure. I thought I might stay in the states for a while." He kissed her on the cheek. "How would you feel about that?"

"I would like to be closer."

When they finished eating, Sigurd took the tray back to the kitchen. He walked back into the bedroom. Mack pulled the covers to one side. He crawled into the bed and pulled her to him. They made love again, this time harder and faster. They slept holding each other like they had years ago. When they woke up the next morning, they made love again, both of them wanting more of the other. After, Sigurd put on his pants and retrieved a duffel bag from his car. She wondered what the neighbors would think of a shirtless man coming out of her house in the early morning. She smiled. *I really don't care.*

They showered together, taking turns slowly washing each other. They took their time getting to know every part of the other's body. When Sigurd grew hard, Mack wrapped her arms around his neck and her legs around his waist. He cradled her back with his hands and pressed her against the wall of the shower. He drove into her. She arched against him. Soon, they both shuddered in relief.

"I could spend every morning like this." He smiled as he got dressed in clean clothes from his duffel bag.

"So could I." Making love with Sean was nice. But they were teenagers, and neither one really knew what they were doing. Making love with Sigurd was beyond amazing.

"I thought I would drive to Coeur d'Alene over the weekend to find a space to live and work. That way when you are finished with the case here, we will be in the same town. What do you think?"

She glanced away. "Sure. Sounds good."

If he had noticed her reticence, he didn't say anything about it. "I should have everything set up by Sunday evening. After that, I could drive back and forth while you are here."

"Sounds like a plan."

Sigurd kissed Mack before he left. "See you Sunday night."

CHAPTER 51

What am I missing? Mack leaned back into the couch cushions and placed her stockinged feet on the coffee table. She'd been rereading all the evidence from the murder investigation for over six straight hours. *I know it's there. What is it?* She placed her face in her hands. "Crap!"

Drao jumped into her lap and, looking into her eyes, meowed.

"I'm sorry. I'm not angry at you, you sweet boy. I'm angry at myself." She rubbed his ears for a few moments.

When her cell phone rang, she didn't recognize the number. She swiped the answer icon. "Detective Anderson."

"This is Susan Brown."

"Oh. Hi."

"Am I disturbing you?"

"I can use a break, so your timing's perfect."

"I was wondering if I could come by and talk to you?"

"Sure. Come on over. I'll order food. Do you like Chinese?"

"Yes. Thanks. That would be really nice."

Mack gave her the address, then changed out of her warm-ups and into jeans. Susan arrived in less than five minutes. Mack kept forgetting that everything in Skaus Lake was so close.

"Hi. Come on in."

Susan looked around the room. "This place is really nice."

"I like it, too. Being here has made me start thinking about buying a house with a yard and a view."

"Where do you live now?"

"I have a townhouse. It's fine, but it doesn't have any space around it, and it certainly doesn't have a view like this." She indicated the lake through the living room windows. "I was just going to pour myself a glass of wine. The only other thing I have to drink is orange juice. And water."

"Juice would be great. Thanks."

She poured both of their drinks and brought them to the living room. "Please, make yourself comfortable."

Susan sat on the couch, and Mack sat in one of the chairs next to it. Drao jumped into Mack's lap.

"Oh, your kitten's so cute. What's her name?"

"His name's Drao."

"That's unusual."

She explained about the Scottish Gaelic origin.

"Can I hold him?"

"Sure."

Susan reached across and picked Drao up. He immediately started to squirm and cry, so she set him back on Mack's lap. The kitten jumped down and ran into the bedroom.

"He's not used to people. I've only had him a couple of days. He wandered into the courtyard and never left." She took a sip of her wine. "How are Ethan and Will doing?"

"Will's still waking up in the night, calling out for mom. Ethan's real quiet. I don't know what I should do to help them. I was hoping you could tell me if there's anything I can do."

"Every person copes with grief differently. One of the best ways you can help them is to give them plenty of hugs."

Susan smiled slightly.

"How are you?

"I talked to Chrissy like you suggested. And, you were right. She thought going to a party would help take my mind off the murders. We both apologized. We're fine now."

"I'm glad." She took a sip of wine. "Have you and Grace talked about what to do with the house?"

"We agreed that the best thing to do would be to sell it, along with all the stuff in it. Grandma contacted someone that's going to take care of it all. That way none of us have to go back in the house. We'll live with Grandma in her home. It only has three bedrooms, but Tom and Will are used to sharing a room. And, one of them can move into my room when I go off to college." She shrugged. "It'll be fine."

The doorbell rang. "I bet that's the food." Mack opened the door, paid for the food, and tipped the delivery boy. She unloaded the bags onto the dining room table and retrieved two plates from the kitchen. "Come and eat."

Between bites, Susan asked, "Do you have any leads in the murders?"

Mack debated with herself. "You're going to hear this soon enough. I suppose it's better if you hear it from me. A man came into the police department and confessed to the murders."

"What. That's amazing!"

"Wait. Before you get too excited. I believe it's a false confession."

"You do? Why?" Susan looked and sounded deflated.

"I can't explain it. I just do."

"I don't really understand. But I trust you. So, if you say he's not the murderer, I believe you."

"Thanks. I appreciate your trust."

"But if he's not, then who is?"

"I don't know for sure. I'm getting close to figuring it out though."

CHAPTER 52

Mack dreamed about the Brown-Caldwell murders Saturday night. It was like she was an invisible observer, silently watching the horror as it occurred. She saw the murderer come in the back door of the house, then quietly close it. She couldn't see the murderer's face. It was a black hole covered by the hood of a sweatshirt. The murderer took the butcher knife from the kitchen and went into the living room. The three victims were lying on the living room floor in random locations. One at a time, the murderer grabbed the victims' legs and dragged them into place. Then the murderer stabbed Patricia and Alan and slit Aaron's throat. In the dream, Mack kept thinking, *Don't kill them. Please don't kill them.*

She woke up to Drao was licking her face. When she opened her eyes, his nose an inch from hers. She grabbed him and hugged him to her chest. "I need to get out of this house today and clear my mind."

She put on her running clothes. She ran along the lake, then around the edge of the neighborhood, extending her run to four miles. She showered, then made coffee. She put it in a large insulated travel mug that she always brought when she was away from home. After saying goodbye to Drao, she loaded the mug and her handbag into her sedan and started driving, with no destination in mind. She'd explored the different neighborhoods of Skaus Lake for about an hour when she realized that she was hungry.

She drove to the same restaurant that she'd eaten breakfast at ten days ago. It felt like it had been a year ago. She ordered, then she sat back and took a deep breath, trying to release some of the tension in her body. She felt weighed down by the dream, so she ate a light breakfast of granola and yogurt.

When she started driving again, she decided to go to the Browns' neighborhood. There were only two other streets in the area. Skyline Road was in the center of the other two. The three streets were spread out, with large trees in between, allowing for complete privacy. She drove up and down the streets, looking at each house. She started on the farthest street and worked her way back toward town. *Every one of these homes has an incredible view. And, each one's spectacular. That's it. It's decided. When I get back to Coeur d'Alene, I'm selling the townhouse and buying a house with a view.*

Mack smiled as she drove up and back down the last street in the neighborhood. She thought about what she would like her new house to look like. Her subconscious woke her up from her daydream. She stopped the sedan and backed up. The house closest to the lake had a security camera pointed toward the main road into the neighborhood. "Excellent."

She parked in the driveway, got out, and knocked on the door. A good looking older man with salt and pepper hair and green eyes opened the door. "May I help you?" he asked in a crisp British accent.

"I'm Detective Anderson." She held out her badge so that he could read it. "I'm investigating the three murders that happened on Skyline Road."

"Oh yes. I knew I'd seen you before. You were on television a couple of times."

She smiled. "That's correct. I'm here because I saw that you have a security camera on the outside of your house. Is there any chance that I could look at the recording from the time of the murders if you have it?"

"I believe that I can do better than that." He held out his hand and shook hers. "I'm Lawrence Ivan. Please come in." He walked into a room to the right of the front door. "This is where I keep the security equipment." He motioned for her to come inside.

The room was small and dark, without any windows. Ivan turned on an overhead light. "The security camera has night vision capability and motion detection. I actually have it to watch the wildlife in the area. I record a week at a time, and I keep each disk for a year. Then I start recording over them. Unless there's an unusual wildlife sighting on the disk."

She saw that there were dozens of discs. Each one was neatly stacked in a row on built-in shelves. Each disk had a label with dates on them. "I'm very impressed."

Ivan smiled. He looked through the discs for a few seconds, then pulled out one. He handed it to Mack. "This is the one you're looking for."

"Thank you. We'll make a copy and return it to you."

"That would be perfect." Ivan led Mack back to the front door. "I hope it helps."

She shook hands with him. "Thank you so much." She got back in her sedan and drove to the police department. She walked up to the front to let the dispatch officer know that she was in the building.

Dave was on duty. "How's the investigation going?"

She held up the disc. "I may have caught a break."

"Things are slow here today. Let me know if I can help."

"Do you want to take a look at this with me?"

"That would be sweet."

She handed him the disc. He loaded it into the computer on the desk. She pulled up a chair and sat next to him. He tapped on the keyboard, and the disk started playing. The recording was date and time stamped.

"Can you speed through to the Friday evening before the murders?"

"No problem."

Images moved quickly by. They saw a couple of raccoons and a skunk. He slowed the recording when they saw a large grizzly bear. They watched as the bear walked out of the woods, drank from the lake, then slowly wandered back into the forest. "That was awesome." He sped the recording up again.

She pointed at the monitor. "There." He paused the recording. Mack leaned in. She saw Chris Purvis and Floyd Rupp came into view. They walked along the main road from town. "Can you blow up their faces?"

"Sure. No problem. Do you know who those guys are?" When she didn't say anything, he nudged her. "Mack?"

"Sorry. What did you say?"

"Do you know who these two guys are?"

"Yes. One of them said they were casing the area. We haven't found the other man."

"Oh, I heard about that." He chuckled. "That's the guy you chased down, making a fabulous tackle."

She gave him a quick smile.

"Can you print out a blow-up of the faces?"

"Sure." He pressed a few keys, then handed Mack the printouts.

She stared at Chris Purvis' face for a minute, then she stood.

"Don't you want to watch the rest?"

"Oh. Yes." Mack sat back down. "You can go forward at normal speed."

They watched Purvis and Rupp walk up the main road, then turn and walk up the first cross street. The men stopped walking at Ivan's house and looked around. Mack and Dave could see that the two were talking to each other, but they couldn't make out what was being said. They watched the two men walk up the street until they were out of range of the camera. The next recording of the two men showed them walking back down the street. Time was five twenty-two Saturday morning. The next sighting of the men was at six thirty-eight. The two walked down the main road toward town.

Mack said, "The time on the recording corresponds to when one of the Browns' neighbors saw the two men walking on Skyline Road. Another neighbors' dog barked around quarter to five and again at quarter past five. Those two times are probably the men walking past their house. The dog also barked around three-thirty and again at four-thirty. That could have been the murderer coming and going."

They saw Nora Nelson driving out of the neighborhood at five thirty-one that morning. "That's the neighbor that saw Purvis and Rupp on Skyline Road," Mack explained. "One of the Browns' neighbors heard a car door slam about five-thirty. Probably Mrs. Nelson leaving. Let's fast forward through the rest of the day and see if there's anything else."

He played the rest of recording. There was very little traffic in the secluded area. Mack recognized the logo on a truck that drove in at nine thirty-four and out at ten forty-seven. The logo was the same yard maintenance company that Patricia had used. A man drove by at two-fourteen in the afternoon and back again at five thirty-seven that evening. There were no recordings of any of the murder suspects.

But now Mack had a photograph of Chris Purvis that she could compare to Luke Adler.

CHAPTER 53

Mack knew she couldn't get too distracted by the idea of finding Adler. She needed to continue to work the murders. She drove back to Skyline Road to speak to each of the Browns' neighbors again. She was hoping that one of them would have remembered something else. She was grasping at straws, but she had run out of ideas.

She started at the Taylors' house at the bottom of Skyline Road. When Mr. Taylor answered the door, she held up her badge. "I'm Detective Anderson. I'm investigating the murders that occurred at the Browns' house. I know you spoke to Lieutenant Swartz before. I'm following up to see if you or your wife remembered anything else that we should know about."

"Please come in." Taylor held the door open for her. "My wife's in the kitchen. Let's go in there so that you can speak with her also."

"Thank you." She followed him through the living room.

"Edna, this is Detective Anderson. She's checking to see if either of us remembered anything else that might help with the murder investigation."

The Taylors were both in their seventies, trim, and tall. They had nearly identical haircuts that were short on the sides and in the back, and spiky on top. They looked more like brothers than husband and wife. It was all Mack could do not to stare.

Edna said, "I'm sorry, but I didn't hear or see anything."

"I only woke up that one time when the car door slammed," Mr. Taylor said.

"Is there anything unusual about the Browns themselves or any visitors they had that either of you can think of?"

The Taylors looked at each other for a few seconds. She said, "Nothing I can think of." He shook his head. "Sorry. I can't think of anything either."

~~~

The next house up the street was the Browns'. As Mack drove by, she saw that a real estate agent had placed a 'For Sale' sign in the corner of the yard. She stopped at the house north of the Browns', which was where Mr. and Mrs. Lee lived.

She knocked. When Mr. Lee answered the door, she identified herself and explained that she was following up. He didn't invite her in. "My wife and I told the other officer everything we know. We're tired of this entire incident. We want to get back to our normal lives."

"I'd imagine that Patricia Brown, Alan Brown, and Jack Caldwell would like to get back to their lives too. I'm so sorry that you've had such a rough time of it." Turning, she stormed back to her sedan, flung the door open, and slammed it shut after she got in. "Asshole."

She drove up the road to the Nelsons' house. She went through the same explanation. The Nelsons invited her in but didn't have anything further to add that they could think of.

"Mrs. Nelson, I thought you'd like to know that we identified the two men you saw. We've verified that they didn't have anything to do with the murders."

"Thank you for telling me. I've been wondering about them."

~~~

Cameron Smith, Chrissy's father, answered the door when Mack knocked. She identified herself and held up her badge.

"Please come in. Chrissy and Winnie are watching TV. Why don't we go on back and all talk together?"

"Thank you." She followed him as he led the way.

After introductions, Chrissy asked Mack, "Have you found the murderer?"

"We have several leads."

"So, no."

"Chrissy!" Mrs. Smith said. "That's very rude."

"Why? My best friend's traumatized."

When Mrs. Smith started to object again, Mack held up her hand. "It's fine. I understand your frustration, Chrissy. Believe me, I'm frustrated too. That's one of the reasons I'm here. I was hoping that there's something one of the three of you might tell me that would help."

"Like what?" Chrissy asked.

"Did you ever see Patricia, Alan, or Jack arguing with anyone?"

The three Smiths looked at each other and shook their heads.

"Chrissy, was anyone at school upset with Alan or Jack that you knew of?"

"Not that I can think of. They both were quiet. They didn't cause any trouble. I can't think of anyone that would've been upset with the boys."

"What about someone who might have been bothered that they were gay?"

"Nobody at school would mention anything like that to me. They all know that I'd call them out for being a homophobe. My older brother's gay, and I don't put up with any of that shit."

Mrs. Smith said, "Language."

Chrissy rolled her eyes.

"What about Aaron Paul? I know that he sells pot at school. I'm not a narc. I'm not concerned about that. I just thought Alan or Jack might owe him money."

"Oh, that's just great," Mr. Smith said.

Mrs. Smith covered her mouth with her hand. "Oh, my."

"It's no big deal." Chrissy looked back and forth between her parents. "Aaron's purely small time. He has a few plants that he grows in his house. From what I've seen, he smokes the majority of his own stuff. If they owed him money, it couldn't have been very much."

"Okay, thanks. That's very helpful." Mack handed Chrissy a business card. "If you think of anything else, please give me a call."

"I will."

Mr. Smith walked Mack back to the front door. She got back in her sedan and drove up the street, turning around at the end. She stopped and looked down at the five houses. She sighed. *Tomorrow's another day.*

~~~

Sigurd arrived at the cottage that evening, arms loaded with bags of groceries. "I thought I would make Fårikål." He set the groceries on the kitchen counter and drew Mack into a kiss.

"Yummy." Mack hugged him. "Both you and dinner." She chuckled.

They chopped cabbage and peeled potatoes together, occasionally taking a moment to kiss each other. While the food simmered on the stove, they sat on the couch and sipped cold white wine.

"Were you able to find a space and the equipment you need?" she asked.

"I did. I think I have everything."

"Not everything." She grinned.

"True." He pulled her into his arms. They frantically made love on the couch. "These past two days I missed you and that," he said, panting.

"Me too." She sighed loudly. "I'm hungry."

He grinned. "I thought I satiated your hunger."

"Braggart."

He laughed. He filled their glasses with wine and handed one to her. He leaned down and kissed her on the lips. "Stay right here. I will bring you a plate of food."

Mack took the opportunity to admire Sigurd's narrow hips and broad back as he walked to the kitchen. She watched the way the muscles in his chest and arms bulged slightly as he loaded two plates with food.

He turned and saw her looking at him. "What are you smiling about?"

She knew she'd been caught in the act of ogling him. She tried to cover. "I was thinking how nice it is to have someone wait on me."

He carried their plates to the couch and handed one to her. He'd set each of the hot dishes on a potholder so that it wouldn't burn their hands. They chatted as they ate. He told her about the place that he'd found to live and work in. It sounded similar to his building in Boise, where they'd first met.

"I found a recording of the night of the murders," she said. "It clearly shows Chris Purvis' face. I made a printout." Setting her plate on the coffee table, she pulled the photograph of Purvis out of her briefcase and handed it to Sigurd.

"We can digitally compare the images we have of Purvis and Adler to determine if they are the same person. I can do that tomorrow if you would like."

She nodded. "I need to know."

"I have an appointment to sign the papers on the building in Coeur d' Alene at eight in the morning. I will work on the comparison once I am set up tomorrow."

She kissed him on the cheek. "Thank you." She ate more Fårikål. "I need to be at the police department early tomorrow. So, I guess we'll both have early mornings."

He smiled. "Since our time together tonight is so short, you better hurry up and finish that food, so that I can take you into the bedroom and have my way with you."

Mack set her plate on the coffee table. Taking Sigurd's hand, she stood. "I'm finished."

CHAPTER 54

By the time Nick walked into the bullpen at seven on Monday morning, Mack had already completed yesterday's report. He sat at his desk. "What's up?"

She handed him the copy of her report.

He read it. "Damn. Too bad that camera recording didn't pan out."

"There was a nice shot of a grizzly drinking out of the lake."

"Well, that would certainly be helpful if our murderer had four legs."

She chuckled and stood. "I need more caffeine." She headed toward the coffee mess. She carried her cup of coffee back to her desk. "How was your mom's birthday party?"

"It was nice. Thanks for insisting that I go."

"A son's mom only turns sixty once. That shouldn't be missed."

He held up the report. "It looks like you worked all weekend."

She blushed. "Not all weekend."

"Ah ha. Thus the need for the coffee, huh?" He grinned.

She changed the subject. "And Susan came over to talk this weekend."

"You're not getting too close, are you?"

Mack shook her head. "She needs to talk to someone that understands how she feels."

"Her grandmother lives in the same house as she does. You'll be leaving town soon, and she won't have you to talk to anymore. She should be talking to her grandmother."

"It's fine."

He held up both hands in surrender. "Okay. If you say so."

When Mack's desk phone rang, she picked it up. "Detective Anderson."

"Detective, this is Elaine Bader. I'm a reporter with the Idaho Statesman in Boise. A reliable source told me that a man confessed to the three Skaus Lake homicides, yet that man hasn't been charged. Would you like to comment on that for the record?"

"Ms. Bader, the police do not comment on ongoing investigations."

"Suit yourself. But this is going to be our headline for tomorrow's paper."

She set the receiver back in the cradle. "Crap. Someone at the sheriff's office leaked that Jergins confessed, but hasn't been charged."

"Damn it! We have to let the chief know. Now."

She followed him up the hall to Davis' office. Nick knocked and entered. "We have an issue." He took a seat.

Mack repeated the phone conversation she'd just had with the reporter.

"Barbara!" the chief yelled.

She came into the office. "What's all the yelling about?"

"Call a press conference for two this afternoon."

"You got it."

Davis looked between Mack and Nick. "We have to break this before someone else does. Get over to the sheriff's office and charge Jergins." Mack started to speak, but he held up his hand to silence her. "This is not up for discussion. I understand how you two feel. But we don't have any other choice now. Get it done."

"Yes, sir," Nick said.

The two went back to the bullpen. Mack said, "I have to call my captain and let him know. I don't want the first he's heard of the arrest to be on the news." She took her cell phone outside and placed the call. She explained what had occurred.

"Good. You can get back here and help with our own workload. When I sent you over there, I didn't think you would be gone this long."

"Captain, Jergins isn't the murderer. It's a false confession."

"I read your daily summary. I know that you believe he's not the murderer, but you don't have a shred of evidence on anyone else."

"Cox is the perp. I'm sure of it. I just need more time to prove it. Give me the time I need. We owe it to the victims."

Wilson sighed. "You've got a week. I want you back here first thing Monday morning. Is that clear?"

"Yes, sir. Perfectly. Thank you, sir."

"You may have to let this one go, Mack."

"I refuse to accept that. The victims deserve better from me."

Nick phoned Grace, the Caldwells, and Ethan Williams' parents to tell them that Jergins confessed and would be charged with the murders. Grace said she would tell the three Brown children when they got home from school. Ethan's parents said they would do the same. They all sincerely thanked Nick for all his hard work on behalf of their loved ones.

Mack and Nick agreed that they wouldn't tell them they believed Jergins' confession was false. She didn't tell him that she'd already told Susan.

~~~

Mack put on her best blank face for the press conference. She stood behind Chief Davis in her usual position, with Nick beside her.

"The Skaus Lake Police Department has charged Marvin Jergins with the murder of Patricia Brown, Alan Brown and Jack Caldwell," the chief announced. "Detective Anderson and Officer Moore interviewed Mr. Jergins, and he confessed to the murders. He also provided details of how and why he committed the crime. We cannot and will not discuss any of those details. Thank you for coming today."

Chaos erupted, as reporters shouted questions at the chief. Davis turned and started walking back into the building. Mack and Nick followed.

Reporters squeezed them from both sides. One stuck a microphone in Mack's face and yelled, trying to be heard over the fray. "How did you get Jergins to confess?"

She shoved the microphone away and kept walking, face devoid of emotion.

That same reporter tried Nick next. "Officer Moore, how long did you interview Jergins before he confessed? Come on. Give us a little hint of what you had to do to get him to confess."

Nick gave the reporter a withering look. He kept quiet and continued to walk toward the building.

Seeing that he'd gotten a reaction out of Nick, the reporter continued to bait him with questions about pressuring Jergins into a confession.

When Nick walked through the police department's front door, Barbara stepped in front of the reporter. She had her arms crossed over her chest, with an 'I'd like to see you try it' look on her face. The reporter stopped dead in his tracks, took one look at Barbara, and turned around.

Nick sat heavily at his desk. "Well, that was fun. The chief set us up by insinuating that Jergins confessed after we interviewed him. This damn case just gets worse and worse."

"Unfortunately I have something to tell you that's going to make it even worse."

He groaned, dropping his head into his hands.

"Captain Wilson wants me back at work in Coeur d'Alene in a week."

He sat back in his chair and shook his head. "Honestly, if he gave you another two weeks, I don't know if it would help. There isn't any evidence against Cox. Which isn't surprising. He'd probably been planning how to get to Susan for years."

"I'm not giving up yet. We have a little more time. There's something that we've missed. It's been nagging at me for days, but I can't grasp it."

"Well, I haven't had that feeling. I've scrolled through the database of my meager brain, and I've come up with nothing. So, where do we go from here?"

Mack shrugged. "I don't know. I guess when all else fails, we start at the beginning."

CHAPTER 55

By the time Mack opened the front door of the cottage that evening, she had a headache, and her feet felt like they were made of lead. She hated to admit it, but she was glad that she didn't have to come home to an empty house. Drao greeted her as she walked inside. She picked him up and put her face in his fur, letting the softness soak in. He purred, rubbing his head on her face. "How are you, my sweet boy? I hope your day was better than mine. Today was pure crap for me."

The kitten followed her to the kitchen. She unholstered her Glock and set it on the kitchen counter. She took a cold bottle of Chardonnay out of the refrigerator and opened it. She took a wine glass and the bottle out to the patio. Sitting in her favorite chair, she curled her legs under her. Drao jumped into her lap and began to purr. She poured some wine into the glass and sipped it. The light faded to dusk. The combination of the wine, the crisp air, the view, and Drao's purring started to calm her.

A car pulled up in front of the house and parked. She saw that it was Susan. Mack said hello when Susan reached the front gate.

"Hi." Susan sat in the other wicker chair. "Grandma told us that you arrested that Jergins guy. I didn't tell them that you said you thought he didn't do it."

"That's probably best." She held up the glass of wine. "I'm having a drink. Go inside and help yourself to some juice."

Susan went into the cottage and came back out a few minutes later with a water glass full of orange juice.

Mack drank wine and Susan sipped her juice. Neither of them talked. They both looked at the lake, lost in their own thoughts.

"Do you think you'll ever find out who the real murderer is?"

Mack shook her head. "I've scoured everything on the murders, and there isn't a drop of evidence. I'm sorry, Susan." She paused. "And, my boss wants me back in Coeur d'Alene on Monday morning."

Susan finished the glass of juice and set the empty glass on the side table. "I'd like to see you one last time before you leave. Would you meet me for dinner next week?"

She smiled. "I'd like that."

~~~

Mack had given Sigurd the extra key to the cottage so that he could come and go when he wanted. Walking into the house, he found her sitting on the floor, paper spread out all around her. Drao was curled up in her lap, softly purring.

She set the kitten on the floor and stood up. She tiptoed around the piles of paper and over to Sigurd. She embraced him and gave him a long kiss.

"Mmmm. I like being welcomed back by you."

"Wine?"

"Please."

She poured him a glass and refilled hers. They sat on the couch together. He put his arm around her shoulders and kissed her on the forehead. He motioned to the mess of papers with his head. "What is all that?"

"Everything we have on the homicides. I just can't quite grasp onto who the murderer is. The answer's right there, but every time I try to bring it to the front of my mind, it flutters away. Does that make sense?"

He nodded. "It does. I have found that when that happens to me, the best thing to do is not force it."

She sighed. "Unfortunately, I don't have the luxury of time." She told him about only having a few days to solve the case.

"It will come to you. Trust yourself."

She kissed him on the cheek. "Thank you."

"How does crepes for dinner sound?"

"Wonderful."

226

As he cooked, she set the table and filled up their wine glasses. After they finished eating, they cleaned up the kitchen together and took their wine out onto the patio. The air smelled of rain. Within minutes, the cloud filled sky opened up. Mack could see rain falling in the shafts of light from the moon.

Drao jumped into Sigurd's lap and curled up.

She chuckled. "You and I seem to be the only two people he likes."

He smiled and petted the kitten. "He has good taste."

They sat in companionable silence, enjoying the rain. Sigurd took her hand in his. "You were right. Purvis and Adler are the same person."

"As soon as his sketch was on TV, he disappeared. Again. Nobody's seen or heard from him since."

"You mean, nobody has admitted to hearing from him."

She looked at him. "If I gave you Adler's phone number, would you see if you can track him down?"

"I will set up the trace tomorrow." He stared into the night. "Have you decided what you are going to do if you find Adler?"

She shook her head. "There's no evidence against him, so putting him behind bars is out."

"I want to make sure that you consider all of the consequences," he softly said. "There is a lot at stake. Your job. Your freedom. And, us. I just found you again. I do not want to lose you."

She was silent for a full minute. "I can't just let him walk around, while my husband and daughter lie in the ground. I have to do something."

Sigurd stood and gently kissed Mack on the top of her head. As he walked back into the house, he said, "No. You are choosing to do something. There is a difference."

CHAPTER 56

Mack dreamed about Sean and Samantha's funeral. She woke up from the dream to find Drao standing on her chest, his face close to hers. "I'm okay," she whispered, wiping the tears from her face. She sat up and looked down at Sigurd sleeping. She did not like the feelings that she was beginning to have for him. Drao rubbed his head on her chest and purred.

Looking at her cell phone, she saw that it was a little after five. She carefully got out of bed so she wouldn't wake Sigurd. She made coffee and took it out on the patio to soak up the peace. "I'm going to miss this view when we go home," she said to Drao.

A few minutes later, Sigurd came outside. He set his cup of coffee on the side table, bent down, and sweetly kissed Mack. "Are you alright?"

She didn't say anything for a few seconds. "I'm afraid, Sigurd."

"Do you want to tell me what you are afraid of?"

"You. Having feelings for you, with the possibility of losing you. The pain of that. I barely survived losing Sean and Samantha. I don't know if I'd make it through that again."

"I understand. I felt that way after losing my wife and son. But one day I realized that if I did not take the chance on loving and losing, I would not really be alive anyway." He took both of her hands in his. "You know as well as I do that there are no promises in life. I hope you will take a chance."

~~~

Nick nodded at Mack as she walked in the back door of the police department later that morning. "You look like someone kicked your dog," he said.

"I feel like that, too."

"What's going on?"

She shook her head. "Nothing."

228

"Okay. Good talk."

"Let's talk about the case."

"Fine by me," he mumbled. "You said that we should start over. At the beginning. Where is that exactly?"

"The way I see it, we both believe Cox is the murderer. So, we look at all the evidence again with that in mind. Maybe that will change the way we look at things. There has to be something we've missed."

He sighed. "Okay. I'll look at the evidence we collected at the house."

"I'll look at the autopsy reports."

Two hours later, Barbara walked into the bullpen. "Mr. Chris Purvis and his very expensive lawyer are here."

Mack had been asking herself over and over what she'd do the first time she came face-to-face with Luke Adler. She'd never found an answer. *I guess I'll get my chance to find out.*

"Are you coming?" Nick asked her when she gave no indication of moving.

"Oh… yeah. Sure"

As they walked up the hall to the front lobby, he asked, "I wonder if he's come to confess, too?"

She tried to act normal, but she could barely pull off a small smile.

In the lobby, a man stepped forward and said, "I'm Glen Holloman. I'm Mr. Purvis' attorney." Holloman was dressed like he'd come from a board meeting at a Fortune 500 company. "We've come here today because we understand that you wish to speak with Mr. Purvis."

She felt light-headed. She didn't hear a word that Holloman said. All she could hear was the rushing of her own blood in her ears. She stood completely still and stared into the face of her husband's and daughter's murderer. Slowly, as if it had a mind of its own, her right hand reached toward her Glock.

Suddenly, a third man that Mack hadn't noticed before stepped forward. "Well, well. Fancy meeting you here," he said to her.

She felt like she'd taken a punch to the head and was trying to clear cobwebs from her brain. David Ridley was standing there smirking at her. Sweat trickled from her armpits and rolled down her sides beneath her shirt. She tried to keep the tone of her voice calm as she said, "Mr. Ridley. I thought you were in prison."

Three months after Sigurd took Mack to Scotland, Ridley was arrested on drug trafficking charges. Because of that, Mack felt that it was safe to come back to the states. By then, she'd made the decision to become a police officer, so she went back to college in Boise.

"I got out a couple of months ago." Ridley's face showed his disdain. "Now I'm just an honest businessman."

She smirked. "I bet you're on the Neighborhood Watch committee too."

He took a step toward her. Intimidation had always been his go-to. To a nineteen-year-old girl, he had been terrifying. But she was no longer a girl, or easily intimidated. Ma took a step toward him. She jutted out her chin. Her hazel eyes shot sparks.

Adler frowned. "You two know each other?"

Ridley said, "We've had the pleasure. Long ago."

Holloman cleared his throat. "Well, shall we get started?"

"This way." Nick motioned down the hall toward the interview room. "What the hell was that about?" he whispered to Mack as they followed Adler and Holloman.

"Nothing."

"Right. We could all see that."

Nick opened the door to the interview room. "Have a seat."

Adler and Holloman took their seats.

Nick looked questioningly at Mack when she didn't sit down. He sat across from Adler and turned on the recorder. "We'll be taping this interview."

Holloman said, "My client agrees to be recorded."

Mack stood next to the door, staring at Adler. She wasn't sure she trusted herself to get close to him. She imagined reaching out, wrapping both hands around his neck, and squeezing until his face turned blue. Sigurd's face suddenly came to her.

Holloman said, "As I noted in the lobby, my client's here because he heard that you wanted to speak with him."

Nick asked, "What took you so long to get here?"

"I went on vacation in the mountains. I was out of cell phone range and didn't have a TV." He shrugged. "I wanted to get away from everyone and everything. When I got back into town last night, Mr. Ridley contacted me and let me know that you wanted to ask me some questions."

Holloman said, "We understand that you're seeking my client to ask him questions about a triple homicide that happened the same morning he was in the vicinity of the crime scene."

Nick nodded. "That's correct."

"Please proceed with your questions."

"We have a witness and a video that places you walking on Skyline Road at five-thirty in the morning two Saturdays ago. Mr. Rupp told us that you were there casing the neighborhood."

Holloman interrupted. "Officer, even if that were true, you know you can't arrest my client for thinking about committing a crime."

Nick held up his hand. "Of course I know that. What we want to know is if you saw anyone walking around or driving around while you and Mr. Rupp were casing the neighborhood."

"Officer!" Holloman looked like he'd bitten into a lemon. "My client's definitely not admitting to casing the neighborhood."

Nick grabbed onto the side of the table. "Okay. Got it. So, did you see anyone?"

Adler propped his elbows on the table, hands beneath his chin. "A lady drove by in a car."

"Anyone else?"

Adler furrowed his brow. He looked like thinking was causing him pain. "No. I don't remember seeing anyone else."

"You sure?"

"Officer, my client said he didn't see anyone else. Do you have any other questions?"

Nick looked at Mack. She shook her head.

"No. No more questions."

"Well then, we'll take our leave." Holloman stood up.

Nick led them to the lobby. Mack followed behind, taking deep breaths to calm herself.

Ridley walked toward her. "Should I call you Mack?"

Clearly, Barbara had been talking while she and Ridley were alone. Mack placed her hands on her hips. "You can call me detective, and I'll call you asshole."

His face flushed. He balled up his fists and stepped closer to her.

Nick moved between the two. "It's time for you to leave, Mr. Ridley." He turned toward Adler. "We'll be keeping a close eye on you and Mr. Rupp."

"Let's go." Holloman took Adler's arm and led him out.

Ridley backed away from Mack, smirked, then turned and walked out the door.

Nick asked, "What the hell's wrong with you?"

Mack glared at him. She rushed back to the bullpen.

He followed close behind. "I'm your partner! I deserve to know what's going on."

"It's personal. It doesn't have anything to do with the Brown-Caldwell case. It's from my past. And, I don't want to talk about it. So, let's get back to looking for evidence against a murderer."

Nick held up both hands then dropped them to his sides. "Okay. If you say so. Just know that I'm here if you need something."

She realized that the edge between tears and composure was thinner than she thought. "Thanks," she whispered, blinking back tears. She picked up the autopsy reports again, trying to concentrate on reading them. She read the same line three times without having any idea of what it said. Mack pinched the bridge of her nose and sighed. "I'm going to call it a day." She stood and grabbed her handbag off of the back of the chair.

"Okay. Just remember what I said."

"Thanks. I appreciate it."

Nick watched Mack leave. "Damn it!" He slammed his palm on the top of the desk.

CHAPTER 57

Mack walked to her sedan and drove to the cottage on autopilot, her mind numb. She picked up Drao when she walked in the front door. She hugged him to her chest and put her cheek on his head. He meowed.

She changed into sweats and poured a glass of wine. She took Sean's jacket out of the coat closet by the front door and put it on. She picked up Drao and took him and the wine out to the patio. She hoped that the view would lift her mood. It was a forlorn hope.

The wind started blowing a storm in. A gust of wind rattled a window in the cottage. Within a few minutes, rain wept like tears down the rock face of the courtyard wall.

Mack remembered Sean walking up the sidewalk to the convenience store, with Samantha in the pack on his back. He stopped, then turned and waved at her. She pondered the fleeting nature of life and the unpredictability of the future. *The world doesn't change in front of your eyes. It changes behind your back.* She felt like pain and suffering were permanently imprinted on her.

She took her glass into the house to refill it. Out of the corner of her eye, she saw movement at the front door. Thinking it was Sigurd, she turned with a smile on her face. The smile died when she saw Ridley and Adler. She lunged for her Glock. Before she could grab it off of the kitchen counter, a bullet shattered the wine bottle. There was only the sound of a small pop. *Silencers.*

Ridley pointed his gun at her. "The next one goes through your skull."

She straightened and wiped her wine covered hand on her pants. "What's the matter, Ridley? Are you mad because I called you a name?"

He smirked. "You know why we're here."

She turned toward Adler and gave him a look that could have killed on its own. "Is he here to apologize for murdering my husband and daughter?" She looked back at Ridley. "Are you here to apologize for giving the kill order that resulted in the death of my family?"

Adler walked toward Mack. "Where's my brother, bitch?"

"How does it feel to lose someone you care about? Huh? Does it hurt? Well, multiply that by two for me, asshole."

Adler waved his handgun at her. "You've got balls. With both of us pointing guns at you, do you think talking to us like that's smart?"

Ridley walked up to Mack and hit her on the side of her head with his gun. "What did you do with Ernie?!"

She fell sideways onto the kitchen counter and grabbed her Glock. *Got you, asshole.* She instantly dropped to the floor.

Ridley fired, hitting the wall behind her head. She whirled and fired twice in rapid succession, hitting him in the chest. He dropped like a bag of concrete.

Adler fired before she could turn toward him. The bullet grazed her right side. She hurled herself forward, twisted to the right, and fired at him. She hit him on the left shoulder. His arm dropped to his side, but he continued to shoot with his right hand. A bullet whizzed past her forehead. She quickly fired twice more. This time she hit him on the right side. He dropped the gun and grabbed the wound. She sprang to her feet and backed away.

He pulled out a kitchen stool and heaved himself into it. "Okay, bitch." He groaned. "Call an ambulance."

She shook her head. "Why would I do that?" She pointed her gun at his head.

Sigurd burst through the door, handgun held at chest height. He looked between Mack and Adler. "Are you okay?" he asked her.

She nodded.

"Oh good. A witness." Adler laughed. "You know, when I shot your husband, he begged me not to hurt your daughter. But the bullet went through him and into her. I told him it was too late. I just stood there and watched until they were both dead."

Mack could see that he hadn't been touched by the humanity that inhabits most people. She saw only blackness in his eyes.

"Call that ambulance, bitch."

She didn't respond. She stood there pointing her gun at Adler and thinking. *Now would probably be her only chance to get justice for Sean and Samantha. Could she live with herself if she killed him? Was she even the type of person who could kill someone in cold blood?* She looked at Sigurd. *Did she want to take the chance of losing him?*

"I know you're not going to shoot me, bitch," Adler said, pulling her attention back to him. "You're a cop. You're sworn to uphold the law, not break it. Even if I did kill your precious family."

She looked at the floor for a few seconds. When she looked back up, she said, "Wrong, asshole." She fired.

The bullet hit Adler in the center of his forehead. He fell backward off of the kitchen stool, knocking it over.

She slowly walked over, picked up the stool, and placed it back under the island. She set her Glock back on the counter. She took her cell phone out of her back pocket and called the Skaus Lake emergency number.

Bob White asked, "What's your emergency?"

"This is Mack. Two men broke into my house."

"Are you okay?!"

"I'm fine. They're both dead. I'm going to need Nick and the coroner. You probably should call Chief Davis and let him know, too. He may want to be here."

"You got it."

She disconnected. She hadn't realized that Sigurd had moved to her side. He stuck his handgun in the back of his pants. Then he pulled her into his arms. She flinched and sucked in her breath.

236

He saw the blood on the right side of her shirt. "Shit, you are hit!"

"It's just a scratch." She could see the fear in his eyes. She placed her hand on the side of his face and gave him a small smile. "I'm fine. Really."

His head dropped, and he took a deep breath. When he looked back up, he had tears in his eyes. "I had been coming back early to tell you that I traced Adler's phone to Skaus Lake. When I drove up and heard shots, a ball of fear hit me so hard that I could hardly breathe."

She put her arm around him and laid her head on his chest. He gently held her in his arms. They stayed that way until Nick burst through the door.

He looked confused when he saw the two together. He scowled at Sigurd and rushed to Mack, trying to pull up her shirt to look at her side. "Are you okay?"

She brushed him off. "I'm fine. It's superficial." She turned to Sigurd. "Nick, this is Sigurd. He heard the shots as he drove up and came in after I'd killed both men."

Nick looked down at Adler, then over at Ridley. He rubbed his hand down his face. "Damn."

Mack said, "Exactly."

He sighed. "Well, I better get to the business of taking photos and stuff." He paused. "Then I'm going to need to take statements."

"Why don't you sit on the couch," Sigurd said to Mack. "I'm going to get some things from the bathroom to bandage that wound." He gathered alcohol, gauze, and tape and sat next to her. He helped her shrug off Sean's jacket.

She saw the slit in the leather and the blood on the lining of the coat. "Crap."

He lifted her shirt and started cleaning the wound.

Charlie burst through the front door. When he saw the bloody wound on Mack's side, he said, "Ah, geez!" "Are you okay? I got here as soon as I could."

It was the first time she had seen him dressed in civilian clothes. She gave him a small smile. "It's just a scratch."

Charlie seemed to suddenly realize that Sigurd was there. "Hi." He gave Sigurd a curious look.

"Charlie, this is my good friend, Sigurd."

He nodded, then walked toward Nick who was taking pictures of the bodies. When Charlie reached Adler and saw the bullet hole in his forehead, he didn't say anything. He looked over at Mack, then back down at Adler.

She closed her eyes and leaned the back of her head against the couch.

Sigurd finished bandaging the wound on her side, then turned his attention to her head. Mack hadn't even realized that it was bleeding.

When Nick finished the photographs and sketches, he told Charlie to go home.

"Thanks for coming, Charlie," she said as he came over to say goodbye.

He nodded. "See you soon."

The deputy coroner arrived a few minutes later. Mack introduced Joe Bonner to Sigurd. Bonner looked at the bloody gauze, then at Sigurd. "Need any help with that?"

"Thanks. But I've got it."

Nick said, "It's all yours, Joe. I'm going to talk to these two while you do your thing."

Bonner nodded and got down to work.

Nick sat in the chair next to the couch. He pulled out his tape recorder and turned it on. He identified himself and Mack. Then Nick turned to Sigurd. "Last name?"

"Norgaard."

"Occupation?"

"Owner and operator of Unite Investigative Services."

"Okay, thanks." He turned toward Mack. "You know the drill. Please describe what happened tonight in as much detail as possible."

She went through the events of the evening, leaving out the delay in shooting Adler.

"Why did they come here to your house?"

Sigurd said, "They may have been looking for me." He paused. "Mack and I met just after her husband and daughter were killed. The police gave up on finding the murderer, so she contacted me to see if I could help find him. We were unable to do so." He shrugged. "Mack was with me one evening when I had a run-in with Ridley's nephew, Ernie Adler. Neither Ridley nor Adler knew our identities. Shortly after that incident with Adler, Mack went to Scotland to spend time with her parents. And, I went to Norway to spend time with my father, who was sick. Today was the first time Ridley and Mack had seen each other since the run-in with Ridley's nephew."

As Mack listened to him, she realized that everything he said was true. She nodded. "They must have followed me home." Following Sigurd's lead, she added, "When I saw Chris Purvis, I realized that he's actually Luke Adler, Ridley's other nephew, and Ernie Adler's brother."

"Why didn't you tell me that at the police department today?"

"It didn't seem pertinent. We know that Adler isn't the perp in our three murders." She shrugged. "And there aren't any outstanding warrants for his arrest."

Nick rubbed his forehead. "Anything else I should know?"

Sigurd and Mack glanced at each other and shook their heads. She said, "No. Nothing else."

"End of interview." Nick turned the recorder off and stood. "I know you're aware that you'll have to find another place to stay."

He paused. "I'm going to recommend a determination of a clean shoot. It should only be a few days before you can get back in."

She stood and patted him on the arm. "My gun's on the counter. We'll go pack."

When she walked into the bedroom, Drao crawled out from under the bed and meowed. She picked up the kitten. "Poor baby. I'm sorry you were scared."

Sigurd rubbed Drao's ears. He held the kitten while Mack changed clothes and packed. Then she held him while Sigurd packed.

The two took the backpacks they'd packed, along with Drao, back to the living room. The kitten cried and tried to get free, so Mack zipped him inside her sweatshirt. She hugged him to her chest.

Dave was standing by the front door. "Hey, Mack. How are you doing?"

"I'm okay." She walked over to him and gave him a one-armed hug.

He said, "I'm going to follow the transport vehicles to the coroner's office."

"I'm sorry to pull you away from your family."

"It's my job." He shrugged. "I'm sorry you had to go through this."

Mack gave him a small smile "It's my job."

He patted her on the back.

"Oh. I'm sorry," she said. "Dave, this is my friend, Sigurd." The two shook hands.

Joe Bonner said, "Okay. We're ready to go." Mack and Sigurd stepped back as the bodies were removed. Dave nodded at her and followed the bodies outside.

She and Joe shook hands. "Thanks, Joe."

"You got it."

Sigurd picked up both his and her backpacks off of the couch. The two walked out the front door. Nick followed, turning off the lights. Mack locked the door and Nick attached a crime scene seal to the door.

"Please tell your friend, the landlord, that I'll pay for all the repairs," she said. "If he has a contractor he prefers, just let me know."

"I'll call him and explain. It's pretty minor. A few holes in the walls." Nick paused. "You going to be okay?"

"I'll take care of her," Sigurd said. "I promise."

She smiled at him and said to Nick, "I trust Sigurd with my life. I'll be okay."

He nodded. "Chief Davis was informed. He's waiting at the police department, so I'll go talk to him now."

"I'll call Captain Wilson," Mack said. "Our office will set up the internal investigation. They'll want you to be the lead, of course, as you're the on-scene investigator."

"Do you want our office to take the lead on notifying next of kin?"

"Since the shootings occurred in Skaus Lake, that's probably best."

"No problem. The chief will want to have a media release after the normal forty-eight-hour release hold."

"I'm sure Captain Wilson will want to be part of that."

"We'll have Barbara coordinate the details with your department."

"Thanks, Nick," she said. "I appreciate it."

"Why don't you take a couple of days?"

Mack shook her head. "I can't. There's still a murderer out there."

CHAPTER 58

"**W**here to?" Sigurd asked Mack after he loaded their bags into his new white king cab truck. He reached across and took her hand in his. It was ice cold. "Why don't we go to my place in Coeur d'Alene?"

"Okay." She unzipped her sweatshirt a little so she could rub Drao's ears. He meowed and turned his head right and left, glancing around the truck cab. Then he ducked his head back inside her sweatshirt.

As Sigurd drove, she took out her cell phone and called Captain Wilson. "Sorry to wake you, sir."

"What's happened?"

She gave him a quick synopsis of the shootings and what she and Nick had agreed upon for the investigation and media release.

"Are you safe?"

"Yes. I'm going to stay at a friend's place." She paused. "I plan to keep working on the murders in Skaus Lake through the weekend, as we agreed."

"Do you need to talk to our on-call psychologist?" Wilson paused. "Do I need to be concerned about your readiness to return to duty?"

"No, sir. I'm fine. I don't need to talk to the psychologist. I want to get back to trying to find the murderer."

"Okay. I'll take your word for it, for now. But just know that I'm going to be keeping an eye on you."

"Understood. Thank you."

The two rode the rest of the hour in silence, holding hands. Drao was softly snoring inside Mack's sweatshirt.

When Sigurd pulled up in front of his new place in Coeur d'Alene, Mack looked over at him and smiled. "Reminds me of your place in Boise. Where we met. I liked that place. It felt like a safe harbor for me."

He nodded. "I hope this place will feel like that too. Let's get our things inside." He carried their backpacks to the front door of the industrial building. He set his bag down and punched in a code on the keypad next to the door. The door's lock clicked and popped open a couple of inches. He grabbed the handle of the heavy, steel door with both hands and pushed it open the rest of the way. "Go ahead." He followed Mack inside with the backpacks. The lights automatically came on. He grabbed the handle on the inside of the door and pushed it closed. The lock clicked again. "Come on. I'll show you around."

The front door led into a large living room, which was open to the dining area on the right and the kitchen beyond that. To the left of the living room were two additional rooms. The first was the bedroom and the second was the bathroom. Mack saw that the bathroom had two doors, one into the living room and one into the bedroom. The entire space was bright. It was painted off-white and decorated in a modern, sleek style. Large abstract paintings hung on all the walls. The room-spanning, exposed ductwork enhanced the design. All the floors were polished concrete.

The living room had a navy L-shaped sofa, adorned with numerous throw pillows in differing prints and shades of blue. The coffee table was white acrylic with a glass top. A light wood media suite filled the wall across from the sofa. The towers held beautiful hand-blown blue glass vases in different sizes and shapes. A collection of small gold glass boxes sat next to the TV.

The dining room table was white acrylic with a wood top that matched the bookshelves. The dining room chairs were upholstered in a vibrant navy, cobalt, and pale blue striped fabric

The kitchen cabinets were flat-panel, high gloss white, with tubular stainless steel pulls. The countertops were navy quartz with cobalt and pale blue specks.

"It's stunning. How did you have time to do all this?" Mack set her briefcase on a console table to the left of the front door.

"I did not do any of it." He shrugged. "I hired someone to get it all done quickly. I told them what I wanted, and they did the rest."

"Well, they did an amazing job." She unzipped her sweatshirt and set Drao on the floor. He meowed once, then starting exploring. She looked around the room. "I don't have a single thing hanging on any of my walls. I spend most of my time at work." She shrugged. "I guess it's just been a place to sleep."

He led the way into the bedroom. The furniture was also modern, with a light wood headboard and side tables. The bedding had the same blue hues as the rest of the home. He set their backpacks on the floor next to the bed. "Do you want to unpack?"

"No. I'll just stay here until the cottage is released." She paused. "I need to spend as much time as I can in Skaus Lake, working the murders. I only have five more days."

He placed his hands on her shoulders. "I understand. But I want you to take care of yourself, too." He kissed her forehead.

"Thanks for caring."

He went back outside and retrieved Drao's litter box and food from the back of the truck. They set up the litter box in the bathroom and the food and water bowls in the kitchen. "Are you hungry?"

"No, but I could use a large, stiff drink."

"Scotch?"

Mack nodded. She leaned on the kitchen island counter and watched him pour the amber liquid into two crystal glasses. He added ice and handed a glass to her. Taking her by the hand, he said, "I have not shown you the best part of this entire place." He led her to a wall of the living room that was covered in screens the same color as the walls. He picked up a remote off of a side table and pressed a button. The screens retracted to the sides, revealing a wall of glass. He led her through double glass doors and out onto a deck with a view of Lake Coeur d'Alene and the national forest beyond.

"Oh, Sigurd, this is breathtaking."

"I thought you might like it." He kissed the back of her hand. "Let's sit." They sat next to each other on a sleek teak wood outdoor sofa with blue striped cushions. The sides of the deck were glass, so the spectacular view was uninterrupted. He put his arm around her. She pulled her legs under her and laid her head on his shoulder.

Drao came outside and meowed. He looked down through the glass on the patio. Then he hopped up into Mack's lap and started purring. She rubbed the kitten's ears. "How are you doing, little guy?" He meowed in response.

Mack and Sigurd sipped their drinks in silence. Cloud cover rendered the night sky completely dark. Suddenly, lightning streaked across the sky, followed by a clap of thunder that exploded across the mountain peaks.

"Samantha and I would sit at her bedroom window and watch for lightning strikes. We'd count the seconds between the strike and the thunder that followed." She paused for a few seconds. "I wonder why that memory just now surfaced, after so many years."

He rubbed her arm. "Sometimes memories need a chance to breathe. Like red wine."

"And, sometimes they're deliberately suppressed. Because they're too painful to remember."

"Or, maybe now is the right time for them to be remembered."

The day's events suddenly overwhelmed Mack. She realized that her emotions were raw. "All I know at this moment is that I wish I could stay right here and not have to deal with the real world ever again."

CHAPTER 59

Mack hadn't bothered to set her alarm clock. She didn't wake up until eight, not having fallen asleep until the early morning hours. She and Sigurd hadn't talked about the shootings the night before. They sat on the porch for an hour, then went to bed and held each other. She knew that he wouldn't push. He'd wait until she was ready to talk. Sigurd wasn't in bed. She picked her cell phone up off of the bedside table and called Nick to let him know that she would be in around ten.

He said, "Take your time."

She put on a pair of warm socks and padded into the living room.

Sigurd and Drao were in the kitchen. "I have a quiche in the oven. It will be done in a few minutes." He gave her a long hug. "Coffee?"

"Yes. Please."

He filled a mug and indicated a sugar and creamer set to her. "Help yourself." He refilled his cup.

Mack admired the dishware, which was a modern graphic design in differing blue hues. "I'm going to take a quick shower before breakfast." She kissed Sigurd on the cheek.

"Okay. You need anything?"

"Nope. Got it all." She took her coffee with her to the bathroom. As she dried her hair, she realized that even the bathroom towels coordinated with the décor in the rest of the place. *I have one set of tan towels that I got on clearance at Target. Hey. They do match my tan down comforter.* "I'm never letting Sigurd ever come over," she mumbled. She dressed and went into the kitchen.

Sigurd had her to sit on a barstool. He had started to put a fresh bandage on Mack's side, when she said, "I stood in the bathroom and thought about the color of my towels. I killed a

246

man in cold blood last night, and I thought about towels." She rubbed her forehead. "What the hell's wrong with me?"

"You are probably in shock. Is this the first time you have ever killed someone?"

Mack nodded.

"It is not an easy thing to forget."

"Have you killed anyone?"

"Yes. It was necessary." He put a clean bandage on Mack's temple. It was clear to her that he didn't want to talk about it.

~~~

They sat on the porch, ate quiche and fruit, and drank coffee. Shafts of morning light filtered through the thick canopy of trees, casting shadows across the lake. Mack recognized the call of a nearby jay. She watched as ducks swam around the edges of the lake below. She sipped coffee and soaked in the peace. Suddenly, she asked, "Hey, where's your office?"

"Come on. I will show you." Sigurd motioned inside. He led her by the hand to the front door. He turned toward the wall to the right of it. A large mirror hung there. He took his cell phone from his back pocket and tapped on the screen. He heard the click of locks, then the mirror swung inward. He gave her a crooked smile and stepped inside the hidden room.

She followed. She saw that the mirror was attached to a vault style door with steel shear pins and an electromagnetic locking system.

"The door is bulletproof, and the locking system is fail-secure, so even if the power goes out, the locks work." He shrugged. "It is the only kind to have."

She raised her eyebrows and grinned. "Of course." She walked around the room, looking at all of the electronic equipment. She counted four computers and monitors. "I guess with all your electronics, you do need a vault."

"The most important thing is that nobody is able to access the data I have on the computers."

She nodded. "Makes sense."

He secured the office door as they left. "It is also a safe room. Let me show you how you can get in if you ever need to." He walked over to the television and picked up the remote. "Looks like a regular remote. But if you press the colored buttons in the correct sequence, the office door will open."

"Okay."

He said, "Red, yellow, green, red, red."

She repeated the sequence. "Red, yellow, green, red, red." She repeated it silently to herself several more times. "Got it." She put her arms around his neck and kissed him.

He wrapped his arms around her waist and returned the kiss.

She sighed. "I have to get back to Skaus Lake. I told Nick I'd be in by ten."

He nodded. "Unfortunately, I have to be here all day. I am meeting with the parents of a missing child. So, I have arranged for my friend and colleague, Connor, to drive you back. I hope you do not mind."

"Not at all, but I hate to put him out."

"He is driving to Cranbrook, British Columbia to talk to a potential client. So, dropping you off on the way is no problem." Sigurd took out his cell phone and made a call. "Ready here."

~~~

Every bit of Connor Fitzpatrick's five feet, eleven inches was sinewy muscle. He had ginger hair and pale skin that was covered with freckles. His nose was somewhat flattened at the bridge. His stance and walk demonstrated his confidence, without him having to say a single word. "Miss Mackenzie." He smiled and shook her hand. With an Irish brogue, he said, "It's good to meet you." "This big lug's been telling me about you." His green eyes twinkled.

She liked Connor immediately. "Oh, has he? Anything I should know about?"

"We'll talk on the drive." He winked at Mack and smiled mischievously at Sigurd.

"Behave yourself." Sigurd slapped him on the back.

He laughed. "Absolutely not."

Sigurd walked Mack to Connor's car and kissed her on the forehead. "See you tonight."

She nodded and kissed him on the cheek. The vehicle was a shiny black two-door sports car with black, leather interior. Mack got inside and looked around the interior. "This is a very nice car. What kind is it?"

He started the car. "It's a Jaguar F-Type S." He glanced at her. "Do you know cars?"

She shook her head. "Not even a tiny bit."

He chuckled. "It has a top speed of about one hundred seventy miles per hour, and it will go from zero to sixty in under five seconds."

She raised her eyebrows. "Wow. Have you ever needed to drive that fast?"

He began to drive. "Several times. Unfortunately." He didn't elaborate.

"Have you and Sigurd known each other long?"

"I guess it's been nine years."

"How did you two meet?"

"The first time Sigurd saw me, I was bussing tables at a restaurant in Boise. An obnoxious, drunk customer called me an Irish shant. I ignored the guy and kept working. But the guy stood up and shoved me, causing me to drop the dishes I was carrying. The restaurant's manager fired me on the spot." He shrugged. "The two guys went around to the back of the restaurant and waited for me to come out. I told them that I didn't want to fight, but they were drunk. Suddenly, Sigurd was standing next to me, making the odds even. The guys came at us… and, well… they didn't have a chance. When the police showed up, Sigurd told them that the two guys had started the fight." He chuckled. "After the police left, Sigurd asked me if I wanted a job."

"Are you from Ireland?"

He nodded. "I was born in Donegal. I came to the states when I was eighteen."

Mack and Connor talked about Scotland and Ireland for the rest of the drive to Skaus Lake.

CHAPTER 60

Mack got in her state police sedan and drove straight to the Skaus Lake Police Department.

"You good?" Nick asked when she walked in the back door.

She nodded.

"I made a timeline of the Friday night and Saturday morning of the murders. I included everyone who is, or might be, involved." He handed a copy to her. "Again, the only two people without alibis are Barbara and Cox."

She took off her jacket, hung it on the back of her chair, and set her handbag on the floor next to her desk. "This is great. Thanks." She studied the timeline, looking for any possible discrepancies in alibis. She shook her head. "The problem is we have too much missing information. We can't prove that Cox, or any other suspect for that matter, was at the crime scene. I hate to say it, but we need to go back and speak to everyone again. And that includes Barbara."

"Damn. She's going to be angry for a week."

"Tough shit. It's Wednesday. I go back to work in Coeur d'Alene on Monday morning." She rubbed her forehead. She could feel a headache coming on. *Too little sleep and too much caffeine.* "If we don't solve this case, it will weigh on me forever."

Nick nodded. "Agreed."

"Sorry. I know you're feeling as frustrated as I am. I shouldn't take it out on you."

He waved his hand. "No biggy."

"Okay." She sighed. "Let's get going."

"Who do you want to start with?"

"Let's start with Jergins. See if the details he gave us when he confessed have changed any."

~~~

Mack and Nick waited in an interview room while a sheriff's officer went to get Jergins.

"Hey, I forgot to tell you," Nick said. "We released your cottage this morning. The cleaning and repairs are being done as we speak. You can go back there tonight if you want."

"That's great. What did the owner say when you talked to him?"

"He was amazed by what happened there." Nick shrugged. "I made the arrangements for the cleaners and repairman, so he didn't have to bother."

"That's going above and beyond the call of duty. I appreciate it."

"That's what friends do. They help each other out."

She smiled. "Thanks. I stayed at Sigurd's last night in Coeur d'Alene. But the hour drive back and forth is time that I could be working the case."

"So. Sigurd seems. Capable."

"He's the most completely whole person that I know."

The door opened, and Jergins was ushered in. The sheriff's officer locked Jergins' cuffs to a ring in the floor, then left. He closed the door behind himself.

Mack questioned Jergins about the details of the morning of the murders, but he didn't waver from the confession that he'd first volunteered. She used every technique and trick she had in her arsenal to no avail.

"Where to now?" Nick asked when they were back in his sedan.

"We might as well get the interview with Barbara over."

He rubbed his forehead. "Damn."

Barbara was not happy when Nick told her that they wanted to talk to her again. "You arrested a guy that confessed! What the hell do you want to harass me for?"

He rubbed his hand down his face. "We just want to talk for a few minutes."

Barbara leaned back in her chair and crossed her arms over her ample chest. "No."

His brow furrowed. "What?"

"I said no! I told you I was home alone. I told you I didn't do it. There's nothing else to talk about. If you want to talk to me again, do it through my lawyer."

~~~

Barbara wasn't the only person that wasn't happy to be reinterviewed. Nobody they spoke with was pleased to see them again. They didn't want to dredge up the details of the murders.

Mack and Nick visited Pastor Beck first and asked him if he could tell them anything.

He merely said, "No."

After school, they went to Ethan Williams' home. Joe was at work. Alice agreed to let them speak with Ethan on the condition that they didn't mention the fact that Susan was his half-sister. They agreed.

"Ethan, is there anything you can think of that you didn't tell us before," Mack asked. "Anything at all? Even it seems unimportant or insignificant."

He was quiet for a few seconds. "Sorry. I can't think of anything."

She smiled at him. "Okay. Thanks"

Next, they went to Grace's house and talked separately with each of the Brown children. None of them had any new details to add that they could think of.

"I've already talked a second time to all of the Browns' former neighbors," Mack said. "There's no point bothering them a third time. We got everything we could from them."

"I don't know where to go from here," Nick said.

"Neither do I." She sighed. "Maybe if we sleep on it, something will come to us."

He drove them back to the police department. Neither of them went inside. They both got in their cars, calling it a night.

Mack called Sigurd on her cell phone. "The cottage is done already, so I'm going to stay there tonight. That way I don't have to drive back and forth. I've got an early court appearance tomorrow morning."

"Do you want me to drive over tonight?"

"I would like to see you. But I've run into a wall on this case, and I need some time alone to see if I can come up with any answers."

He hesitated. "I hope you are not shutting me out because of Adler."

"I'm not. I promise. I just need a little time alone to work on the case. Why don't you come over tomorrow night?"

"See you then."

As Mack drove back to the cottage, she wondered how she'd feel when she returned to the place that she'd committed murder.

The inside of the cottage looked like nothing had happened. She looked down at the spot on the floor where Adler's body was. She waited for feelings of guilt or remorse or sadness to come, but none did. She also didn't feel joy or happiness that he was dead. What she did feel was relief. Relief that it was finally over.

She took her Glock out of the side holster and set it on the kitchen counter. She went into the bedroom and changed into warm-ups and fuzzy socks. Taking a wine glass from the cabinet and an open bottle of Chardonnay from the refrigerator, she went out onto the patio. Even though Drao had only lived with her for a little while, she missed him not being around. That feeling elicited an immediate rush of fear in her. She mentally shook herself. *This fear of loss has to stop.*

She sat back in the wicker chair and soaked in the view of the lake and tree covered mountains. She let her mind wander through the Brown-Caldwell case, hoping that her subconscious would spit out what her conscious mind was unable to grasp.

When her cell phone rang, she saw that it was Nick. "What's up?"

"I wanted to let you know that the shooting investigative team set your interview for tomorrow at one in the afternoon. It's going to be in our interview room. The media release is set for nine on Friday morning. The formal decision of the investigative team will be finalized by then. It's pretty much a formality since you shot them in self-defense."

"Thanks for letting me know." Mack disconnected and sipped wine. She thought about the evil that she'd seen in Adler's eyes, just before she put a bullet between them. *I was able to murder a man, so what kind of evil lives in me?*

CHAPTER 61

Mack and Nick met at the courthouse the next morning. They sat behind the prosecutor's table, where Deputy Prosecutor Ivan Archer was laying out paperwork. Archer was prosecuting this case himself because it was high profile. The two investigators had met with him the day before to review the evidence and confession.

Archer shook hands with them. "Thanks for coming."

Mack said, "Ivan, I want to reiterate that we both believe Jergins' confession is false and he isn't the murderer."

Nick nodded his head in agreement.

"Understood."

The proceedings drew numerous spectators, including members of the press. Ida and Frank Caldwell were present. Mack spoke to the Caldwells and Grace on Monday. She told them that at this first appearance Jergins would be advised of his rights. She also explained the procedure that would be followed. Jergins would not be allowed to enter a plea at the first appearance. This would be done at the arraignment. Grace said she didn't know if she possessed the strength to attend. But the Caldwells adamantly said they would attend every day that Jergins was in court.

As they waited for the defendant and judge, Mack's mind wandered. She was always reminded of a church when she was in a courtroom. Like a pulpit, the judge's bench was elevated at the front of the room, looking down on the proceedings.

The back door of the courtroom opened, and Jergins was ushered to the defendant's table by two sheriff officers. Jergins seemed indifferent to the stares of the spectators in the courtroom.

Magistrate Judge Tucker Black entered, and everyone rose. After the judge took his seat, the rest of those in the courtroom also sat.

Without preface, Judge Black read Jergins his rights. "Mr. Jergins, you have the right to a jury trial. You have the right to confront your accusers and to compel favorable witnesses to testify on your behalf. You shall not be compelled to be a witness against yourself."

While the judge read, Jergins hung his head and kept his hands folded together, as if in prayer.

When Judge Black finished reading, he said, "Mr. Jergins, I see that you do not have an attorney present and I understand that you are unemployed. Will you be obtaining an attorney or do you need the court to appoint an attorney to represent you?"

Jergins looked up at the judge. "I don't have any money."

"Very well, then. The court will appoint an attorney to represent you."

The proceeding lasted a little over an hour. As Mack walked back to her car, a reporter stuck a microphone in her face and asked if she had any comments. She ignored the man and kept walking. She felt the crushing responsibility of trying to find real justice for the victims. She drove back to the police department thinking of the three bodies lying on the floor of the Browns' living room.

When Mack parked at the police department, she laid her forehead on the steering wheel and closed her eyes. Between thinking about the case and the internal investigation, she'd only slept two hours the night before. She was startled when Nick tapped on the drivers' window.

"You okay?" he asked as she got out of her sedan.

"I feel like I've let everyone down."

As they walked to the back door of the police department, Nick said, "You know what? You're a human being doing your best. Like the rest of us. You can't expect to be more than that."

She didn't respond. Inside, she headed straight for the coffee pot and filled a large cup. She sat heavily on her desk chair and sipped coffee. She picked up a copy of the transcripts of the children's interviews and started reading them, for what seemed like the hundredth time. She didn't know what she was looking for. Maybe inspiration. None came.

Barbara came to Mack's desk at precisely one o'clock. "They're ready for you."

Mack's mind went blank as she walked up the hall. Turning toward the door into the interview room, she paused and took a deep breath. Entering the room, she saw that Captain Wilson was sitting at the head of the table. Chief Davis sat on his right and Nick on his left. It was common for a representative of the local prosecutor's office to be a member of the team investigating officer-involved shootings. So, she wasn't surprised to see Ivan Archer sitting next to Nick. She shook hands with the four men.

"Take a seat." Captain Wilson indicated the chair at the opposite end of the table.

Mack sat and, under the table, wiped her sweating hands on the front of her pants. She hoped she didn't look as nervous as she felt.

"We'll be recording this interview." Nick turned on the machine. For the record, he identified the people in the room, the date, and the time.

She watched the reels inside the tape recorder turn round and round. The tape started on one side and moved to the other side. *Pretty much just like I did when I shot Adler. I moved from the side of the law to the side of crime.*

Wilson said, "In your own words, please describe the events of Tuesday evening that resulted in the fatal shooting of Mr. David Ridley and Mr. Lucas Adler, also known as Chris Purvis."

She went through her version of the evening and Sigurd's version of how she knew the two men. She explained that both men had fired at her first. When she finished talking, she was immensely relieved that nobody asked her any questions.

Wilson and Davis thanked her and said they would let her know the team's findings by the end of the day.

She walked out of the interview room and straight into the ladies room. She splashed cold water on her face and neck until she felt her body temperature start to cool down. She straightened up from the sink. Water dripped onto the floor as she stared at her reflection in the mirror. She leaned into the mirror, looking into her own eyes for a few seconds.

~~~

Mack was glad to see Sigurd's truck sitting in the driveway of the cottage when she pulled up that evening. Smiling, she opened the front door. Drao meowed and rubbed his head on her legs. She picked him up and snuggled him. Sigurd was in the kitchen, drinking a glass of wine. The cottage smelled heavenly.

"Hi." He set his glass down and walked toward her. "I missed you."

She set Drao on the floor and walked toward him. They met next to the couch in the living room. She threw her arms around his neck and kissed him passionately. She ran her hand down his chest to the front of his pants. She took him in her hand. "I missed you, too."

He picked her up and carried her to the bedroom. They tore at each other's clothes, unable to get them off fast enough. After they were both satiated, they lay in each other's arms until he said that dinner would be ruined if they didn't eat soon. They both pulled on sweats and went into the kitchen, where he filled their plates. She poured wine for both of them. They took their plates and glasses to the dining room table.

When she took her first bite, she said, "Mmmm, this is delicious. What is it?"

"Coq au vin. The way my mother makes it."

"Do you cook when you're with your mother?"

He shook his head. "No. My mother will not have it. One, she loves to cook. Two, she thinks nobody can cook as good as she can."

Mack grinned. "It's a good thing you can cook because I can't. I spend so much time at work. I get take-out on the way home or order pizza to be delivered."

"I like cooking. It relaxes me."

"But it isn't fair for you to do all of the work. How about if when you cook, I'll clean up?" Mack chuckled. "I know how to do that."

"Deal."

He continued to sip wine as she cleared the table and washed the dishes. When she finished, they took their wine out to the patio. Drao followed, hopping into Mack's lap, then curling into a ball.

She petted the kitten and listened to him purr. The purring seemed to blend perfectly with the night sounds around the cottage. Crickets chirped. Frogs croaked. A coyote howled in the distance. The night sky was clear for a change and stars twinkled overhead.

She sipped her wine, then leaned back in her chair. "The investigative team for the shootings found that due to the threat to my life, the use of deadly force was reasonable."

"I'm happy to hear that."

Mack was quiet for a few moments. "I've come to believe that there may be good in the worst of us and evil in the best of us."

CHAPTER 62

When Mack sat at her desk the next morning, Nick asked, "How are you?"

She shrugged. "Pissed at myself. I hate not being able to solve this case."

"I know the feeling." He paused. "Charlie's back on patrol. He asked me to say goodbye for him. You'll be back for Jergins' arraignment, so I'm not going to say goodbye."

She nodded.

Barbara came into the bullpen carrying an arm full of empty boxes. "I have more if you need them." She set the boxes on Nick's desk.

Mack and Nick spent the rest of the day boxing up all of the evidence and records from the Brown-Caldwell case. They worked in silence, labeling each box with the case name, along with what was in the box. When they were finished, Barbara helped them store the boxes in evidence lockers that were along one wall of the main corridor.

As they placed the last box inside and Barbara turned the key in the lock, a feeling of sadness filled Mack. She slammed her open palm on the front of the locker.

"Come on, let's get out of here," Nick said.

She took a last look around the bullpen, picked up her handbag, and walked out the back door for the last time.

The two arranged to meet at the Sports Bar. Nick changed at the restaurant again. When Mack arrived, she locked her handgun in the trunk of her sedan. She walked inside and saw that he had already ordered two shots. When she sat on the bar stool next to him, he pointed at the glasses. "Good scotch."

She picked up one of the glasses and held it up. "Cheers."

They both drank their shots. Nick raised his hand to the bartender. "Another round." After the bartender filled their glasses, he raised his. "To a great partner. It's been an honor."

"Thank you." She drank the shot in one swallow, then called the bartender over. "One more round, please."

The bartender filled their shot glasses again. After he walked away, she raised her glass and said, "May we always part with regret and meet again with pleasure."

~~~

Mack had arranged to meet Susan that evening at First Avenue Pizzeria to say goodbye. Susan was already at the restaurant when she arrived. As she sat in the chair across from the girl, the owner brought a glass of white wine.

"I ordered before you got here," Susan said. "This is my treat. I wanted to thank you for helping me make it through all this."

"I appreciate that."

Tears glistened in Susan's eyes. "I'm going to miss you." She swiped at them with her napkin.

"My leaving Skaus Lake doesn't have to mean goodbye," Mack said. "You have my cell number. You can call me anytime you need to talk."

Susan wiped tears. "Thanks. That would be great." The waitress delivered their pizza. "I ordered the works. Figured we could use some vegetables for a change."

She chuckled. "Good call."

"Oh no. I asked for no tomatoes. I don't really like tomatoes. Oh well, I'll just pick them off."

With her wine glass mid-way to her mouth, Mack stared at Susan for a heartbeat.

"Is something wrong?"

Mack shook her head. "No." She took a drink of her wine. She felt dizzy and lightheaded. She nibbled at the pizza, but her stomach was queasy.

"Are you okay?" Susan asked. "You haven't eaten much."

"I had a couple of drinks with Officer Moore before I came here. I think I need to go home and lie down."

"Oh, okay."

She stood and picked up her handbag off of the seat next to her. "Sorry to cut our visit short."

Susan stood and drew her into a hug. "This isn't goodbye."

Mack drove back to the cottage as quickly as possible. She jumped out of her sedan, opened the front door, and sat on the couch. She rifled through the copies of paperwork on the murders that she'd brought home. When she found the transcript of Ethan Williams' interview, she started skimming it. When she got to the part that she was looking for, she read it twice. It all came together. "Oh, no."

"Oh, yes."

Mack jumped up and whipped around.

Susan stood in the doorway with a handgun pointed at her chest. Susan reached behind her and pushed the front door shut. "I knew you'd figured it out in the restaurant."

"Don't do this. You're only making things worse for yourself."

Susan laughed. "Oh come on. The police in this hick town will never solve the murders. They're not nearly as smart as you are. The first time I saw you, I knew I needed to keep an eye on you." She motioned with the gun. "Sit back down. I want you to tell me what you figured out. I'll fill in the gaps." She waved the gun and smiled. "Go on, have a seat. Let's talk."

Mack slowly sat on the couch as she watched Susan. Drao peeked around the bedroom door, ears back.

Susan saw the kitten. "That stupid cat of yours is a better judge of people than you are." She looked back at Mack. "So, go on. Tell me what you know." She sat in the chair farthest from the couch.

"You cooked dinner for everyone Friday night. You made spaghetti with meat sauce. You mixed either Rohypnol or GHB into the sauce. I figure it was GHB because it's a powder that quickly dissolves into a clear, odorless substance. It has a salty taste. Other than that, it's barely detectable. The ingredients are inexpensive, and recipes are readily available online." She paused. "After ingesting GHB, an individual starts to be affected within thirty minutes or so, and the effects last six to seven hours. The effects include slower motor coordination, dizziness, and unconsciousness. GHB's even harder to detect than Rohypnol and remains in the body for an even shorter amount of time. That's why it wasn't found during the autopsies."

Susan nodded. "Very good, so far. I knew the effects would differ for each person. I also knew the younger boys would eat less than the grown-ups. So, they would be fine. When Chrissy ate dinner that night, I reminded her of her weight. She didn't eat that much either."

"Chrissy was unconscious, so you didn't have any trouble sneaking out of her room and back in after the murders. You took an extra set of clothes to her house. You brought those with you to change into after the murders. You have a key to get in. Your DNA and fingerprints are all over the house, so you didn't have to worry about that. The Lees' dog barked both times you walked by their house."

"I thought that yapping thing was going to give me away."

"You dragged your mom, Alan, and Jack from where they'd passed out in the living room to the center of the floor. Probably hoping that would make the investigators think the scene was staged by some psychopath. You went into the kitchen, got the butcher knife and stabbed your mom and Alan. Poor Jack just happened to be in the wrong place at the wrong time. You slit his throat. You changed clothes, walked into the woods and buried the bloody clothes, and went back to Chrissy's."

"It was so easy."

"You didn't count on Ethan not liking spaghetti sauce. Because he was the only one, besides you, that didn't eat it, he was awake. Probably worried you when you heard that he saw you."

"It did. A little. But I actually wore some of Alan's clothes. In case someone saw me, they'd think I was a man. And, it worked."

"You got rid of your computer because you'd done research on GHB with it. It's probably buried in the woods with the clothes. Did you take your mom's laptop and Alan's phone to throw us off?"

"I took mom's laptop to throw you off, but Alan actually lost his phone the week before. It couldn't have been more perfect." Susan laughed.

"I don't think Alan and Jack actually smoked pot. I think that was another plan of yours to confuse us."

"Right again."

"Did you call the reporter at the Idaho Statesman and tip her off about Jergins confession?"

Susan nodded. "I couldn't believe my luck. But then you told me that you didn't believe him. I thought if I told the press it would put pressure on you to close the case."

"Why? Why did you do it?"

"Well. That's an interesting story. It started when I was twelve. The disgusting excuse for a human being that called himself my dad started raping me. The third time it happened, I told dear mom. You know what she said? She asked me why I'd make something like that up. She told me to stop being so dramatic. Nice, huh? Come to find out, that piece of shit Greg wasn't really my biological father. Did you know that?"

Mack nodded. "Yes. I found your birth certificate in your mom's desk."

"That's where I found it too. A couple of years ago. I was looking for some paper for the printer, and I saw my birth certificate. Imagine my surprise. Although, I was glad to find out that I hadn't been having sex for three years with my real father."

"Why kill your brother?"

"The story continues. One night I put a chair under the doorknob of my bedroom door, to keep Greg out. I couldn't stand it anymore. When I got up the next morning and moved the chair, he was there, just waiting. He picked me up and slammed me face down onto my bed. He shoved my head into the mattress and raped me. When he finished, he told me not to ever lock him out again. I lifted my head and saw Alan watching through the partially open door. He looked me in the eyes and ran away. He never looked me in the eyes again, and I never spoke to him again. He could have helped me. But that pussy was too afraid. He let it continue. Just like my dear mother."

"Oh, God, Susan. I'm so sorry that happened to you."

"I know you mean that. You've been really nice to me. That's why I feel bad that I have to kill you."

"You don't have to do that. I can help you get treatment to deal with the trauma you suffered all those years."

Susan laughed dryly. "Talk to a stranger? Tell them the intimate details? Sit around in a circle and talk with a group of strangers about it? I don't think so. I talked to Pastor Beck about it when we first moved here. But it didn't do me any good. I hated my mother and Alan more and more each day."

"I can help you get into a place where there are specialists that know how to help victims of sexual abuse."

"A psychiatric hospital? Come on. Do you really think they'd ever let me out after I killed four people?"

Mack's brow furrowed. "Four?"

"Yeah. I killed dear old Greg too. Nobody would help me, so I took care of it myself. I used GHB on him too. Mixed a bunch of it into his food at dinner. I stood over him and watched until his heart gave out. Oh, you should've seen the look of fear in his eyes when he realized what was happening. It was fabulous! Although, it didn't even come close to making up for what he'd done to me."

"A judge will understand why you killed them."

Susan shook her head. "I've heard enough about trying to save me. It's not going to happen. Stand up. Come on. Get up, Mack." She motioned with the gun. "Over there. On the rug."

The front door opened and Sigurd came in. "How does pasta sound for…" He didn't get the rest out. Susan whirled and shot him. He grabbed his side with both hands and fell to the floor.

Before Susan turned back around, Mack lunged and knocked her onto her back. She wrenched the gun out of Susan's hands and threw it aside. Then she slammed her fist into Susan's face. The girl screamed. Blood began to pour from her nose. Mack flipped her onto her stomach. She took two pairs of plastic handcuffs out of the utility pocket of her pants and secured Susan's hands and legs.

Mack ran to Sigurd. He was unconscious. Blood dripped from his side onto the floor. Memories of Sean and Samantha washed through the shores of Mack's mind like the debris from a shipwreck. She ran to the bathroom and grabbed a large towel off of the towel rack. She ran back to Sigurd and knelt next to him. She folded the towel and pressed it into his wound. She pulled her cell out of the back pocket of her pants and hit the 'Emergency Call' button.

She recognized Dave's voice. "What's your emergency?"

"This is Mack. I need an ambulance at my house! Hurry, Dave, hurry." She threw the phone on the ground. She could hear Dave yelling. "Mack! Are you okay? Mack!"

She pressed on Sigurd's wound with her left hand and cradled his face with her right. "Helps on the way. You're going to be okay." She gently pressed her lips to his. Tears ran down her face. She heard a siren and the squeal of tires in front of the house. She ran outside and waved her arms in the air. "In here!"

The emergency medical attendants hurried to the back of the ambulance and opened the doors. The pulled their equipment out and rushed into the cottage. One technician put an oxygen mask on Sigurd, while the other checked his vital signs. "Breathing shallowly. Skin pale and cool. Hang bag and run saline." One attendant inserted an IV, while the other secured a pressure bandage over the wound.

Mack said, "Sigurd. I'm here. Hang on. You hear me. Hang on."

"Ma'am, please step back."

She shook her head. Tears streamed down her face.

"Ma'am, step back. Let us do our jobs!"

She crabbed backward on her hands and knees.

Suddenly, Nick was there. He helped her to her feet. She looked at him with vacant eyes.

The technicians loaded Sigurd onto their portable stretcher and wheeled him to the ambulance. Mack followed on their heels. As they loaded him into the ambulance, she continued to talk to him. She tried to get into the ambulance, but they wouldn't allow it. The technicians closed the doors of the ambulance and drove away.

The blaring siren almost drowned out Mack's words. "Susan's in the living room. She's the murderer. She was going to kill me. Sigurd interrupted her, and she shot him."

"Jesus. What the fuck?"

Charlie and Bob arrived within seconds of each other. Nick asked them to secure the prisoner and the crime scene. They looked at Mack with concern as they entered the cottage.

Nick said, "Come on. I'll drive you to the hospital."

She let him lead her by the arm to his sedan. They arrived at the hospital a few minutes later. Sigurd was already in surgery. Nick went to get coffee for them. They had the long and dreadful task of waiting ahead.

Mack paced back and forth. She told Nick how Susan had committed the three murders. "She also admitted to murdering her step-father. She poisoned him, but the death was classified as natural heart failure."

He sat on the edge of a chair with his elbows on his knees, chin resting on his entwined fingers. When she relayed what Susan had said about the physical abuse, he mumbled, "Jesus Christ."

"Man's civility is inspiring, isn't it?" She saw a doctor coming down the corridor toward her. She stared at him, but she couldn't read his face.

When the doctor reached them, he said, "Mr. Norgaard came through the surgery. We just have to wait and see now."

Mack asked, "Can I see him?"

"Who are you?"

Nick quickly answered. "This is Mr. Norgaard's sister."

"Alright. But only for a few minutes."

She followed the doctor down the corridor to Sigurd's room. When she stepped inside, she saw that he had an IV in his hand and an oxygen cannula in his nose. The color of his skin sent every ounce of fear that she had into the void of her stomach. She pulled a chair up next to the bed and took his hand in hers. "I'm here." She kissed him on the forehead. "Please come back to me. Please. I can't stand to lose another person that I love."

CHAPTER 63

Mack and Nick followed an Idaho state police Officer who was watching his four-legged partner work. The police dog sniffed back and forth along a narrow stretch of pine needle covered ground.

The officer said, "We've got a hit." His partner stopped and dug at a spot that looked like every other inch of ground. "Good boy." He patted the dog and led him away.

A state police crime scene investigator snapped photographs while he and Nick dug. They uncovered the bloody clothes that Susan had been wearing when she killed Patricia, Alan, and Jack almost three weeks before.

Nick looked at Mack. "We've got a black hoodie, t-shirt, jeans, socks, and tennis shoes." He brushed at the soil. "Got the two laptops. They're under the clothes." He helped the state police investigator bag and tag each item.

When they finished, the investigator said to Mack, "I'll take these back and process them."

"Thank you."

Nick asked Mack walked down to their sedans, which were parked at the top of Skyline Road. He asked, "How's Sigurd doing?"

"Good. He was lucky. That bullet could have caused a lot more damage than it did. Since he no longer has a spleen, he'll need a couple of immunizations. Pneumonia and meningitis. Just to be on the safe side. Otherwise, he should be fine."

"That's great. I'm glad to hear it."

"He's getting out of the hospital tomorrow."

"That's quick."

"He wanted out, so he hired a private nurse. That's the only way the doctor would agree to release him. We'll stay in the cottage until he's well enough to go back to Coeur d'Alene." She stopped and looked at Nick. "You were right about me getting too close to Susan. I let my emotions get involved in the investigation. Both my sympathy for Susan and my dislike of Cox."

"Don't beat yourself up. We both had Cox pegged as the prime suspect. I still have a hard time processing that Susan is the murderer."

"Without any acknowledgment by Susan's family that the abuse was happening, she probably felt that the very essence of her existence would be destroyed if she didn't respond," Mack said. "In Susan's case, violence was predictable. And perhaps preventable."

EPILOGUE

Mack stood in front of Captain Wilson. Her badge and Glock sat next to each other on top of his desk.

"I hate this," Wilson said. "You're one of the best detectives I've ever worked with. I wish you'd reconsider."

"I appreciate that, sir. But after everything that happened in Skaus Lake, I just can't go back. I realize now that I only became a detective because of my husband and daughter. In my new job, I'll be helping people that are alive. Not trying to be a champion for the dead."

~~~

Mack and Sigurd held hands as they walked up the small hill in the cemetery. They stopped in front of two headstones, one large and one small. She dragged in a ragged breath and let it out. He squeezed her hand.

"I'm here because I wanted to tell you that I'm finally okay." She paused. "I was lost without you for so long." She sighed. "I lived every day as a victim. But I was only a victim of my own thoughts and actions." Mack looked at Sigurd. "I'm making a choice. A choice to take a chance."

The End

Acknowledgements

I would like to thank you, the reader, for purchasing this book. You make the storytelling worthwhile. If you enjoyed it, please take a few minutes to leave a review on Amazon. Unfortunately, Amazon doesn't recognize star ratings, only reviews. Even two words count.

~~~

I hate typos but sometimes they slip through. Please send any errors you find directly to me at gillean@gilleancampbell.com. I'll get them fixed ASAP. I'm very grateful to eagle-eyed readers who take the time to contact me.

Gillean